A DIVINE EXPERIENCE

– the secret life of
Florence Nightingale

by

Elizabeth Johnson

A Divine Experience

– the secret life of Florence Nightingale

by

Elizabeth Johnson

Copyright 2017 Elizabeth Johnson

ISBN: 978-0-9996801-0-0

This book is produced by Elizabeth Johnson Publishing in conjunction with **WRITERSWORLD**, and is produced entirely in the UK. It is available to order from most bookshops in the United Kingdom, and is also globally available via UK based Internet book retailers.

WRITERSWORLD
2 Bear Close Flats, Bear Close, Woodstock
Oxfordshire, OX20 1JX, England
☎ 01993 812500
☎ +44 1993 812500

www.writersworld.co.uk

The text pages of this book are produced via an independent certification process that ensures the trees from which the paper is produced come from well-managed sources that exclude the risk of using illegally logged timber while leaving options to use post-consumer recycled paper as well.

Dedicated to the memory of Ben Lloyd

without whom this story may never have been told.

ACKNOWLEDGEMENTS

Everlasting gratitude to my dear family and friends whose support kept me going through times of doubt – in particular to my daughters Caroline and Kate and grandsons Samuel, Dominic and Devon.

Also many thanks to my special team of 'critical friends' who gave so generously of their time and for their invaluable words of wisdom and encouragement:

Ruth and John Armstrong, Heather Catchpole, Tessa Holland, Katherine Lynch Brown, Karen Nimmo Scott and Tony Toller.

May you all be proud of this book and of the important part you played in its completion.

Front cover illustrations from top left – Sidney Herbert, Florence Nightingale, David Herbert Llewellyn

Illustrations of Florence Nightingale and David Herbert Llewellyn by Heather O. Catchpole.

Back cover illustrations – Wilton House, CSS Alabama

SHADOWS

By Richard Monckton Milnes, Lord Houghton (1809-85)

They seemed to those who saw them meet
the casual friends of everyday.
Her smile was undisturbed and sweet
his courtesy was free and gay.

But yet if one the other's name
in some unguarded moment heard,
the heart you thought so calm and tame
would struggle like a captured bird.

And letters of mere formal phrase
were blistered with repeated tears
and this was not the work of days
but had gone on for years and years.

Alas that love was not too strong
for maiden shame and manly pride!
Alas that they delayed so long
the goal of mutual bliss beside!

Yet what no chance could then reveal
and neither would be first to own,
let fate and courage now conceal
when truth could bring remorse alone.

Chapter 1

During the first few weeks of the Nightingales' European tour, Florence gazed with little interest at the passing scenery as the great carriage, drawn by six horses, travelled through the flat French countryside. She'd held her son for only a short time before kind hands had borne him away but the image of his pale face, grey blue eyes and shock of dark hair stayed with her day and night. Florence turned to watch her father absorbed in a book at the far end of the carriage, while her mother and sister sat on top wrapped in fur rugs, taking in the air of the fine autumn morning.

Florence had disgraced her family; the subject was closed but disappointment and accusation still lurked like dark shadows beneath the interactions of everyday. The vision from God haunted her and she must find redemption by devoting her life to His service, not an easy prospect for a girl of seventeen. While the carriage rumbled on down interminable dusty roads, Florence sighed as she allowed her thoughts to return over her life and the events leading to the uncertain future she now faced.

After their marriage in 1818 her parents, Fanny and William Nightingale, had spent an extended honeymoon travelling through a Europe once again accessible following the Napoleonic wars. Florence was named after the glorious Italian city of her birth in May 1820, while her elder sister had been christened Parthenope, the ancient Greek for her birthplace of Naples, where their father told them was to be seen the most beautiful bay in the world.

After three years abroad, Fanny suggested it was time to return home. William would have been content to stay in Italy for the rest of his life but Fanny insisted and the Nightingales returned to England with their two small daughters. Florence was too young when they left to remember her early life in the warmth of the Arno valley, the palaces, domes and spires – her first memories were of a cooler climate and isolation in the heart of Derbyshire.

Florence's father was originally named William Shore. His mother Mary was the niece of Peter Nightingale who, in 1784, with his partner John Smedley, had founded Lea Mills, specialising in the lucrative production of cotton and muslin, set up on a hilly site straddling a brook near Matlock.

One winter's evening, grandmother Mary Shore recounted the story of "Madman" Uncle Peter to young Florence as they settled in the parlour of her farmhouse home.

'We never understood him, so wild and reckless,' she said. 'Money from the mills went to his head – he sold out to Mr Smedley and gave up working. Horses became his passion, midnight steeplechases his favourite sport and none so dangerous.'

'But why was he called "Madman"?' Florence asked, kneeling down to toast bread in the glowing embers of the fire.

'Peter and his unruly friends drank too much, made wagers and gave themselves handicaps, riding bareback blindfolded or with one hand tied behind their backs,' said her grandmother. 'Off they'd go, tearing into the pitch black in hunting clothes with night wear on top, trying to jump fences they couldn't see, lucky he never got killed. No wonder he didn't marry – what woman would be brave enough to take him on?'

Florence laughed as she spread butter and jam on the hot toast.

'After Peter died,' grandmother Shore continued, 'his estate was left to me, to be passed to my son, William – now your father, of course – when he came of age but only on condition he changed his name to Nightingale. My uncle was a strange one, right enough.'

William Edward Nightingale, known to everyone as WEN, became friendly with Fanny's brother, Octavius Smith, while they were at school together and for years was welcomed as a regular visitor to the Smith family home. An awkward young man, tall and thin with a keen sense of humour and a thirst for knowledge, WEN continued his education at Trinity College, Cambridge.

On leaving university, he inherited Uncle Peter's fortune – a lead mine discovered on the property greatly increased its value and a large sum was invested, allowing WEN to be unencumbered with the burden of earning a living for the rest of his life.

Although Fanny's father, William Smith, was groomed to join the family firm, a grocery business importing tea, sugar and spices, he had other ideas. In his mid-twenties, he decided to become a politician and, being a member of the trade classes, bought his way into Parliament at the cost of £3,000 for the Whig seat of Sudbury. Soon he married the daughter of a wealthy Nottinghamshire family and the couple produced ten healthy children, five boys and five girls.

Fanny described her childhood to Florence as being 'hurly burly – we children never thought about anything much more than our own comfort and pleasure. None of us were fond of the schoolroom and our exasperated tutors soon gave up the struggle to teach us anything.'

Fanny loved dancing and shopping and was considered to be the most attractive of the sisters, slim and vivacious with rich brown wavy hair. Many suitors wooed her but by the time she'd reached her late twenties none had come up to her high standards. Then Fanny fell in love with James Sinclair, a dashing but impecunious captain in the Ross-shire Militia with a small pay packet, no expectations and almost ten years her junior.

His daughter's choice did not impress Mr Smith and he pointed out to Fanny: 'It's absurd of you to contemplate marriage with an income of only four hundred pounds a year. I'm certainly not prepared to support your engagement or finance your future.' Both families were against the match and, despite Fanny's pleadings, the affair ended a year later.

By now Fanny was nearly thirty and WEN only twenty four –

they became engaged and married the next year but were not a well-matched couple. Fanny loved entertaining and social gatherings, she was the perfect hostess, while WEN preferred solitude and leisure to read and reflect.

Uncle Peter had lived in Lea Hall, a tumbledown Jacobean manor set in over one thousand acres of magnificent parkland on high ground, fourteen miles from Derby. WEN fancied his skills as an architect and on their return to England set about designing and building a new house a mile away in the park.

Lea Hurst took several years to complete, was solid, unpretentious and pleasing to the eye, set on a broad terrace in a perfect landscape overlooking hills and woodland. Above the fine oriel window in the drawing room was a balcony where Florence often stood to admire the glorious views; she loved the purity of the air and the peacefulness of upland solitude.

In a quiet corner of the garden was a summerhouse where the girls would work and play. Florence's dolls were constantly in need of medical attention – she never tired of tending to their various ailments, wrapping them in bandages and applying lotions concocted from flowers growing in the tall hedgerows, where wild roses mingled their sweetness with the fragrance of honeysuckle.

The family attended Sunday services in the local village of The Hollow, sitting in their reserved high-backed pews with Florence dressed in her best attire, completed by sandal shoes and a leghorn bonnet turned up under the brim with poppies. Her father became one of the main supporters of the village school and had his own quiet way of helping the poor folk on his estate, but often warned people requesting money for local charities, 'I was not born generous.'

The girls looked forward to the annual Summer Feast Day, when children came in procession to Lea Hurst carrying wreaths and garlands, accompanied by the music of a marching band. Florence and her sister helped the maids to serve a sumptuous tea as the excited children sat at long tables set out in the fields below the house. The day ended with organised games and merry dancing until, happy and exhausted, each child returned home clutching a gift from the Nightingales.

From time to time, Fanny accompanied her daughters on visits to the cottagers in The Hollow. 'Families like us are known as "Sunday people",' she told the girls. 'We are fortunate to have the luxury of time and wealth and it's improving for you both to help others less well off than yourselves.'

To enter the cottages was forbidden for fear of infection, but that did not prevent Florence from delivering beef-teas and jellies with nosegays of flowers, carried in her pony's saddlebag and left by their doors. The cottagers became her friends, their homely wit matched her own and their simplicity and kindness made a great impression on her. 'We look forward to Miss Florence's visits,' they would say. 'She has a way with her that makes us feel better.'

Lea Hurst became WEN's favourite home but Fanny was not happy.

'This house is too small with only fifteen bedrooms,' she complained, 'isolated, inaccessible from London, cold and uninhabitable in winter.' She convinced her husband that Derbyshire, except in summer, was impossible, they must have another home, larger, in a warmer part of the country and nearer to the social life she craved.

In 1825, WEN bought Embley Park in Hampshire, a good-sized Georgian manor set in nearly four thousand acres of land on the borders of the New Forest and with exceptionally fine gardens. The hunting and shooting were first class, London was reasonably close and Fanny's two married sisters both lived within easy reach.

Embley could accommodate many visitors for long periods, suiting Fanny's determination to turn the house into a social centre for the intellectual and aristocratic elite of the time. Fanny was the ruling spirit of the house; directions to the staff, down to the most minute particulars, were issued from her sitting room –

she well understood how to receive and entertain a house full of guests.

By the time Florence was six, the pattern of the Nightingales' year was fixed. Summers were spent at Lea Hurst, the remainder of the year at Embley and in spring and winter shorter visits were made to London. Fanny would have loved a house in the city but WEN would not agree and set about turning himself into an English country gentleman. He took an active interest in local politics, was a Whig in favour of parliamentary reform and became High Sheriff for Hampshire.

'How I hate the Tories,' he remarked to his wife. 'Nothing seems to concern them more than beer and money.'

Florence soon came to know the countryside from Derbyshire to Hampshire end to end and found the drive a joy in both summer and autumn. Servants were sent ahead with the luggage as the family travelled in their own carriage, or sometimes by coach, taking the journey at leisure and putting up at inns along the way.

As the prettier of the two sisters, Florence was tall, slightly built with a pale oval face and a head of shining hair, brown and red with a glint of gold like the colour of fallen leaves. Her dark grey eyes critically observed the world and her sweet smile showed a set of perfect white teeth. Full of spirit with an enquiring mind and pining for excitement, Florence tried to organise everyone around her. Such a strong-willed child could also be an obstinate one and her parents attempted to improve her behaviour by promising rewards if she managed to survive for one week without being disobedient.

Florence tried hard to behave but soon she'd be found grooming her pony when supposed to be perfecting her needlepoint, or absorbed by a book in the library still wearing her day clothes when important visitors were expected. Fanny considered her youngest daughter to be a strange creature from another world, calling her "a wild swan in a family of ducks".

WEN maintained decided views about the education of his two daughters. A governess was employed for music and drawing – classical and modern languages, maths and philosophy were taught by their father, based on the syllabus he'd followed as a student.

Florence enjoyed her father's lessons, as a teacher he was patient, kind and never patronising although the timetable was strict; slackness and disorder in the classroom were not permitted. Outdoor exercise, dancing classes and deportment lessons, with household affairs taught by their mother, became part of the girls' routine.

Solemn and languid with little sense of humour, Parthenope contrasted unfavourably with bright-eyed Florence's quick wit and lively conversation. Both daughters learned easily but Florence was the more intelligent and dominated in the classroom, causing her governess to remark, 'There is no likelihood that this child will ever become giddy or trifling.'

Parthenope's envy of her sister made her bored and resentful, she didn't know her horizontal from her perpendicular but her memory for poetry was prodigious. She played the piano with accomplishment while Florence thumped. Florence possessed a pleasant singing voice while her sister could sing no better than an owl.

Florence was neat and methodical, Parthenope's lack of discipline irritated her and she considered her sister's love of drawing and flower arranging to be trivial occupations. As time went on the temperamental differences between them made it impossible for the girls to become the devoted sisters that Fanny would have liked.

The family divided. Parthenope helped her mother with entertaining and domestic matters, while Florence spent her days in the library with her father – these were the times she enjoyed most as he was a great one for jokes and loved the odd and curious. Partly by disposition and partly by being married to

Fanny, WEN was a lonely man but father and daughter found solace in each other's company.

A complicated network of uncles, aunts and cousins played a prominent part in the girls' early lives; they were often sent off to stay at different houses while Fanny and WEN were away or relatives would arrive to look after them.

Aunt Mai was WEN's younger sister and should he have no son, Uncle Peter's estate would pass to her. When Florence was seven, Aunt Mai married Fanny's brother, Sam Smith, and soon gave birth to a son they called Shore. Fanny was now nearly forty and unlikely to have another child, which meant that Shore was accepted by the family as the future heir to the Nightingale fortune.

As she grew older, Florence began to find the rich smooth life of home distasteful. She disliked the constant socialising, the endless small talk, was uncomfortable with meeting new guests and disappeared to be on her own whenever possible. Escaping into an imaginary world, she invented stories in which she played the heroine's part and constantly poured out her feelings on to paper into what she called her private notes.

'I crave,' she wrote, *'for some regular occupation, for something worth doing instead of frittering time away on useless trifles.'*

At Christmas time, Florence would be seen riding on her own round the neighbourhood of Embley wearing an ermine tippet, muff and beaver hat, distributing gifts of tea and warm petticoats to the older cottagers. On Christmas Eve she joined in with the village choir to sing carols and afterwards shared mince pies with them in the hall.

Florence became a young woman within a life seemingly simple and peaceful, yet beneath the surface there was no peace. The Nightingale girls were brought up in a hothouse of emotion as the wave of romanticism sweeping Europe now penetrated English domesticity.

While Florence's view on life was clear and realistic, she also possessed a romantic nature and through reading books by her favourite writers – Jane Austen, Wordsworth, John Keats and Lord Byron – she soon became well versed in tender passion. All three of the Nightingale women prided themselves on being martyrs to their excessive sensibility and delicacy was frequently observed. WEN often told his friends, 'I am surrounded by a whole litter of women and have plenty to put up with.'

In the summer of 1834, WEN was invited to stand for Parliament as Whig candidate for the Andover division. The election, the first to be held since the Reform Bill of three years earlier, had resulted in constituencies being restructured, half a million more Britons given the right to vote and a new House of Commons becoming established. WEN was not only defeated but also disillusioned, explaining to his wife, 'The seat was lost because I refused to grease the palms of the voters. The main object of the Reform Bill was to end bribery, but the newly enfranchised men of Andover still seem to think the possession of a vote means hard cash.'

WEN's first contact with practical politics left him disgusted and he resolved never to enter political life again. Her father's reluctance to channel his intelligence in ways to change the world disappointed Florence, while Fanny was forced to give up her idea of becoming a politician's wife with a house in London, transferring her plans and ambitions instead to her daughters.

On their visits to London, the Nightingales were invited to society functions and it was during the Christmas festivities of December 1836 when Florence and a handsome young aristocrat called Sidney Herbert were to evade her chaperones and enjoy intimate time together – the outcome of this liaison would profoundly affect the rest of their lives.

Chapter 2

Sidney Herbert spent much of his time during breaks from parliamentary duties at the family home of Wilton House, an easy carriage ride from the Nightingales at Embley. His mother, the Countess of Pembroke, associated Wiltshire with her husband and since his death was not keen to visit, preferring instead to spend her time in London. As Sidney's sisters were busy with their own lives, he was often on his own in the great house and happy to accept invitations to dinners and parties with local families.

Sidney had been born into a family with aristocratic roots spreading deep into the sixteenth century. His early ancestor, William Herbert, was a young, hot-headed Welsh nobleman forced to flee the country after killing a man during a Bristol brawl and had joined the French army, earning commendation for bravery from King Francis. After returning to England, William married Anne, younger daughter of Sir Thomas Parr and soon an unexpected event projected the Herberts to fame and fortune when Anne's sister, Katherine, became the sixth and final wife of Henry VIII.

The Herberts gained favour with the King and were granted extensive estates belonging to the dissolved abbey of Wilton in Wiltshire where William built the family home. After King Henry's death, William became involved in the struggle for power, joining forces with John Russell to suppress Seymour. For his support of Dudley he was raised to the peerage, becoming Earl of Pembroke and Baron Herbert of Cardiff and thus began the dynasty to which young Sidney Herbert now belonged.

Sidney surprised his mother by being born a little earlier than expected on 16th September 1810, during a visit to his grandmother's house – Pembroke Lodge in Richmond Park.

Countess Elizabeth had moved to the lodge following the breakdown of her marriage to Henry, 10th Earl of Pembroke, after he'd embarked on a series of affairs resulting in at least two illegitimate children.

Sidney's birth was intended to take place at the Pembroke's London home in Grafton Street; no preparations had been made in Richmond and clothes for the baby were hurriedly borrowed from the local workhouse. When, in later years, her son's generosity threatened the family's fortunes, his mother often remarked, 'Workhouse clothes were the first he wore and will clearly be those in which he will die.'

Sidney was the only son of George, 11th Earl of Pembroke, and his wife Catherine, the beautiful daughter of Count Woronzow, Russian Ambassador in the Court of St James.

Lord Pembroke already possessed two children – his first wife Elizabeth died shortly after giving birth to their third child who'd survived her by only a few hours.

George sought distraction from his grief by volunteering for active service with the army in Flanders, but the death of his father a year later required him to return to England to manage the neglected Wilton estates. His second marriage to Catherine proved ideally happy, although she was twenty four years younger, and the couple soon celebrated the safe arrival of a daughter they christened Elizabeth.

Now their son was born and adored by his parents. Sidney resembled an angel in an Italian painting, with curly golden hair and large brown eyes shaded by long thick lashes. When he was four years old, his proud mother entered him in a fete and wrote to his grandmother:

'Sidney looked so beautiful dressed as Cupid with a garland of roses and green leaves, a pair of duck's wings mounted with wire on his head, a bow and quiver complete with arrows tied round his sweet neck on a broad blue ribbon.'

Sidney was probably too young to mind but if he did hate being dressed up, he bore the whole charade with good grace, just to please his mother.

Sidney's father, George, spent many months altering the neglected family estates at Wilton, increasing revenues and trebling rent rolls. The house was in need of extensive alterations and after an investment of over two hundred thousand pounds, Wilton once more became a beautiful country home. Catherine too loved the place and with her husband's encouragement, she designed a new formal Italian garden with broad gravel paths, graceful fountains, elegant statues and stately cypresses.

A tutor was employed to teach Sidney basic studies at their London home but he found academic work taxing and much preferred outdoor activities. While in Wiltshire, he learned to ride his pony, shoot and fish, took walks with the dogs and played games in the grounds of Wilton House.

When he reached the age of ten, Sidney's parents decided it was time to prepare their son for the future by learning to cope without them. They chose to send him to Mr Bradford's school at Hall Place, Beaconsfield, a large Georgian mansion set in beautiful gardens on the edge of the Chiltern Hills overlooking the Thames Valley.

On the evening before he was due to leave, his mother called him into her sitting room. 'My dearest boy,' she said. 'Tomorrow is a momentous day when you will be starting out alone on your life's journey. Do you remember once I showed you a portrait of the person your father and I named you after?'

'Yes, Mamsey, he was called Sir Philip Sidney.'

His mother nodded. 'Sir Philip lived when Queen Elizabeth was on the throne and his sister Mary married your ancestor Henry, 2nd Earl of Pembroke.'

'Was he a good man, Mamsey?'

'Sir Philip was charming and chivalrous, everyone loved him and we're proud of his connection with the Pembroke family,' said his mother. 'He was clever, wrote beautiful poetry and was one of the Queen's favourite courtiers but he died while young, fighting for his country in the Netherlands. So, Sidney, as you go off into the world, I want you to think of Sir Philip, the kind of man he was and try to live your life in the same gentlemanly way.'

'Of course I will try, Mamsey.' Watching him standing there, so young and vulnerable with his lower lip trembling, Catherine could no longer speak; she pulled her son towards her and stroked his golden curls.

'Oh my dear child, we shall miss you dreadfully,' she whispered. Sidney put his arms round his mother's neck then wiped away the tears that had begun to fall down both their faces.

Since its foundation in 1572, Harrow School had managed to survive a colourful history of scandals, rebellions, drunken headmasters and slack discipline. When Sidney became a pupil at the age of fourteen, he was anxious his academic standard might not be as high as some but after a short time on trial he was placed in the first remove of the fourth form, which was better than anyone had anticipated. In his weekly letter home he proudly reported this remarkable news, making sure his mother would not think he was mistaken by spelling out his success three times: 'first, f-i-r-s-t- or in figures "1st".'

One warm summer's evening at the end of the school holidays, just before Sidney's fifteenth birthday, Lord Pembroke invited his son to walk with him in the gardens, accompanied by an assortment of excited dogs.

'Now listen Sidney, I have some important things to tell you about Wilton and your future. You will know that when I die your half-brother, Robert, will become the 12th Earl of Pembroke?'

'Yes Father, I understand,' replied his son, throwing a stick for the dogs to chase.

'With the title, he should take responsibility for the running of our estates. However, Robert has informed us he is not interested in returning to England and wishes to remain living in Paris with his mistress and their children.' This was shocking news to Sidney.

'Your mother and I have discussed the situation and when the time comes, we should like you to undertake the care of Wilton. We know that you love the place as much as we do and consider you would be the ideal custodian for future generations.'

Sidney was concerned – would he be capable of taking on such a huge responsibility?

'Don't worry too much,' his father reassured him. 'I promise to leave the estate in good condition and the agent at the time will ensure you are given all the help you require.'

'Well, sir, if that is your wish, then I should be honoured to agree,' Sidney replied.

'I am delighted to hear you say so. Let's hope it will not be for a long time yet but to know the estate will be in good hands is a great comfort to me. Come on now dogs, it's time for dinner,' and they walked together back to the house, through the beautiful gardens and across the magnificent Palladian bridge.

Sidney was familiar with the story of his elder half-brother, but had not until now realised its full implications. During a holiday in Italy when Robert was twenty one, he had been seduced by an older woman, Princess Octavia Spirelli, the wife of a Sicilian nobleman. When a few months later her husband died, the princess had persuaded Robert to marry her. Lord Pembroke hurried to Italy to intervene, arriving too late to stop the ceremony but managed to have the marriage declared clandestine and, after an appeal to the authorities, both Robert and Octavia were arrested.

Several months in prison were enough to cool Robert's ardour and on release he returned to England. The princess instituted proceedings for reinstatement of conjugal rights and the court decreed the marriage, although illegal, was valid. Octavia was Robert's lawful wife and refused to divorce him, leaving him unable to marry Alexina Gallot, the mother of his illegitimate children with whom he was now living in Paris.

Lord Pembroke died when Sidney was only seventeen. His mother, Countess Catherine Pembroke was a remarkable woman – beautiful in youth and distinguished with age, a lady by nature as well as birth. After the death of her husband, she took on the responsibility of her son and five daughters in a kind and capable way but her strength of will allowed the children no deviation from the behaviour she expected from them, in consideration of their aristocratic background.

The death of Lord Pembroke was a heavy blow to Sidney; theirs had been a loving relationship and he keenly felt the loss of his father's wise counsel. At his mother's suggestion, he left Harrow and went to board with a private tutor, Reverend Francis Lear, rector of Chilmark near Wilton, who continued Sidney's tuition to prepare him for entry to Oxford University.

Sidney's stay at Chilmark was a happy one. Reverend Lear was sympathetic to his loss; he had known Lord Pembroke for many years and as he guided Sidney with kindness and compassion through this sad time, the two men developed a close friendship.

From Chilmark, Sidney wrote to his mother in London:

'My dearest Mamsey: you cannot think how comfortable it is to be in a nice little country church after that great noisy chapel at Harrow. Everything is so quiet and the people all so attentive that you might hear a pin drop when Mr Lear is preaching.

I like too being so near Wilton, many things here bring to mind all he said and did – all the places where I have ridden with him and the home where we used to be so happy. In short there is not a spot about Wilton now which I do not love as if it were a person. I hope you will be coming there soon and get it over for seeing that place again will be a dreadful trial to you.'

Early in 1829, Sidney went up to Oriel College at Oxford University, a masculine stronghold fostering great men and loyal ns. His rooms were some of the best in college, comfortably furnished with brown leather armchairs and colourful Turkish rugs on the wooden floors. Light streamed in through tall, narrow, round-head windows on two sides of the room – one side overlooking the quadrangle, the other across the street towards the back of Christ Church.

Sidney was aware a freshman's reputation would depend on the selection of his companions and joined a small group of able young men of good character, avoiding contact with the low idlers and blackguards to be found at all colleges. Knowing his mother would worry about the company he was keeping, Sidney set her mind at rest by writing:

'The wine parties I attend are really quite harmless and free from all intemperance. In fact most of the conversations I find boring and trivial.'

Sidney soon settled into the routine of university life and became admired as a speaker at the Union Debating Society. His original intention had been to take honours and read for them but he was unsuited to academic work and left Oxford with a fourth-class degree, having decided his future lay in politics.

Some years earlier Viscount Fitzwilliam, an intimate friend and distant relative of Sidney's father, had died leaving no heir. After bequeathing to Cambridge University his fine collection of pictures, marbles and manuscripts, the viscount had left the bulk of his property to Lord Pembroke with the remainder to Sidney, who at the age of twenty one was to inherit extensive estates in Ireland and Shropshire.

In September, when Sidney attained his majority, he took on the responsibility of running the Wilton estates and a few months later paid his first visit to Ireland.

After the passage of the Reform Bill in 1832, parliament was dissolved and in the election that followed, Sidney became Tory

MP representing South Wiltshire.

Although now aged only twenty-two years, Sidney was better prepared to enter politics than many others older as for her son's sake, the countess gathered round her the most eminent members of London society, especially those of the Tory party. Sidney moved in select circles and as one of the most handsome and charismatic young men of the day soon became a conspicuous and popular figure.

On the day of the election, a magnificent procession of four hundred horses, with Sidney in its midst, left Wilton accompanied by a drum major, to arrive at the hustings in Salisbury.

Sidney wrote to his mother: *'It was a wonderful day. I delivered an enthusiastic acceptance speech, followed by a radical agitator who spoke for nearly one hour, despite dead rabbits being hurled at him and not a word being heard above the racket of the crowd.'*

Sidney entered politics with no personal objective or selfish ambition to gratify, but merely a desire to do his duty and use his privileged status to help others. Although showing little sign of future oratory distinction, his maiden speech in the House was certainly a more creditable performance than those of most young aspirants for parliamentary fame.

The Whig government of Earl Grey was dismissed in 1834 by William IV, who appointed Sir Robert Peel as the new prime minister. Peel was a brilliant politician with twenty-five years' experience, a tall man with a huge frame and slightly wobbly legs. He was impressed by Sidney, recognised his potential and wrote offering him a training role in the Board of Control.

'This office would afford great opportunity of acquiring political knowledge and an insight into the complex machine of government,' wrote Peel to Sidney.

'It is easy to find a Lord of the Admiralty but not easy to

find one capable of discharging such duties as I now propose you undertake. Believe me, my very dear Sidney, that neither for my sake or your own would I propose them if I did not feel satisfied that you are capable of understanding them.'

Sidney's official training was short. In the Tamworth Manifesto addressed to his constituents but distributed widely in the press, Peel outlined his support for the Reform Act, explaining his desire for a more enlightened conservatism and, as a result, the Tory party divided.

Although still in power, Peel's Conservatives remained a minority in the House of Commons, a situation Peel found increasingly intolerable and he resigned in 1835. Sidney became a regular member of the Peelite opposition, embarking on a long and bumpy political career to be shortly overshadowed by dramatic and unforeseen events in his personal life.

Chapter 3

Mrs Fanny Nightingale spent much of her time arranging elaborate dinner parties at Embley Park in an effort to encourage the friendship of aristocratic and influential county families.

Although WEN had rejected the idea of becoming an MP, he still took an interest in the business of politics and his wife invited to their house gentlemen supporting various political persuasions, leading to lively and sometimes heated debates. One of the regular names included on Fanny's invitation list was that of Mr Sidney Herbert. The Nightingale girls were called on to entertain the guests after dinner, with Florence reluctantly singing selections from the popular songs of the day accompanied by Parthe playing prettily on the piano.

Florence was now, at fifteen, a talented and fearless horsewoman and begged her father to allow her to go hunting. Fanny and Parthe did not approve but she was determined to go anyway. The next lawn meet of the season was to be hosted by Sidney Herbert at Wilton House and WEN agreed she could accompany him.

On the morning of the hunt Florence was up, dressed and ready to go well before it was time for them to leave. The groom had taken their horses to Wilton the day before to ensure they would be fresh for the chase and Florence's anticipation grew as their carriage arrived outside the great house.

Members of the hunt in coats of red, black and navy blue mingled as the stirrup cup was handed round. Their excited horses, with gleaming tack and coats brushed to silky perfection, pawed the ground, snorting with impatience for the day to begin and the pack of leggy foxhounds ambled round the melee, sniffing the air, waiting to be summoned by the horn.

Sidney Herbert was already there, dressed in a finely-cut red coat fastened with three brass buttons, tight white breeches and black boots topped with mahogany leather, riding through the crowd on a spirited grey mare and greeting everyone with a special word.

Florence was smitten. The excitement of the hunt thrilled her – the sound of the huntsman's horn and the cry of "Tally-ho" as the hounds took off, giving tongue as they caught scent of their prey, followed in hot pursuit by the mounted field flying over open countryside, hedges and ditches.

She was secretly pleased when the foxes went to ground but when the hounds were quiet and the scent was lost, the huntsman would recast. The field moved off again in a different direction, until after some hours they returned slowly home, exhausted but invigorated by the day's sport. Florence found herself riding back to Wilton beside Mr Herbert.

'And how did you enjoy your day, Miss Nightingale?' he asked.

'It was wonderful, Mr Herbert, thank you so much for allowing me to join in.' Florence smiled with bright eyes and patted her horse's neck.

'My pleasure and how is life at Embley?'

'I'm working hard at my studies. Mama considers classics and mathematics too taxing for a woman, although Papa is keen to teach me. She would prefer I sat planning menus preparing to be the perfect hostess but I loathe having to conform. Why should women not have every right to use their talents in the same way as men?'

Sidney listened patiently as she explained her ideas of how to improve the world with exciting new inventions and discoveries. Or she might be an explorer, travel to exotic places and study tribes in the Brazilian rain forest.

Florence concluded, 'Mama says I don't look at things from the proper feminine angle and am too young to know what is good for me.'

Sidney smiled. 'You certainly have a courageous spirit, Miss Nightingale, which I'm sure will serve you well in whatever your future holds.'

He had never before met a young woman with Florence's rebellious nature and admired her determination to follow her own path with little regard for conventional womanly image. Her enthusiasm and self-belief he found attractive, reminding him of his own dear mother.

Sidney noted with pleasure the ease and grace of Florence's posture in the saddle, with her knee resting elegantly on the mane of her horse. The fitted black riding habit showed off the delicate undulations of her slim figure and she looked so pretty with her face glowing from the day's hunting, strands of golden brown hair straying loose from her hat.

'How about you, Mr Herbert?' Florence asked. 'It must be exciting to be elected a Member of Parliament and have such influence over other people's lives.'

'Sometimes politics can be rewarding but usually the work is quite boring and frustrating, individuals have very little power over the huge churning machine of Westminster.'

'What would you change if you did have the power?'

Sidney thought for a moment. 'My father was a soldier who served overseas as well as at home. He wrote a diary describing the terrible conditions endured by his troops and how badly they were treated, in spite of the great sacrifices they were making. His words deeply affected me so one of my ambitions would be to improve the lot of the British soldier.'

Sidney's voice was low and harmonious – he spoke with such sincerity that Florence was held by his words as if under a spell.

'I hope very much that one day you will succeed, Mr Herbert,' she replied and they spurred on their horses to catch up with the rest of the hunt.

During the carriage ride home, Florence was lost in thought. She had enjoyed the hunting but it was Sidney Herbert's presence that from now on filled her waking and sleeping dreams.

Sidney escaped from the stresses of parliamentary life in London to Wiltshire as much as possible – his days were filled with the business of being an MP, attending local functions and dealing with constituency matters, as well as handling the running of the Wilton estates. He and the Nightingales began to see more of each other at social gatherings held in the grand country houses of the county set.

Accompanied by WEN, Florence and Sidney spent hours riding through miles of the stunning Wiltshire countryside, while the two men often met at shooting parties hosted by themselves and other local landowners.

When his favourite spaniel had puppies, Sidney sent a message inviting the Nightingales to see the litter. Florence, Parthe and WEN drove over in the carriage to Wilton House where Sidney greeted them and they walked together to the stable block.

There, in a low hamper in a nest of wool and flannel, lay five warm bundles of tan and white plumpness, nuzzling with contentment on their mother's teats. Florence was enchanted – she loved animals and knelt down to examine the puppies more closely. The Nightingales' old family dog had recently died and she couldn't wait for a replacement.

'So Florence, what do you think of my babies?' Sidney asked.

'They're beautiful, could we please have one Papa?'

'If you'll be sure to help look after the puppy and allow me to train it for being useful at shoots, I'm sure that would be in order,' her father replied.

Florence was delighted and chose a bitch puppy with a distinctive tan star in the centre of her white chest, deciding to call her Venus.

'I'll bring her over to you when she's ready to leave her mother in a few weeks' time,' Sidney promised. He sensed Parthe and WEN were becoming bored and offered to show them round his home.

The mellow stone of Wilton House glowed in the bright April sunshine. The Nightingales marvelled at the elegant architecture, luxurious furnishings with magnificent paintings, porcelain and sculptures displayed in every room. On the journey home Parthe talked of nothing but the wonderful house, while Florence could think only of her new puppy and Sidney.

On the morning of 12th May, Florence's sixteenth birthday, Sidney rode over to Embley carrying Venus in a small basket. Round her neck was tied a golden ribbon with a label which read: *'Happy Birthday – please look after me.'*

Sidney and Florence began to seek each other out whenever occasions allowed; a special friendship formed between them with Florence suffering more and more from the anxieties of her young passion.

Sidney was ten years older with charm in everything he did and a gentle sympathetic manner. His face was handsome, lightly freckled over the bridge of his aristocratic nose, a lock of soft thick dark blonde hair fell forward across his forehead and the corners of his mouth turned up naturally in a smile. He possessed the assurance customary for a man of his high social background but showed no hint of arrogance.

Florence felt able to confide in him her innermost thoughts, without worry that he would disregard or laugh at her. She talked to him with more freedom than she had felt with anyone before, looking to his opinion on almost every subject. Sidney soon became the object of her adolescent sexual obsession – an emotional condition so strong that nothing could prevent her from achieving her desire.

Sidney was well aware they could become too fond of each other if he went on taking notice of her and what could come of it? Florence was young and not from the kind of family background to be approved of by his aristocratic mother. Sidney was inexperienced with affairs of the heart and showed an uncharacteristic shyness by avoiding ladies who appeared interested in him. Perhaps he should keep out of Florence's way to prevent deceiving her of his concerns? But he felt happy and relaxed when they were together – there was a vitality and warmth about her that he could not resist.

The Nightingales travelled to London at the beginning of December 1836 to take part in the Christmas festivities and, as was their custom, occupied a suite of rooms at the Burlington Hotel. The whole family had been invited to a private ball at the Bracebridges to which Florence was greatly looking forward, as she knew Sidney would be there.

The Bracebridges were a wealthy couple with no children, who loved socialising in London and at their home, Atherston Hall, near Coventry. The dance floor provided one of the few places where young people could meet and courtships might blossom; under the cover of the music and dance, intimate talking and touching could legitimately take place.

Florence was now an attractive young lady of sixteen, possessing the confidence and poise of someone older. She was not usually interested in fine clothes but had chosen her gown for the ball with great care, the deep midnight blue satin shimmered as she moved, flattering her pale skin and accentuating the dark grey of her eyes which sparkled with excitement.

Even Fanny was impressed. 'Really dear, the colour of that dress suits you so well. I could never wear such a shade of blue but it is very becoming to your complexion,' she told her daughter.

The wide neckline accentuated Florence's small breasts and the long skirt fell gracefully to the floor from pleats high on the waist, with short puffed sleeves reaching to the elbow, accessorised by white mid-length gloves, square-toed blue satin slippers and an ivory fan. Her golden brown hair was parted in the middle, dressed each side with elaborate corkscrew curls, the back was braided and fixed with a single red rose.

The ball was just beginning as the Nightingales walked up the grand staircase, lined with flowers and footmen in smart green and black uniforms. From the ballroom came a hum of conversation and rustle of movement as the orchestra struck up for the first dance.

Fanny acted as her daughters' chaperone on these occasions, well aware of the reputation and character of the men who asked for their attentions and would nip in the bud any undesirable friendships. When a gentleman was worth encouraging, she was adept at disappearing or becoming distracted at strategic moments.

Florence entered the ballroom with her family in a high state of anticipation, tonight was a good night – she felt in complete possession of her forces. She moved across the floor in her long skirt with the unhurried gliding motion perfected at home – her head held high on her slender neck, her back as straight as a ramrod, conscious of composure and free grace in her movements. She did not dare look round to catch Sidney's eye but became aware he was there observing her.

Most of the dances were lively – country dances, Scottish reels, cotillion, quadrille and the newly popular waltz. Other gentlemen asked Florence to dance on a number of occasions, but, although she could now see Sidney, he had not yet made himself known to her and it was not until the supper dance, halfway through the evening that he approached.

'Mrs Nightingale, would you allow me the pleasure of the next dance with your daughter?'

Florence's excitement was intoxicating; Sidney's smile melted her heart. Everything about his face and figure looked elegant from his shining blonde hair and freshly shaved chin, to his white frilled high collar shirt, black tailcoat, slim black trousers and black satin waistcoat.

Sidney was bowled over by Florence's beauty that night – here she now appeared the feisty country girl, transformed into a glorious young woman, emerging like a butterfly into the richness of London society. Florence handed her fan to her mother, who smiled encouragingly as the young couple took to the floor.

'You are a delight to dance with Florence – so light on your feet,' Sidney murmured. Florence thrilled at his praise, relishing the pressure of one warm hand in hers, the other holding her firmly in the small of her back as they spun round the floor, their eyes so absorbed in each other that they could have been alone in that crowded room.

After the dance he led her into the dining room where they sat together and ate supper with other members of the family and friends. Florence had never felt so happy – she charmed all around her with her wit and vivacity. Afterwards they danced once more and Sidney asked if he might call on her at the Burlington the next day.

Florence overlooked to mention their assignation to her family and when the time arrived for Sidney's visit, she was alone. Her mother and Parthe had taken off in the carriage, eager to complete their Christmas shopping, while her father was examining the collection of the Elgin Marbles at the British Museum – he'd invited Florence to accompany him but she had feigned a headache.

Sidney was shown into the drawing room where Florence waited with her heart pounding.

'Good afternoon, Sidney. I trust you are rested from last night's exertions?'

'Quite recovered, thank you, Florence. And you're looking radiant. Is your family not here?'

'No, I'm afraid we're alone.' A rare blush touched Florence's cheeks as her eyes shone with the fire of youthful joy.

Sidney had never felt so passionately for her as at that moment, he experienced a rush of tenderness at the sudden belief that this sweet, beautiful creature was in love with him and could resist her no longer.

Sidney folded her in his arms and murmured her name – his kisses were gentle, searching and deep. Florence felt an ecstasy aroused by his physical presence – her whole body tingled with an overwhelming, delicious thrill of anticipation. She knew quite well what she was doing as she led Sidney to her bedroom and soon gave herself completely and willingly to him, with no thought for the future consequences.

Her favourite present that Christmas was a small black velvet box which arrived with a short note – '*To my dear Florence from your loving friend Sidney Herbert.*' Inside was a turquoise and pearl heart-shaped pendant on a fine gold chain.

Chapter 4

In February 1837, the doctor was called to Embley to visit Florence who had been feeling unwell and in hushed tones he announced the shattering news that she was expecting a baby. Fanny went pale, slumped in the bedside chair and dissolved into hysterical crying. WEN whispered comforting words and led his wife to her room, where she collapsed on the bed in a state of shock. Florence dropped to her knees, buried her face in her hands and sobbed.

Her father returned and knelt by her side murmuring, 'Poor child, oh my poor child.' She reached up her arms round his neck and covered his face with kisses as large tears fell down his cheeks.

'Oh Papa, please don't cry. I'm so sorry to have disgraced you and Mama, will you ever forgive me?'

'Listen Florence – there's no question of asking us to forgive you,' his voice shook with emotion. 'Only God is able to judge your behaviour and grant atonement for your sins. We are shocked and disappointed by the way you have let the family down, but you're our beautiful daughter and of course we shall stand by you.'

WEN wiped his eyes and blew his nose. 'We must now think of the future and decide what is best to do for all of us. I need you to tell me the name of the father of your child and how this came about.'

Florence cried that Sidney was not to blame, she had planned for them to be alone, her hands had caressed and guided, her words encouraged until their passion had reached the point of no return. When she'd finished speaking, her father tucked her into bed as he had when she was a small girl, said a short prayer and bade her goodnight leaving Florence lying stilled by shock, gazing at the ceiling and immersed in sombre meditation. After some hours in that attitude, she knelt by the bed and called on her religion for help.

Florence had been brought up as a Protestant and attended church services with her family each week, bible stories of God choosing sinners to carry out His work on earth were familiar to her. Now it was her turn – she was the fallen and she had been chosen.

The next morning, her father came to check on her progress and was surprised to find her sitting up in bed looking bright and calm.

'Papa, I didn't sleep a wink last night. A vision came from God chastising me for my sins, I heard His voice – it was so beautiful. He said to earn atonement I must achieve worthiness by devoting my life to His service. What could that service be? Will you help me to discover what those words might mean?'

'Of course my dear, I'll help you all I can. Now are you able to eat a light breakfast?' Her father reached out and rang the bell for Mrs Gale, who came straight away.

Mrs Gale was a woman in her early fifties of such stunted growth she was known by the family as "Little Gale" and often referred to by others less kindly as a dwarf. She was devoted to the Nightingales and had worked with the family for over twenty years. She and Thérèse, Fanny's French maid, were the only members of the female servant household trusted to accompany the family on their travels between Derbyshire and Hampshire.

Fanny was still distraught – the doctor's pronouncement constituted her worst nightmare. Marriage was not an option as she knew that Sidney's mother, the Countess of Pembroke, would never approve the match. The Nightingales were a genteel middle-class family, grown wealthy on the proceeds of the industrial revolution and would not be considered as a suitable family to be linked with the aristocratic Herberts. Sidney was twenty six, at the start of a promising political career, while Florence was only sixteen and considered too young to be married or ready for motherhood.

Later, when they were alone in the drawing room, Fanny turned in despair to her husband.

'What are we to do? No one must find out about this. Imagine the ruinous gossip – we should have to leave the country, I could never face anyone again. After all we have done for her, the ungrateful child. I knew she'd cause trouble, she's always been so wilful.'

Fanny began pacing the room while her husband stood with his back to the fire, gold rimmed eyeglasses perched on the bridge of his nose. WEN tried to calm her.

'Now then Fanny, we can rely on Mrs Gale and Thérèse, they need be the only ones outside the family to know. We will soon travel up to Lea Hurst where Florence can rest in peace and quiet, away from prying eyes. Our daughter needs our support and we must give it.'

Fanny snapped, 'You have indulged her too much William, and now she is out of control.' WEN looked at the floor and kept silent.

'And what about Parthe?' Fanny went on. 'Her prospects too will be ended if this gets out. No respectable man would want to marry her either. What would the future hold for them both without husbands? Living in service on the charity of some crusty old woman, despised by her and her servants? Or maybe as governess to someone else's ghastly children? It's all too horrible William, you must do something.'

'Florence tells me she had a vision from God – seems to think she now has to do some kind of service as penance for her sins,' said WEN.

'Penance, penance?' Fanny cried. 'No penance could make up for what she has done. And as for Mr Herbert, I have no words to describe how I feel about him.'

WEN sighed. 'I know how hard this is for you my dear and I too am most unhappy, but our concern now must be for Florence. I have sent a letter to Mr Herbert asking him to call tomorrow. Whatever you may think, I believe he is an honourable man and no amount of anger you inflict on him would help Florence now.'

He took his wife's hands in his own and continued. 'We can totally rely on Mr Herbert's discretion and be assured he will make sure the child is given a secure future. The whole sad affair can then be forgotten, left in the past and normal life will eventually be resumed. You'll see my dear, all will be well,' but Fanny was not at all convinced.

WEN was a kind and considerate husband who held his wife in high esteem. He'd married Fanny for love but his suspicion was that after her broken affair, she'd chosen him as a prudent match to provide her with the prestige of a genteel family life. Fanny had always before shown the strongest will in their marriage but now she could not cope. WEN must take control and with speed bring to an end this disgraceful chapter in their lives, no matter how much he too was suffering.

Parthe became hysterical at the certain knowledge that Florence's bad behaviour and indiscretions would ruin her own reputation. Secretly, she was envious that her sister had been intimate with a man and intended to find out the full details.

Although angry and disappointed with her daughter's misconduct, Fanny could not help but have a little sympathy. Sidney Herbert was certainly a charming man and in different circumstances she would have been delighted to welcome him as a son-in-law. At least Florence could not be said to have descended below her rank, but young ladies who set their caps at men above their station must also encounter disappointment.

Fanny well remembered the grand passion she'd felt for the love of her life, the dashing James Sinclair and how devastated she'd been when their affair was ended by her family. No one knew better than Fanny how difficult it was for a young man to go far enough without going too far. She sighed and thought, 'Poor Florence – there but for the grace of God I too could have gone.'

When Sidney came to visit Embley the following day, WEN showed him into the library and the two men discussed the situation. Sidney was humiliated and ashamed about what had happened, his feelings for Florence were warm and genuine but he had taken advantage of a young girl's innocent love and now he must face the consequences.

No legal requirement existed for him to be further involved, but his strong sense of moral obligation dictated he should help as much as possible to ease the situation for the Nightingale family.

The two men agreed that Sidney should assume responsibility for the child after it was born, find a suitable home and provide financial support as required. The whole terrible affair must be kept a strict family secret and Sidney and Florence would not meet again until circumstances became appropriate for them to do so.

As Sidney rode away from the house with the reins slack on his horse's neck and his head bowed in thought, Florence watched him from her window moving into the distance of unknown years. If she ever saw him again they would be a very different couple, their young love was ended to be remembered only as a treasure of the past. She leaned on her elbow, gazing after him as he disappeared behind the great cedar tree and spent the rest of the day in gloomy reverie, with her beloved spaniel Venus lying by her side.

As head of the household, WEN put plans in action to distract his wife and daughters from the traumas they were experiencing. Fanny had for some time complained the facilities at Embley were not suitable for the amount of entertaining she planned as the girls came out into society. Now WEN agreed designs for major alterations to the house, which would take several years to complete, and during that time they would embark upon a tour of Europe.

The family returned to Lea Hurst in the early summer and Florence spent the rest of her confinement in the peace of the

Derbyshire countryside. She helped her father to plan the itinerary for their trip, while Fanny and Parthe discussed new colour schemes and furnishings for Embley.

For once Florence allowed her parents to take control of her life with no argument, her senses were dulled to the sights and sounds that most used to interest her. She took long walks with Venus in the grounds of Lea Hurst, tormented by her vision and worried about how she was expected to earn redemption by serving others. A great deal of her time nowadays was spent reading the Bible, as though searching for some crumbs of comfort and revelation amongst its heaped-up mass of words.

The affair with Sidney was over – although heartbroken, Florence well understood the reasons why and she was confident that arrangements would be made to ensure the child was given a secure future. She had let the family down and it was now her duty to behave as an obedient daughter but the world was turning hateful and ugly – her future seemed to be a dark tunnel with the door at the end shut fast.

One warm summer evening, the two sisters were alone in the drawing room with their heads bent over their embroidery, when Parthe looked up and said, 'You know Florence, all this business is very upsetting, you have dreadfully disappointed us. I cannot think how it all came about – was it very wonderful?'

Florence rested one hand on her swelling belly and replied, 'If you knew how this came about it would not seem wonderful to you.'

'Can you not tell me?' her sister pleaded.

'No I'm sorry Parthe – not everything can be explained. One day you'll experience something similar for yourself,' and she returned to her sewing.

Parthe stitched a tendril of honeysuckle into the pattern of her embroidery and gave a little sigh. After a while she asked, 'Flo, how will you bear to give away your baby?'

Florence paused for a moment. 'It's a strange trick of nature and my misfortune that women are able to conceive babies before they are ready to look after them,' she said. 'I don't think of it as my baby, only as a child I shall bring into the world. Some other family will love it and be responsible for its life.'

'Well I think when the time comes it will be very hard for you,' her sister replied.

'I could never keep the child – Mama and Papa would disown me. I have no husband and no means of support, so how would it be possible? My suffering will be punishment for my bad behaviour but I have you to help me dearest Pop, don't I?' Parthe nodded, then as tears began to fall, she crossed the room and hugged her sister.

Following the death of William IV in June 1837, the country moved into a new era with young Queen Victoria taking the throne. Sidney took advantage of the dissolution of parliament by visiting the Wiltshire estates where his task was to select a family to provide a suitable home for his child.

Sidney turned for help to his friend, the Reverend Lear at Chilmark and he recommended a stipendiary curate who'd spent time in neighbouring parishes and was well-known to him. The Reverend David Llewellyn was forty two, his wife Elizabeth some sixteen years younger and they had two sons, John who was six and Arthur aged four.

Sidney and the Reverend Lear visited the Llewellyns at their home in Urchfont. Sidney was impressed by the humility and quiet demeanour of the couple and the loving comfort they provided their children. An arrangement was agreed, the child would be brought up within the Llewellyn family with financial support from Sidney, a more secure living would be sought for Reverend Llewellyn and a scholarly education provided for the boys.

In late summer, the party of the Nightingales, Fanny's maid Thérèse, a courier and Mrs Gale the girls' trusted nurse, crossed from Southampton to Le Havre, with Florence well wrapped up in the folds of a voluminous dark green travelling shawl. The group continued on to Rouen where, a few days later, Florence safely gave birth to a son in one of Europe's most modern hospitals.

As soon as she was recovered, the family set off for their tour in a large specially built carriage designed by WEN. The inside was fitted with devices for eating, resting, reading and writing in comfort; on the roof were seats for the family and servants to enjoy the air and admire the scenery, six horses drew the carriage ridden by liveried postilions.

At the end of September 1837, a nurse arrived back in Wiltshire with the baby born in France. Registration of births had become mandatory that year and the Llewellyns visited the office in Lavington in the district of Devizes on 5th October. The date of birth was recorded as 9th September, the place of birth as in Urchfont and the parents as David and Elizabeth Llewellyn.

The name of the child was not entered at the time of registration but at his christening on 24th November the boy was called David Herbert Llewellyn.

Chapter 5

It was a grey misty afternoon in the late November of 1845 and David Herbert Llewellyn sat in the parlour of Lower Farm at Easton Royal struggling with his arithmetic. The silence of the room was broken by the screeching of a dozen slate pencils as students copied down work dictated by the schoolmaster, Mr Sparkes. Three younger children were sitting cross-legged on the floor, practising numbers and letters with their fingers in a large sand tray.

David enjoyed reading and writing but found sums more difficult, although he tried hard to please Mr Sparkes, who possessed a wicked looking cane and was not afraid to use it. At last the announcement came for the end of lessons and the children filed out quietly, grabbed their outdoor clothes then ran laughing and shouting into the street. They climbed the grassy banks, where rows of thatched cottages perched and turned off in different directions to the refuge of their own homes.

The village street was muddy from the constant traffic of carts and horses, not helped by herds of cows with pendulous pink udders plodding up and down from field to dairy twice each day, splattering the road as they passed.

Up ahead at the southern end of the village, David could see that the top of Easton Clump was hidden in mist. He opened the door of the vicarage, hung his cap and coat on a peg in the hall and removed his boots. The house seemed quiet now his brothers were away at school but he was pleased that it would soon be the Christmas holidays.

David pulled a face as he noticed the grubby cuffs of his shirt – his mother was always asking him not to use them for cleaning his slate. What was the point of giving him a cloth if he never used it?

She was in the warm kitchen stirring something that smelt delicious in a big black pot on the range and his younger sister, Sarah, was conducting a dolls' tea party on the kitchen table.

'Here I am, mother, please may I have something to eat?'

'Oh good, David, you're home. We've rabbit stew for later but for now you can just have an apple. By the way, there's a present for you in the parlour from Mr Herbert – Lady Bruce brought it.'

David liked Lady Bruce, she lived up in the Big House. Sometimes she came to school to help with lessons and talked to them about things like the importance of good manners, punctuality and always having respect for their parents. She had a pretty face and when she smiled at David, he couldn't help but smile back. Mr Herbert was Lady Bruce's brother – David thought he was very lucky to have such a lovely sister.

He selected the largest apple from the bowl, went into the parlour and found the package, unknotted the string and removed the brown paper. Inside was a leather covered book with the title 'Oliver Twist' by Charles Dickens.

On the flyleaf was written, *'To my dear godson David on the occasion of your eighth anniversary. May God keep you safe and bless you. From your loving godfather Sidney Herbert.'*

Mr Herbert sent a present every year at this time. David's mother had explained that a godfather was a special grown-up who gave spiritual guidance. With a vicar for a father, David thought he'd enough spiritual guidance for one person but if a godfather meant presents, he was happy to have one. He'd only met Mr Herbert a few times but he seemed nice, he was busy working in London helping to run the country which was a very important job. David settled down by the fire, took a large bite out of his apple and began to read his new book.

Easton Royal was a village of some five hundred inhabitants, part of a large estate owned by Charles Brudenell-Bruce, the

Marquis of Ailesbury, who lived in Tottenham House, four miles away. The farmers were tenants, paid their dues to the estate agent and did not aspire to be squires. The Marquis was for the most part an absentee landlord, although the family did attend occasional Sunday services, occupying their reserved pew marked with a brass plate and handsome crimson cloth cushions.

In 1837, Charles' only son and heir, George William Frederick, Earl Bruce, married Mary Caroline, one of Sidney Herbert's younger sisters and the couple moved to Tottenham House. George and Mary Caroline were both much given to good works and took an active interest in the well-being of the tenants on the Savernake estate. Mary Caroline adored her brother and, although shocked when he first confided to her about the child, she was willing to help.

The current vicar of Easton Royal's Church of Holy Trinity was due to retire and clergy appointments were made by the impropriator, the Marquis. When Mary Caroline recommended that the Reverend David Llewellyn be offered the position of perpetual curate at a salary of eighty pounds, her father-in-law was happy to agree.

Sidney was grateful to the Marquis for his patronage; the award of a living in this way was regarded as a favour and a privilege. The curate's family would reside in the vicarage where Mary Caroline could keep a discreet eye on the upbringing of young David Herbert Llewellyn.

When the Llewellyns, with their three sons and maid Anna Ferris, moved to Easton Royal in 1839, the pretty facades of the thatched cottages with roses round the door and honeysuckle scrambling up porches often hid sparse and unhealthy living conditions, where two or three rooms accommodated families of eight or more. The world outside the villagers' own experience was a region of mystery, newcomers were met with distrust and required to accept them as they were or not at all.

The curate and his family soon became acquainted with their

neighbours and were welcomed by most, although some considered the church and clergy as unimportant when all was well but were eager for their services at times of trouble or necessity.

The Reverend David Llewellyn was a man of simple needs and little aspiration, his main asset being his wife Elizabeth. His father, John, was vicar of Llangathen in Carmarthenshire. David showed a characteristic lack of ambition by following him into the church but was not of an academic tendency, choosing to overlook studying for ecclesiastical qualifications.

The parish of Llangathen was not large enough to support the two of them. At the age of thirty, David travelled to Steeple Ashton in Wiltshire, where he was appointed as a stipendiary curate in the Salisbury Diocese and met Elizabeth Beaven, who soon became his wife.

When Reverend Lear had first approached the couple with the proposal to take on a child they'd been unsure they could commit to such a responsibility, but the promises of a secure living and education for the children were too good to refuse. Mr Herbert had impressed them as a kind, charming man, genuinely concerned for the well-being of the baby and when he'd offered to stand as godfather and give the child his name they were happy to agree.

Details of the birth parents were not revealed and it was not their place to ask. Now David was a much loved member of the Llewellyn family, an attractive child with large grey eyes, thick golden brown hair, clear pale skin and a solemn expression as though pondering the mysteries of life.

Reverend David Llewellyn was thin, of medium height with a narrow face, high cheekbones, light brown straight hair and a long nose from which a small dewdrop almost permanently hung. He suffered from the cold and on all but the warmest days wore a black woollen scarf, knitted by his wife, securely wrapped round his neck.

Life was accepted by him as it came with perfect good humour and resignation, never attempting to change what fate had in store or trying to achieve lofty aims. He was tolerant, understood men's failings and was kind and gentle with young and old; there wasn't a soul in the parish that had a bad word to say about him.

His wife, Elizabeth, was small and plump with a naturally pleasing expression, bright brown eyes and long dark hair pulled back under a cotton cap. A loving mother to her three sons, she was bustling and kind, always ready to give of herself and flourished in her role as the curate's wife. A great deal of her time was spent visiting needy parishioners, bearing appropriate gifts of food and words of comfort; other people's problems became her problems. On Sundays she taught the village children Bible stories and played the church organ during services with enthusiasm, if not a great deal of accomplishment.

The vicarage was a two-storey, timber framed and slate roofed construction providing adequate accommodation for their needs. Vegetables and fruit grew in the plot behind the house where the pig was housed, a few chickens scratched and together with the bounty of the countryside, ingredients were plentiful. A vast amount of bottling, preserving, jam making and pickling went on in the vicarage kitchen and the store cupboards overflowed.

Elizabeth enjoyed making fruit and meat pies on a well-scrubbed table, deftly handling the pastry with sleeves turned up above the elbow, an ample, checked linen apron almost covered her skirt and her cap and gown were plain – there was nothing she was less tolerant of than female vanity.

Washing and cleaning were the responsibility of the housemaid, Anna; her wooden tub and clothes horse in the scullery were in constant use. Anna was dark, tall and not unbeautiful, though her skin was harsh and her limbs angular. Some of her happiest moments were spent sweeping the church, polishing the brasses and arranging flowers in vases on the altar and window sills, while humming fragments of her favourite hymns.

One warm summer's day, David and Anna were enjoying the late morning sunshine in the garden, shelling peas into a white china bowl, when David asked, 'What happened to your family, Anna?'

'I don't have no-one now, Master David,' Anna said. 'My pa worked at Manor Farm in Urchfont, he fell off a loaded wagon and broke his neck when I was only young.'

'How sad for you,' said the boy.

'My ma was cook at the manor and I was a dairymaid,' continued Anna. 'We lived in the farmhouse and shared a bed. Then one winter, when I was seventeen, ma was taken with the flu, a long time ill she was and then she died. The farmer said I'd have to leave 'cos they needed my room for the new cook, I'd nowhere else to go. Such a mercy your ma asked me to come to Easton with you, these last six years have been a real blessing.'

'We're your family now, Anna,' said David as he gave her arm a squeeze and popped a pea into his mouth.

Villagers were employed working ten hours each day, six days a week on the seven farms and seven smallholdings of arable, sheep, beef and dairy. The events of their lives were fixed by the seasons. Summer meant working in dusty fields from dawn to dusk, autumn, with its shortening days, gave a sense of drawing in. Winter was a time to be dreaded with sickness and little food or warmth, while spring was a time of awakening and relief at having survived the winter.

The Bleeding Horse alehouse was a few doors from the vicarage and a place of mystery to David; he and his friends were forbidden to enter but would dare each other to peer through the windows and report back on what they saw. The scene was always the same – village men quaffing tankards of ale, puffing large volumes of smoke which wreathed above their heads, enveloping the room in a thick dark cloud.

The village and the surrounding countryside were the entire world of the children. The Llewellyn boys played games with their friends and spent hours exploring fields and hedges for birds' eggs and curiosities – shards of pottery, animal skeletons, fossils and flints.

The local inn, the Gammon of Bacon, stood a mile away on the main road leading to Pewsey to the west and Burbage to the east. Here on the Green, every Trinity Monday, the Feast of the Revels took place and the whole village would be there. Gangs of tough looking lads arrived from all round the county to try their hand at backsword fighting and fierce rivalry existed between locals and incomers. The fighters became David's heroes – he admired their bravery, their athleticism and their determination to win – one day he wanted to be like them.

Not to be outdone, the young women took part in smock races, running barefoot round the Green wiggling and jiggling in various states of undress, cheered on lustily by their lovers and admirers. David begged Anna to join in but she blushed and refused, saying, 'I'm not going to make a show of myself in front of the whole village, not even for you, Master David.' The day concluded with a large bonfire, pig roast, fireworks and copious amounts of ale and cider consumed both by contestants and the crowd of revellers.

On fine summer evenings, the Llewellyn family drove in their pony and trap up the steep slope to picnic on Easton Clump. The view from the top was marvellous, with the spire of Salisbury Cathedral visible on a clear day, shimmering like a needle twenty miles away to the south. Looking to the north was a patchwork panorama of fields, woods and coppices, reflecting a dozen shades of green, stretching across the Pewsey Vale to Martinsell Hill and the dark outline of the Savernake Forest.

Down below, through the trees, were glimpses of white lime-washed cottages lining the village street and black dots of cattle grazing in the pastures where the medieval priory had once stood. After the picnic, the boys played in the beech woods, climbing trees like squirrels and carving letters on the trunks, while their parents relaxed, listening to skylarks surcharged with song hovering high in the blue sky above them.

On the ninth anniversary of his christening, David wrote a letter to his godfather.

24ᵗʰ November 1846 – The Vicarage, Easton Royal

Dear Mr Herbert – thank you for my present. I enjoyed reading 'Oliver Twist' and am sure 'A Christmas Carol' will be just as good, especially at this time of the year. I'm pleased that my brothers will be home soon from school for the holidays.

Last week I went beating for the first time with his Lordship's shoot. We spent hours tramping over ploughed fields and through woods, putting up birds for the waiting guns. Then a cart came to take us up to a barn behind Tottenham House where we had lunch with soup, bread and cheese and pickles. I had a small drink of ale but didn't like it much.

It was nearly dark by the time I got home, muddy and tired. My mother was very pleased with the pheasant Lady Bruce gave me for her. I hope you are well. Yours sincerely, your loving godson David.

The little Elizabethan village church with its whitewashed walls and dark oak benches was well attended. The traditional ritual of Sunday services provided an opportunity to wear special clothes and linger for a gossip under the Parliament Tree, a giant elm with a girth of thirty-two feet, standing between the church and the vicarage. Harvest Festival was a favourite occasion when some villagers, never seen at church at other times, appeared to sing the familiar hymns and pray for prosperity over the coming year.

Reverend Llewellyn preached plain moral sermons, peppered with bible references of nature and farming he was hopeful his flock would comprehend. Standing in the pulpit his usual shy demeanour changed – he became animated with shining eyes and waving arms, his lilting Welsh tones rising and falling with emotion.

Occasionally, he paused to remove a red and white spotted handkerchief from the sleeve of his ample white surplice and blew his nose with a loud trumpeting sound, much to the amusement of the children and waking those who always took a nap during sermon time.

Many of the village families had lived here for generations, there was a strong sense of community and kinship – they took great pride in themselves and their work. So it was in the vicarage of a humble farming community nestling in the far eastern corner of the Pewsey Vale, where David Herbert Llewellyn was to spend his childhood.

Chapter 6

Events during 1837 left Sidney Herbert shaken and humiliated; Florence and her family were constantly in his thoughts. He lost confidence in his own abilities and took little part in parliamentary debate, spending more time in Wiltshire where his sister Mary Caroline supported him through the first traumatic months.

By the spring of 1838, when the child was safely placed with a loving family and the Nightingales were touring Europe, Sidney returned to the House of Commons and soon acquired a reputation as an excellent speaker.

In 1841, the Conservative government led by Sir Robert Peel regained power and Sidney was appointed First Secretary of the Admiralty, responsible for naval business in the Commons.

Sidney attended to parliamentary duties, sat out dull debates and made speeches from time to time, but his overriding pleasure was life as a country gentleman. With a love for Wilton amounting to a passion he spent all the time he could there, not choosing like many of his friends to devote himself solely to the social life of the city.

To plunge into the whirlpool of London society without some loss of singleness of heart was not possible, although probably few were less injured by its seductive influences than Sidney – but with one exception. He once more became fascinated by a woman of rebellious spirit and a careless disregard for social convention.

While his political career was advancing, Sidney began giving his family cause for anxiety by his association with one of the most notorious women of the day – the intriguing Mrs Caroline Norton – but even if Sidney had wanted to marry her, Caroline was not free.

Caroline was the second of three daughters born to Mr and Mrs Thomas Sheridan. Her father had suffered from tuberculosis and obtained a posting to South Africa as Colonial Treasurer in the hope the climate would help his condition. After only a few years he died and his wife returned to England, faced with the task of bringing up six children on a meagre income.

Caroline was a self-willed child and, when she was fifteen, her exasperated mother sent her with her youngest sister to school in Surrey. From here they were taken on occasions by their governess to visit nearby Wonersh Park, at the invitation of the landowner, Lord Grantley and his wife. Before long, Caroline's dark-haired beauty caught the attention of Lord Grantley's brother George, who wrote to Mrs Sheridan requesting her daughter's hand in marriage.

Caroline was shocked, she'd hardly noticed George and was not happy with marrying someone she did not love, but Mrs Sheridan considered marriage was not a business in which love played a part. George seemed a suitable match, as on the death of his childless brother he would inherit the Wonersh estate and title of Lord Grantley, but Caroline was only sixteen and her mother replied to George suggesting he might renew his proposal in three years.

When Caroline's second season drew to a close with no other matrimonial prospects, George renewed his offer. With her mother's encouragement, Caroline accepted and they were married when she was nineteen.

George was dull, slow and lacked ambition – although he'd trained as a lawyer and been called to the Bar, he was not a successful barrister. After being elected as Tory MP for Guildford, George decided he disliked parliament, was bored with law and waited only for the day when he would inherit his brother's title and retire to the country estate.

The Norton's marriage was a disaster from the beginning – two less compatible individuals it would be hard to imagine. George acted like a fish out of water in society, while Caroline was vivacious, egotistical and an outrageous flirt. Lack of money was to be a frequent cause of arguments and Caroline soon found her husband resorted to violence to end disputes, particularly when he had been drinking. Their first son, Fletcher, was born two years after their marriage.

Caroline used her considerable beauty and wit to establish herself as a society hostess but her unorthodox behaviour raised many eyebrows. She made enemies and admirers in equal measure, seeking revenge for her husband's bad behaviour by demoralising him in public and flirting with every man in the room.

Matters worsened when at the election of 1830, George lost both his seat at Guildford and his job, so now they were surviving on a small allowance which was hardly sufficient to pay the rent of their house near Downing Street. As a gifted writer, Caroline turned to prose and poetry as a means of earning money, burying herself in work as a distraction from her unfortunate marriage.

Caroline was a supporter of the Whigs and one regular visitor to her parties was William Lamb, Lord Melbourne, who soon became a close friend, benefactor and patron. At Caroline's request, Lord Melbourne appointed George as a stipendiary magistrate in Whitechapel, earning a generous £10,000 per year.

During 1831, Caroline's friendship with Lord Melbourne developed into something more intimate and he began to visit her while her husband was at work. George encouraged his visits, turning a blind eye as long as their friendship favoured his own interests, but when two further sons were born, their paternity was regarded by George as doubtful.

As Home Secretary, Lord Melbourne was the darling of Whig society – tall and conventionally good-looking, suave and debonair, with a mass of curly hair and beetling eyebrows. His intelligence and keen perception made him a brilliant conversationalist but he possessed dubious morals as far as women were concerned.

Caroline's close friendship with Melbourne was unwise – her reputation became compromised, she heard the gossip but disregarded it; he provided her with the attention she craved and she loved his company. Melbourne was flattered by her admiration but he should have known better than to expose Caroline to the possibility of scandal.

The Norton's marriage began to disintegrate. Caroline was refused access to her house and the children were sent away, so she went to stay in Wiltshire with her sister Georgiana. Private separation was discussed but George insisted on custody of the children and refused to make a financial settlement on his wife. Caroline wrote long passionate letters to Lord Melbourne but now, as Prime Minister, he could not be seen to be involved in the breakdown of the marriage and urged her to seek reconciliation.

Lord Grantley was keen to make political capital out of Caroline's romance with Melbourne, while George Norton came to see the affair as a potential source of income. With his brother's encouragement, George brought a case for criminal conversation between Lord Melbourne and Caroline, suing him for £10,000 damages for the loss of George's enjoyment of his wife's body and providing society with the cause célèbre of the year.

In June 1836, after nine hours in court, the case was dismissed but the public exposure threatened to bring down the government. Lord Melbourne's ardour for Mrs Norton cooled with indecent suddenness and, much to her annoyance, he soon moved on to other admirers, notably the young Queen Victoria.

George Norton's situation improved when he inherited a large house in Yorkshire and a considerable private income from a distant female relative. Divorce was now out of the question and George was given custody of the children, while Caroline, distraught at losing her sons, began a campaign to raise awareness of the injustice of the law.

As a result, the Infant Custody Act of 1839 was passed, giving custody of children under seven to their mother and the right of the non-custodial parent to access the child. The change of law only applied in England and Wales, so George sent the children to Scotland to live with his sister and well out of the reach of their mother.

Caroline was reintroduced into society by her sister, Georgiana, Lady Seymour, and was seen once again attending London functions, but was still regarded as a dangerous woman to know.

It was in the spring of 1842 when Sidney Herbert first met Caroline at a party given by Mr and Mrs Henry Pelham-Clinton. Sidney and Henry had been friends at Oxford and both served as MPs in Sir Robert Peel's first ministry.

Sidney was curious about the notorious Mrs Norton and was pleased to find her sitting next to him at dinner. Her appearance did not disappoint. Caroline was wearing a green satin dress with a square necked bodice cut low on her ample white bosom, her glossy violet black hair was piled high and ornamented by a peacock feather headpiece.

Caroline spoke first. 'Well Mr Herbert, how are things at the Admiralty?' her large brown eyes quizzically assessed him from under dark lashes.

'There's a great deal to be done, Mrs Norton,' said Sidney. 'Ships to build and a batch of ancient admirals to be put out to pasture.'

'Quite right, the Navy needs a good shake up,' she replied with a sweet, deep laugh.

'And what are you writing at present?' he asked.

'I'm engaged on a poem with a moral message – never forget the poor so often exploited by the privileged.' Caroline's voice was low and smooth as velvet. 'I find it strange that in a wealthy, civilised and powerful country like ours, there should exist so much poverty and ignorance. The poem was supposed to be published to celebrate the first birthday of Prince Albert but my life has been in turmoil recently.'

At that moment, the hostess interrupted their conversation by posing a question to Sidney, and Caroline began discussions with another guest.

After dinner, Caroline went with the ladies into the drawing room while Sidney remained with the men. Later in the evening, she walked across the room and stood alone by the adjoining door, Sidney became aware of her eyes fixed on him and could not help turning to see her lovely face.

'I'm leaving now,' she said. 'It was a great pleasure meeting you, Mr Herbert, please call on me soon.' She handed him her card.

'Of course, thank you for the invitation, Mrs Norton.' Sidney bowed as he accepted her card and held to his lips for a moment the perfumed hand she offered.

The following week Sidney called on Mrs Norton, now living at her uncle's home, and was shown into the drawing room with its dark walls, downy rugs and polished table gleaming in the light of candles. Caroline, dressed in a simple grey silk gown, greeted him with lowered eyes and a shy smile, motioning him to sit on a brown leather sofa while she settled in a blue damask easy chair opposite him.

'Well Mr Herbert, you're a brave man visiting such a vulgar, shocking woman without a chaperone – have you seen my horns and tail?' she asked.

Sidney smiled. 'I like to make my own judgements and not listen to gossip. I only see a talented, beautiful woman who clearly made the mistake of marrying someone she didn't love.'

'A terrible error of judgement,' agreed Caroline. 'When we first married I believed George had good qualities but I never had romantic feelings for him. To him I was an object, no more than a painting or a sculpture he could admire and show off to his friends. Not a living, breathing woman with a mind of her own and the temerity to disagree with his point of view from time to time.'

Caroline paused, twisting the rings on her fingers. 'I'm responsible for my own destiny and cannot complain, but the most important thing for me is, I must not lose my sons. If you had children you would understand my feelings.'

Sidney looked down at the floor for a moment. 'And how about you, Mr Herbert?' she asked. 'A man so charming and handsome must have a love story to tell.'

He raised his head and their eyes met. 'Yes, Mrs Norton, I did love someone once,' he said. 'You remind me of her. She too has a courageous spirit, the will to challenge injustice and make her own way in the world.'

Sidney fell silent and, understanding the subject was closed, Caroline said, 'Well I hope she succeeds. I'm not a feminist but I do believe women have the right to be educated and the opportunity to be independent, although education should not be confused with emancipation. Women should never dream of equality and of course men know better about everything – except what women know better. Now shall we have some refreshment?'

By the time had come for Sidney to leave, the couple knew they would see each other again. Caroline was two years older, Sidney was fascinated by her and although he did not speak to others of his feelings, before long everyone speculated about the relationship developing between him and Mrs Norton. Sidney became a frequent visitor and Caroline accompanied him to parties and dinners at the homes of his friends.

Disputes over access to the Nortons' children ended with tragedy when their youngest son, William, died from blood poisoning after a fall from his pony. George became contrite – their grief united them and he allowed the boys to spend half the year with their mother.

The uncle, with whom Caroline had been living, died and she had to find a new home. She used five hundred pounds advanced from her latest novel to put down as payment on No 3 Chesterfield Street, Mayfair, with her brother standing security for the lease.

Caroline lived alone with no chaperone or female companions and the gossip once again whirled about her. Undeterred, she continued to write and entertain her growing circle of literary and artistic acquaintances, including her new special friend Sidney Herbert, but she was not in good health and worried about the white plague of tuberculosis which had killed her father.

During the summer holidays of 1844, Caroline took her two boys to stay in a cottage on the Isle of Wight, where the sea air cleared her lungs and raised her spirits. Sidney joined them for a few days and they strolled on the sands together, drew sketches of the scenery and went sailing on a yacht called "Fanny". Sidney and Caroline had become close and from that summer, many were convinced they were lovers.

Sidney was not to remain long at the Admiralty. In 1845, when Gladstone's resignation triggered a reshuffle, Peel appointed him as Secretary at War. He accepted the Cabinet position with a sort of depression, realising this step would make it harder for him to escape the world of politics.

Caroline invited him to take her out to dinner to celebrate his promotion. She raised her glass. 'Congratulations, my dear Sidney, on a great achievement, so well deserved.'

'Thank you, Caroline, but I am not in love with politics and have outgrown personal ambition. Public life is so full of frustration and disappointment. Frankly I'd much prefer to spend more time at Wilton but my conscience tells me I've a duty to stay in town and try to help change things for the better.'

'It's wonderful that you put others before yourself,' she said. 'But you're starting to sound like George. I'm delighted your sense of duty keeps you in London. I loathe the country, all that running round muddy fields killing defenceless animals. Give me the excitements of the city any day.'

Caroline performed a little petulant toss of the wine glass as she lifted it to her lips and sipped swiftly. 'Wilton is like your mistress and I'm jealous of the power she has over you. She is waiting to lure you back to her and one day I'm sure she will succeed,' she said.

Sidney laughed. 'Perhaps she will. Events of recent years have made me think hard about the priorities of life and who knows what may happen in the future.'

In December 1845, the closeness of Sidney and Caroline's relationship landed them both in trouble. A story had appeared in *The Times* declaring Sir Robert Peel was to introduce a bill to repeal the Corn Laws, a decision triggered by a failed harvest and the need to free up more food for Ireland where famine was raging.

The leaked information allowed landowners to prepare to resist in the House of Commons what they considered to be an attack on their interests and the debate lasted for months.

Rumours flew that Sidney had told Caroline in confidence of Peel's plans and she'd sold the story to the paper's editor. No one who knew Sidney could suppose he was capable of betraying any secret entrusted to him, while it was unlikely that Caroline would have been so indiscrete. Lord Aberdeen was discovered to be the culprit but suspicions remained that Caroline had somehow been involved.

Peel's free trade measures were passed with the support of the Whigs but when it was clear no future help would be forthcoming, Peel resigned and Lord Russell became Whig Prime Minister, offering Sidney a post in his Cabinet, which he declined.

Some months later, Caroline's romance with Sidney ground to a halt. Lord Melbourne returned to London after several years in the country and was seen around in society once again with Caroline. Sidney had taken advantage of being out of office to spend more time at Wilton and heard about her flirtations in his absence. When they were together he accused her of ruining her reputation, while she in turn accused him of neglecting her and criticising her friends.

Sidney's family was putting great pressure on him and at thirty-five years old, he knew the time had come to settle down and produce heirs to secure the future of Wilton and the Pembroke dynasty. With sadness the couple talked matters over, deciding finally their affair had run its course and it was time they went their separate ways.

Caroline left England to spend time to recover from her broken romance in Ireland with her sister Helen and arrived feeling weary and dejected. All around was evidence of the famine, fields filled with blackened crops and abandoned houses. The whole scene seemed to mirror her own choked feelings as she gazed out miserably at the drizzling rain.

Not far from Wilton lived Lord Heytesbury, a distinguished diplomat and ambassador at St Petersburg. During his long absences abroad, the family of his brother, General à Court, had occupied the house and become friendly with the Herberts.

As a child, the à Court's daughter, Elizabeth, had been fascinated by Sidney and declared to her family she could never marry anyone but him. Now she was twenty-four years old, a beautiful, petite young woman with dark hair and eyes, an olive complexion and a kind nature. Countess Pembroke had always been charmed by Liz, considering her to be the perfect match for her beloved son.

So it was that on 12th August 1846, Elizabeth à Court had her way when she and Sidney Herbert became man and wife.

Chapter 7

The start of the Nightingales' European tour in 1837 was not a success – the scenery was boring, the family stayed in hotels serving inedible food and slept in unclean beds. It was not until they arrived in Nice, just before Christmas, that Florence's spirits rose and gradually her pretty bloom and light-heartedness began to return. Her father had rented comfortable lodgings and they were soon introduced into the British society of the city, joining in the seasonal celebrations where Florence developed a passion for dancing.

The party moved on to Italy, first visiting Genoa and Pisa before travelling on to Florence where they stayed for some months. Florence loved the city of her birth and everything Italian, especially the opera. Fanny held "at homes" attended by fashionable local high society, WEN took the girls to museums and art galleries and every day there were lessons from the best teachers in Italian, piano, singing and drawing.

The Italian lakes were next on the itinerary and then to Geneva where WEN had stayed before his marriage and was keen to renew old friendships. After a few weeks the Nightingales travelled to Paris, taking over a splendid apartment in the Place Vendôme where they were to stay for four months. The family's time in Paris was enlivened by a meeting with Mary Clarke, a forty-five year old English woman of unconventional dress and manner with a mop of unfashionably dishevelled red hair.

Mary considered herself a solitary female intellectual – she could paint and write but it was as a social hostess and conversationalist that she excelled. She claimed equality with men because of her intellect and longed to spend her life applying her talents in some way for the public good. Florence adored her.

Mary took the excited girls everywhere – parties, concerts, galleries, receptions and balls. She had a long-standing relationship with one of the most charming men in Paris, a well-known scholar called Claude Fauriel. She was in love with him and would have married him if he'd asked her but Claude was known for his many affairs, causing Mary agonies of jealousy. The couple met daily, entertained and travelled together but they were friends and not lovers.

Florence was fascinated by the unconventional nature of their relationship and realised for the first time it was possible for a woman to enjoy, without passion or scandal, a close intimacy and friendship with a man to whom she wasn't married.

Eighteen months after they'd left, the Nightingale family returned to England. Fanny was well satisfied, her husband had been right – the tour had proved the ideal way of putting the unfortunate past behind them. Now they could face English society once more and regain their proud sense of family respectability.

While they were away, Florence had been admired for her beauty and intelligence but her reserved manner had kept potential suitors at bay. She was now aged nineteen and her mother was not expecting her daughter's future path to finding true love to be an easy one.

For Florence the brief halcyon interlude was over. Romance was no longer appealing – she'd loved and lost Sidney and disgraced herself by bearing a child. Her conscience now awoke – it was two years since God had spoken to her. When would He speak again? She'd almost forgotten her sins with the pleasure of balls and operas, she must somehow find a way to make herself worthy of God's forgiveness and devote her life to the service of others. The time had come for her to overcome the temptation to shine and turn her back on society.

As the renovations to Embley Park were not yet completed, the family spent the season in London where Florence was once more caught up in the whirl of parties and dances. She desperately needed a special confidante whom she would have chosen to be her cousin, Marianne Nicolson, but Marianne was absorbed only by her own large family, especially her elder brother, Henry.

At the end of July, the Nightingales returned to Lea Hurst, taking with them Henry who was going up to Cambridge University in the autumn and wished to spend the summer improving his mathematics. By the end of August, Henry was in love with Florence. The love was not returned but for a while she encouraged his attentions, wrongly thinking their relationship would please Marianne and bring her closer.

In September the family moved down to Embley, by now a handsome house decorated and furnished in the latest and most luxurious fashion with all the paraphernalia of gentility. The whole place was a constant flurry of activity with innumerable staff working from their warm and cheerful quarters in the basement to maintain order in the Nightingale household.

By the New Year Florence was miserable and irritable – county society was boring and Marianne unsympathetic, she missed Sidney and worried about their child. The long walks she took with her spaniel Venus cleared her head and allowed her to be alone to think but brought her no closer to understanding how to achieve worthiness. She turned for help to another cousin, Hilary Bonham Carter, eldest of six daughters of Fanny's sister, Aunt Joanna.

Hilary was a year older than Florence and had been devoted to her since childhood. She was pretty with a small, pointed face framed in a mass of wavy brown hair, large eyes and an expression of sweetness and intelligence. When Hilary's father died, she had taken on the support of her mother, a nervous, impractical woman overwhelmed by the responsibility of bringing up a large family unaided.

Florence wrote long letters to Hilary describing her dissatisfactions with life but the secret of her affair with Sidney, the baby and her vision she confided to no one. Her cousin wrote back with sympathetic words of encouragement, giving comfort to Florence that at least one person in the family understood her.

Then a letter arrived addressed to her, bearing the Herbert family stamp. She took it to her room to read in private with her heart pounding and hands shaking.

'My dear Florence – I understand from the Bracebridges you have returned to Embley after your European tour which I hope you found enjoyable. I know you must be anxious about the child so I am writing to reassure you he has been safely placed with the Llewellyn family where he already has two older brothers. He was christened David Herbert and I considered it a great privilege to stand as his godfather to retain some influence on his future.

The family is now settled in a small village in Wiltshire, where Reverend Llewellyn holds the living and my sister Mary Caroline, in whom I have confided, is nearby. I am convinced this family will bring David up with loving care as their own son.

I hope my news helps to calm any misgivings you may have had and if you think it appropriate I should be happy to write to you again to report on David's progress. I know this whole affair has been a terrible trial for you and your family. I am deeply sorry for the suffering I have caused and hope one day you will find it in your heart to forgive me. God bless you. Your loving friend Sidney Herbert.'

There were only these few words in his neatly flowing hand and she re-read the letter many times before the significance of the details became clear. Their child was now part of another family and David must never know the identity of his birth parents. Sidney had chosen to help guide their son through life and was offering Florence an opportunity to be involved.

How should she reply? Would it be less hurtful to accept David was no longer hers and decline news of him? Or would that be too great a sacrifice, when by hearing about their son she would also have Sidney back in her life? She excused herself from dinner that night and went to bed, her head spinning with the questions she had to answer. After a few days she replied to Sidney's letter.

My dear Sidney – I was very glad to receive news of the child and to know David has been accepted as part of a loving Christian family is a great comfort to me. To give him up was a terrible anguish I shall never forget. Of course I forgive you and must also take blame for stepping beyond the accepted behaviour of our society, even in the name of love.

The direction of my life is still unsure, although I'm destined in some way to devote myself to the service of others as redemption for my sins. I'm resolved not to be unhappy about you and would value your help in my search for atonement.

My family have supported me through these last traumatic years and are returning now to their everyday lives as best they can. Although I should be pleased to hear of David's progress, I would prefer to keep any correspondence confidential between ourselves and I hope you will respect my wishes. I remain, dear Sidney, yours very sincerely – Florence Nightingale.'

Florence made the decision that her family was not to be further involved. As far as they were concerned, the child no longer existed and Florence did not wish to disturb their equilibrium. She was not however, prepared to forego the opportunity of keeping David in her life, hugging this secret released a feeling of happiness she had not experienced for a long time.

On receiving her letter Sidney understood Florence's point of view; amongst all his family only Mary Caroline knew of his contact with the child and he intended to keep it that way. He was not sure how he could help Florence with her search for atonement but he hoped some way might be found to make up for all the tears she had shed. From now on, Sidney would write to her each year on the anniversary of David's birth and send news of their son's life.

WEN's sister, Aunt Mai, invited Florence to stay at her home. Florence had developed an interest in mathematics and perhaps life would be more fulfilling if she were to be allowed to study. Aunt Mai wrote to Fanny asking if a personal tutor could be employed but Fanny did not approve, replying:

'Household duties should not be neglected for mathematics – what use would they be to a married woman? Everyone knows a clever wife brings no peace to a house.'

Florence was bitterly disappointed. Fanny continued to exploit Florence's guilt for disgracing the family by controlling her ambitions, while her daughter found the joyless days of distasteful occupation harder and harder to bear. There lay between herself and her mother a barrier of issues on which they could never agree and about which it was better not to speak.

Florence never seemed to have a moment alone – her days were filled with trifling requests and needless tasks, pursued by clutching hordes of servants, guests and relations, when all she wanted was peace and quiet to study.

In March the following year, the Nightingales were in London for the season and took rooms at the Burlington Hotel as usual. Florence, now nearly twenty years old, was becoming a well-known figure in society. Intellectual and witty, she danced beautifully and was an excellent mimic but she continually reproached herself for her social success – the path to redemption must be paved with far more serious challenges. Henry Nicholson continued to pursue her but this time she told him the relationship could go no further, thus abandoning hope of Marianne's friendship and causing a severe rift between the two families.

In May the family attended a party given by their friends, the Palmerstons, and were introduced to Richard Monckton Milnes. Florence was not at first attracted to him – a short, round man with olive blonde hair hanging almost to his collar and a deep dimple where his chin should have been. His appearance was a little dishevelled with a loosely fastened crumpled white cravat and faint stains of last night's soup down the front of his red satin waistcoat.

'I am delighted to meet you all,' said Richard in a warm and hearty manner. 'I hear you are acquainted with Sidney Herbert?'

WEN looked down and shuffled his feet, Fanny coughed, Parthe laughed her nervous laugh. Florence managed to remain calm and replied, 'Oh yes, we've known him for years but have lost touch recently.'

'Charming man – we serve together under Peel – I'm MP for Pontefract,' Richard continued. 'We meet occasionally at Caroline Norton's house. Do you know her?' The Nightingales shook their heads. 'Lovely woman, wonderful writer – going through a bad time with her cad of a husband – think Sidney is sweet on her but she'll never be available.'

Florence felt a little faint and was relieved when Richard changed the subject. 'Understand you know Europe well?' The rest of the conversation was taken up with travel reminiscences. His lively, entertaining chatter distracted from his rather unattractive first impression and as the evening wore on, Florence found him an amusing and clever companion with whom she had a great deal in common.

Educated at Trinity College, Cambridge, Richard had joined the literary set and been elected a member of the Apostles, an elite debating club, where he became friendly with an artistic group including Alfred Lord Tennyson. After Cambridge, he studied in Bonn then travelled extensively in Italy and Greece, visiting many of the places with which the Nightingales were familiar.

Richard was a man of the world by profession and loved

contact with society. The breakfast parties he held at his London home, Effingham House in Piccadilly, were famous for assembling the geniuses and celebrities of the day, with mutton pie served as a favourite dish. Richard tended to see only good in everyone and everything, a characteristic which, although admirable, did not equip him too well for the business of life. He wrote thoughtful, sensitive but uninspired poetry and was quick to appreciate the talent of others, acting as a benevolent patron to many young writers.

Richard was Fanny's idea of an ideal suitor and she invited him to Embley where he entertained the Nightingales with amusing anecdotes of the great characters of the day. After dinner he would stand with his hands half thrust into his waistcoat pockets, quoting extracts from his poems and singing to them in a sweet, clear voice, accompanied by Parthe on the piano.

Florence enjoyed his company although he was eleven years older and did not arouse anything like the passion she had felt for Sidney. On the other hand, he was kind and compassionate with a generous respect for her intelligence and sympathetic towards her aspirations to do something positive with her life. She was fascinated by the complexity of his character – one minute funny and outrageous, the next solemnly explaining his work with juvenile criminals or his recent trip to Ireland to view the impact of the famine.

Richard invited Florence to a conference of the British Association for the Advancement for Science held in Southampton, where they admired the astronomical section, boasting the largest reflecting telescope in the world. He impressed her with stories of his adventures of going down in a diving bell and of flying up in a hot air balloon. The couple were introduced to leaders of the scientific world, who talked earnestly on their own particular subjects but had not much to say on any others.

On their return to Embley, Florence remarked she would need to buy a new bonnet to accommodate her brain, so enlarged by all she had learnt. Richard made her laugh and they talked for hours about science, literature, poetry and important issues of the day. He was falling in love with her and by the end of July, when the family moved up to Lea Hurst for the summer, Richard was treated as one of the family.

He asked Florence to marry him but she was reluctant to commit and told him he must wait for an answer.

Chapter 8

During the family's summer visit to Lea Hurst in 1843, Florence became obsessed by the misfortunes of others, economic conditions were deteriorating, the widespread failure of grain crops created food shortages. The crisis in agriculture was accompanied by industrial and financial collapse, many people lost their jobs. The crime rate was higher than at any other time in the century; workhouses, hospitals and prisons were overflowing.

Residents of the nearby village, The Hollow, were mostly agricultural labourers but also living there were home knitters employed by master hosier John Smedley. Framework knitting had been an attractive occupation for generations, with often whole families working in their homes on hired frames. Now they were reduced from respectable artisans to workers on the edge of starvation, unable to compete with machine powered looms in mills and factories.

Florence was convinced that it was her duty to help them and set to work visiting the needy, taking food, bedding and clothes badgered from her mother. The efficient and reassuring care of the nurses in Rouen during the trauma of childbirth had profoundly affected her and by realising the importance of nursing to help ease the suffering outside her own comfortable life, Florence at last took one step along her path to worthiness.

Simple remedies were made up at home – cough syrup of honey, lemon juice and sage, a balm of beeswax and herbs to soothe rough, sore skin. One sick old woman she washed and dressed in a new nightshift, laying her in a bed of freshly laundered sheets, propped up on pillows filled with lavender, rose petals and chamomile. She smoothed back under her patient's cap the hair sticking to her moist brow, fed her warm milk and lightly cooked eggs, then sat holding her hand until the old lady fell into a peaceful sleep.

When the time came to return to Embley she didn't want to leave. How could she achieve anything worthwhile when she was constantly on the move?

'Mama I'm needed here – can you not return without me?' she implored.

'Of course not, Florence – we have social obligations in Embley and you must be part of them. Now get yourself ready as we leave tomorrow,' replied her mother.

Florence was exasperated. 'It's like talking to fog,' she thought.

Her relationship with her mother reached breaking point, Fanny desperately wanted her daughter to be involved in the society she had so carefully nurtured and secure a suitable husband but Florence wanted none of it – stubbornness and misery resulted on both sides.

'How far from simple is this business of marrying off one's daughters,' mused Fanny. 'Obstinacy endured, decisions brooded over, money wasted, not to mention disputes with my dear husband.'

Whenever the situation seemed most hopeless, Florence reached into a secret drawer in her writing desk for the small black velvet box containing the turquoise and pearl heart-shaped pendant, hidden with her precious letters from Sidney.

Although separated from each other, Sidney was still with her. Tears filled her eyes as she remembered how much she'd loved him, but the knowledge of their child growing up in a caring family consoled her and she prayed his life would be a happy one. Florence could not be a mother to David but she knew Sidney would look after him – her life must now be devoted to helping others less fortunate.

Christmas that year was spent with the Nicholsons at Waverley and Cousin Marianne hardly spoke to her, still annoyed that Florence had rejected her brother Henry. In spite of the noisy family around her, Florence was lonely and needed a friend. She confided her problems to Aunt Hannah, her uncle's sister, a deeply religious woman with the purity of a nun.

The old lady could see Florence was unhappy, not on good terms with her family and believed she could provide the solution – union with God would bring Florence reconciliation with her earthly worries.

'You don't know what it's like when one has sinned as badly as I've done,' Florence explained to her aunt. 'In spite of all my advantages I've still sinned and am constantly tormented. Will I ever be forgiven?'

'God's grace is not guided by human considerations, sometimes it comes to those who are unprepared – not to those who strive for it,' replied Aunt Hannah. 'One has to keep one's eyes open to see the Light. I want you to experience happiness like mine, feeling His presence always in my heart.'

She leant over and took Florence's hand. 'You may consider yourself unworthy but if you truly believe, then your sin will be atoned for by your faith. As a believer you cannot be unhappy, because you're not alone – that is how true faith works.'

Florence was not convinced – in her view passive faith on its own was not enough, more action needed to be taken. She mentioned nothing to Aunt Hannah about her vision, neither did she tell her she sought union with God not as a submission, but as a necessary preparation for her longed-for path to redemption. Her frustrations remained and she was still weary with the monotony of joyless leisure.

One morning at breakfast, Fanny announced she was taking Parthe to London for a few days to buy some new outfits. 'Florence, why don't you ask Hilary over to stay while we're away?'

Florence was eager to see her favourite cousin and wrote at once inviting her. The weather was fine and sunny for March. The two women called for the gig, donned woollen bonnets, warm cloaks and stout boots to take Venus for a walk in the New Forest where the trees started to show the first promise of spring, while a cacophony of birdsong celebrated the end of winter.

'It's such a relief to have someone to talk to, Hilary. Mama and I've quite different ideas of how life should be lived – trying to explain I need to leave home is like shaking a red rag at a bull. Does love for one's mother come quite by nature? Will I ever escape the monotony of domesticity?'

'When I was in Paris recently,' Hilary replied, 'Mary Clarke encouraged me to take classes in fashion design – it's what I've always wanted and it seems I have some talent.'

'Well that's wonderful for you,' Florence said.

'But when I asked Mama if I could continue training in London, she said I couldn't be spared. She mustn't be left alone and I was needed at home.'

Florence was annoyed. 'That's just what I mean – your career wrecked, your talents wasted – how can this be allowed?'

'It's disappointing, but what can I do? You're good with words – your letters are so entertaining. Why don't you take up writing and perhaps earn a little money?' asked Hilary.

Florence smiled. 'That's kind of you but writing as a living doesn't appeal,' she said. 'My thoughts need to be expressed in actions, not words. I want to work and perform good deeds, not sit in some dark study all day, churning out platitudes to end up forgotten and unread on dusty library shelves.'

Hilary laughed. 'You could always marry Richard.'

Florence pulled a face. 'Yes I suppose I could but don't let's talk about that now.' She put her arm round her cousin's waist and the two continued their walk, content in each other's company, followed by an excited Venus barking happily as she chased squirrels through the woods.

Spring flew swiftly by and summer came. In June, Florence reached another important turning point of her life when Dr Gridley Howe, an American philanthropist, and his wife Julia came to stay at Embley. Dr Howe had founded an institute for the blind in Boston and formulated a scheme to enable any American citizen who was old or ill to have access to medicine and nursing.

Florence invited him to take a walk with her in the garden, with the excuse of showing off the roses that were blooming particularly well that year.

After a while she asked him, 'Dr Howe, would you think it unsuitable or unbecoming for a young woman such as myself to devote her life to works of charity in hospitals the way Catholic sisters are able to do?'

'Florence my dear,' the doctor replied, 'there is never anything unladylike about doing your duty for the good of others. If you have a vocation for that way of life, then you should follow your aspirations.'

Dr Howe's affirmation was the spur she needed – her problem now was to convince her parents. A year passed and she was no further forward; at twenty-five years old the strain was telling; she was unhappy and frequently unwell. Then two family illnesses gave her the opportunity to practise her nursing.

In August she went with her father to visit her grandmother, Mary Shore, and, finding her to be seriously ill, was allowed to stay and take care of her. No sooner had her grandmother recovered than the girls' beloved old nurse, Mrs Gale, collapsed at Lea Hurst. Florence arranged for her to be moved down to Embley and nursed her until she died sitting upright in a chair with Florence holding her hand.

In the autumn there was an unusual amount of sickness among the cottagers in the nearby village of Wellow and Florence took an active part in their care. She sponged aching heads with vinegar, plumped pillows, changed bed linen, dispensed homemade remedies and reviving soups, but she could only do so much – she needed to be properly taught nursing knowledge and skills in order to make a real difference but how could this be achieved?

Florence's plan was to persuade her parents to allow her to

spend three months training at Salisbury Infirmary. Salisbury was only a few miles from Embley and the infirmary was a well-known hospital. The head physician, Dr Fowler, was a family friend who held advanced views and she was optimistic that he might support her. In December 1845 the Fowlers came to stay and, over dinner one night, Florence proposed her plan.

Fanny was horrified. 'What an idea! No respectable woman would become a hospital nurse – think of all the terrible diseases you could catch. Nurses are women of the street, drunk and immoral – isn't that so Dr Fowler?'

The doctor agreed that ward conditions were unsuitable for a lady of Florence's upbringing. 'The smell can be overpowering, the sanitation poor with beds crowded together and scant regard for clean bedding,' he told them. 'Nurses often sleep on the wards as they've no other homes. There's little discipline, the women fight amongst themselves and sometimes the police have to be called to restore order.'

Parthe had hysterics at the thought of it and WEN was equally disapproving.

'Florence,' he said, 'nursing is no way for a well-educated young lady like you to spend her life. You must forget the whole idea and concentrate on applying time to your studies and helping your mother.'

Florence was left defeated and depressed; she'd been hoping for her father's support. Surely something should be done to make hospitals better places for the sick?

Florence's life reverted to remorse and frustration. Her guilt trapped her and she was convinced the difficulties confronting her were God's punishment for her sins, but she had brought the sufferings on her own head.

She wrote to Hilary: *'I can see no point in living any more now that my plan for nursing has been refused. I shall never do anything with my life and am worthless. You ought not to care so much for me. I'm not good enough for you to worry about.'*

Florence spent her days behaving as a dutiful daughter, while at night she secretly studied the recently published *Blue Books* on public health and gradually developed knowledge of the importance of effective sanitary conditions. She experienced a gleam of triumph as she realised her understanding was quite equal to these peculiarly masculine topics.

A profound change in her character took place. Florence began to rebel against her lot and detach herself from those around her – love, marriage and even friendship must be renounced. There should be no place in her life for wants of her own, all her energies must now be devoted to achieving redemption by becoming a nurse, but how? That was the question she asked and asked and listened in vain for the answer.

A few months later Florence received from a friend *The Year Book of the Protestant Institution of Deaconesses* at a hospital in Kaiserswerth, Germany and realised here could be the opportunity for the training she'd been seeking. The religious atmosphere, the close supervision and discipline placed the nurses above suspicion – objections to English hospitals would not apply, but she still did not dare mention Kaiserswerth to Fanny who was busier than ever and Embley was filled for autumn parties.

Next spring, the Nightingales stayed in the Burlington Hotel for the season and Richard Monckton Milnes was a constant member of their party. Together they visited the theatre, museums and art galleries and admired the Palm House in Kew Gardens.

In the summer of 1846, the conference of the British Association for the Advancement of Science was held in Oxford.

Whilst Florence and Richard were resting, taking refreshments between lectures, Richard said, 'Saw Sidney Herbert the other day. He's left Caroline Norton and is to be married to Elizabeth á Court – sounds like a rushed kind of affair but seems the countess is fond of Liz and thinks it's time her son was settled.' He bit into a Bath bun, dropping crumbs down the front of his waistcoat.

Florence took a sip of lemonade while she composed herself. 'I'm happy for them – please pass on my good wishes to Mr Herbert when you next see him,' she said.

Richard's words sent a cold shiver through her heart. Although Florence had accepted that she and Sidney could never be together, there'd lingered an iota of hope but now it was gone and she felt strangely alone.

Florence may have thought her destiny did not include marriage but her desire to be loved was still strong. She could not face losing Richard, so avoided the moment when she would have to give him an answer and spent a great deal of time deliberating what marriage to him might be like. He seemed to understand her better than most, she knew he would satisfy her intellectually and be a loyal and sympathetic husband.

Florence could not help wondering what Richard would think of her if he knew about her past misdemeanours. Their occasional hugs and light kisses she found comforting but when he reached to touch her more intimately, she pulled away, experiencing none of the dizzying desire she had felt for Sidney.

Florence could be with Richard if they spent time working on projects together but the chances were she would become a society hostess, helping with his domestic arrangements, having his babies and organising his famous breakfast parties. To lose her independence for such a life would destroy her – she enjoyed Richard's company, craved his love and sympathy but did not want to marry him. She remembered Mary Clarke and Flauvier in Paris; why could she too not have such an arrangement?

Then her resolve began to waver. Maybe God was expecting too much from her? How could she ever achieve forgiveness if she was not given the opportunity to serve others? Life would be so much easier if she were to give in and marry Richard. Sidney was now married, why not her also?

Florence became pale and heavy eyed, filled with gloomy melancholy and worn out with the strains of life; fond as she usually was of walking in the gardens, even Venus could not persuade her to go outside. Her mother blamed her illness on nervousness and moping by which she meant it was imaginary and all the doctor could prescribe for her sorrowful condition were tablespoonfuls of nauseous mixture, but it was not a medicinal remedy she needed.

Their friends, the Bracebridges, heard about her unhappiness and took pity on her. Selina Bracebridge was twenty years older than Florence, a beautiful, intellectual woman with a warm and caring nature. She and her husband, Charles, were planning to spend the winter in Rome and persuaded Fanny it would be good for Florence to accompany them. Joining their party while on a delayed honeymoon were to be Sidney and his new wife, Liz, whom Selina had known since she was a young girl.

When Florence had heard of Sidney's marriage, she was envious of his happiness but knew their child provided a bond which could never be broken. While she willingly accepted the Bracebridge's offer, the real longing was to see Sidney. Over the last eight years she had eagerly awaited his annual letters – now, after a decade apart, she wanted him back in her life and the joy of feeling some nearness to him.

Fanny and WEN were concerned about how Florence would react to meeting Mr Herbert again but considered enough time had elapsed for their ardour to have cooled – he was after all married and the child forgotten.

Florence was now an attractive young woman of twenty seven, the unhappiness of her life concealed beneath a veneer of polite social graces. The day after the party arrived in Rome a reception had been arranged for them followed by dinner and Florence arrived with the Bracebridges, her usual serenity disturbed by the anticipation of this longed-for meeting.

Selina noticed them first. 'Oh good – there are the

honeymooners,' she said.

Florence rarely blushed but when she saw Sidney advancing towards them she felt the tell-tale warmth on her face.

Selina called out, 'Sidney, Liz – over here – you both look so well, marriage must suit you,' and she planted kisses on their cheeks. 'Now Sidney, you remember Miss Nightingale?'

Florence held out an unsteady hand which he pressed to his lips for a moment without speaking. Their eyes met and in that single glance a dozen messages were exchanged.

Then Sidney spoke, 'Good evening, Florence – how delightful to see you again after all these years. May I introduce my wife?'

Florence regained her composure. 'Such a pleasure to meet you, Mrs Herbert – is this your first time in Rome?'

'Please do call me Liz. Yes, this is my first trip – I'm so excited to see the wonders of the city – I expect you know them all well.'

'Oh no, I've not visited before either.' She noted with a sinking heart how beautiful Liz was and how attentively Sidney was behaving towards her – Florence did not enjoy the feeling of exclusion.

'Well maybe you would join us in some sightseeing and we could experience the glories of Rome together.' The new Mrs Herbert spoke in such a friendly manner that Florence could not refuse.

Sidney was as handsome as she'd remembered – tall and graceful, a few grey streaks now visible in his dark blonde hair and his warm smile revealing small creases in the corners of his brown eyes.

Liz possessed a captivating manner and an eagerness to please which made her a delightful companion. When they were alone, she confided to Florence that she worshipped her husband and wanted to share in everything he did although she worried she was not clever or amusing enough for him.

Unable to sleep that night, Florence allowed herself to think back to the few precious hours when she and Sidney had lain together in her bed at the Burlington.

She trembled as she remembered the exquisite touch of his firm young body, the sensual smell of his soft warm skin and the comforting whispered words. She'd cried out when he entered her – then with a shudder and a moan it was over, his arms wrapped round her like a soothing blanket, a divine experience of love and peace – one glorious hidden secret which would never be forgotten.

Chapter 9

In February 1848, David Herbert Llewellyn, aged ten years and a few months, left the comfort of his vicarage home to continue his education at Marlborough College, six miles from Easton Royal. All pupils were required to board so, like his brothers, he was allocated a dormitory in Preshute boarding house, a short walk from the main school buildings.

David faced his future with excitement but also some trepidation as the prospect before him had not been painted in rosy hues. His brothers, John and Arthur, had been two of the first pupils when the school had opened in August 1843 and delighted in frightening him with terrible tales of their experiences. John was now in the sixth form and Arthur in the fourth.

The impetus to set up a school for the sons of clergymen came from the need to build new churches in cities to accommodate the crowds flocking there for employment. Extra priests were required and the conclusion reached that these would most likely come from the sons of those already in holy orders.

The school could have been anywhere in the south of England. The coaching inn at Marlborough had been bankrupted with the coming of the railways and the lease on the site became available. A meeting was called and a governing body formed with the Bishop of Salisbury in the chair. The governors were clergymen, country gentlemen and lawyers – none of them had any previous experience whatsoever in setting up a school. One of the enthusiastic founding governors was Earl Bruce, Mary Caroline's husband.

The school buildings consisted of the old coaching inn and a smaller house lived in by the master, with three adjoining classrooms for the fifth and sixth forms and for the teaching of

German and drawing. The rest of the pupils were divided according to age into forms with two removes, all crowded into one large schoolroom.

The great majority of the pupils had never been away from home before – this was not a privileged or luxurious life, the boys needed to be robust and resilient to cope. Economies were made on everything but teaching – minimum food, heating, comfort and privacy. School terms ran from August to December and from February to June with no breaks. There was no school uniform, the pupils wore coats of all shapes and colours, knee breeches, grey woollen stockings, black boots and stiff peaked black cloth caps.

The first master, Reverend Matthew Wilkinson, was an excellent scholar, a man of an amiable disposition with a sonorous bass voice, but he was not good at delegation and soon sunk under the burden of his responsibilities. He wore a cassock tied round his waist with a scarf, which, coupled with his short, slim figure, gave him a rather effeminate appearance.

The rest of the teaching staff was composed of six masters in holy orders, plus two English masters, a French master and a teacher of German and drawing. There were no organised sports or physical activities, the boys clubbed together to buy equipment for informal games of cricket and football on Marlborough Common.

After being shut up in the classroom all day, pupils drifted by natural selection into groups called "tribes" which herded together in the school grounds and went off on rural expeditions. The excited boys roamed freely round the countryside exploring the Savernake Forest or along the River Kennet and rampaged over adjacent farmland becoming poachers, rat catchers and raiders of henhouses. Their behaviour was initially tolerated by the locals, but patience soon wore thin and fierce encounters with infuriated farmers became commonplace. Some of the boys would go swimming in the river dressed in only their underwear but

David's fear of water prevented him from joining them.

Fights between tribes were frequent, bullying became ferocious and rules were regularly broken. The smaller boys were not regarded with much favour by those larger than themselves and their lives became one long struggle for existence.

David was allowed three pence a week pocket money which he normally spent on extra food as school rations were sparse and he was always hungry. One new boy had the temerity to ask for an extra slice of pie at dinner and was threatened with the cane for his impertinence. David soon learned he must remain content with what the gods provided and no more.

Fines from pocket money were common. Boys queued up on Saturday mornings for the distribution of their long-awaited pennies. On one occasion David received a stony stare from the master who exclaimed, 'Boy, do not expect any pocket money for the next four weeks. You were spotted climbing a tree and have been fined one shilling.' David protested his innocence but the master dismissed his pleas, saying it was his fault for looking like the culprit. David described this injustice to Mr Herbert in his monthly letter and was delighted to receive a shilling enclosed with his godfather's reply.

Canes were produced from the masters' desks at the slightest provocation, descending on the backs of the unfortunate, watched with rapt attention by the other boys. Some of a more sensitive nature gave up the struggle and ran away, causing their whole form to be confined to school grounds. Those who escaped were quickly caught, returned to school and publicly flogged.

David learnt to cope with the hard knocks and harsh words of his school life. He was required to fag for a prefect, Augustus Twyford, a graceful lad of what seemed to David monstrous height with eyes set close together, giving him a rather sinister look.

Augustus possessed fearful appendages on his face called whiskers, which excited general admiration and were supposed to make him irresistible to the opposite sex. He was a friend of

David's elder brother, John, and proved to be a considerate master, requiring David to perform menial tasks like boot cleaning and fetching books, in return for protection from school bullies.

David was keen to do well in his studies, although he was given his share of the cane for not achieving the marks required. His teacher was convinced his inability to grasp Latin conjugations was mere carelessness, warning him, 'Listen boy, if you fail to seize this golden opportunity to learn, you will live to regret it.'

The beatings turned his back all colours of the rainbow. At night he cried himself to sleep with his head under the blankets hoping the other boys would not hear him and prayed, 'God bless my family and please always let me remember my Latin.'

After one particularly trying week, a bright and original idea occurred to David which he discussed with his friend, James Golding. Could they perhaps escape for a few days to the peace of the school sanatorium? Assuming sad faces and a dejected air, the couple arrived at the surgery and rang the bell.

A maid appeared, asking what they wanted. 'Please Miss, we're not feeling well and would like to see Dr Gardiner,' David answered. The good lady gave them a look indicating they would be wise to return to school but instead they sat on a bench awaiting the doctor's arrival.

Kindly Dr Gardiner was not available that day and his young assistant was instead on duty. After eyeing the boys for a few moments, he demanded to know from David what ailed him and on receiving the answer, 'headache and sore throat', the assistant burst out laughing.

He then turned to James asking, 'I presume you have the same complaint?' When James admitted this was true, the assistant laughed again and disappeared to a room where drugs were kept, returning with two large glasses filled with a dark nauseous mixture. Still laughing, he watched while the boys reluctantly swallowed the fearful potion and then ejected them from the surgery.

David wrote to his godfather with news of his progress and life at the school:

'Dear Mr Herbert – I am writing to let you know I received top marks for a science test last week. Science is one of my favourite subjects and is not a hardship like Latin. I'm not sure I will ever understand how to conjugate verbs or write grammar. My teacher is quite despairing and gave me three whips of the cane for my lack of application. The lessons are easy for him and he cannot comprehend why I have difficulty learning them.

The boys are mostly friendly although some of the older ones are best avoided if possible. My brothers try to protect me but they are often not nearby when trouble approaches. Being Lent our food is not plentiful – I feel famished and miss my mother's pies. Quite a few boys have scarlet fever so we may have to go home early this term which would be a good thing. I hope you are well. Your loving godson – David Herbert Llewellyn.'

A few days later David received Sidney's reply.

'My dear David – well done for your excellent science test results. Do not be too concerned about Latin as I am sure you will soon come to terms with all its intricacies. I also found the language hard to start with and never liked it very much. I am hoping you will enjoy the contents of the hamper I have sent and the enclosed pocket money is for you to spend on extra food. Please do your best not to catch scarlet fever as it is a horrible illness which can have long lasting effects.

I am busy with estate business in Wilton just now which suits me much better than parliamentary affairs. I hope to travel over and see you when I visit my sister at Tottenham House. School life can sometimes be difficult but try to be brave, choose your friends carefully and keep yourself out of trouble. God bless you – your loving godfather Sidney Herbert.'

The cases of scarlet fever increased, the school was closed and the Llewellyn brothers returned home for a welcome holiday until their return in August.

The great rebellion in the autumn of 1851 was the result of growing anarchy and demoralisation, the school was totally out of control. One privilege after another had been removed and each blow brought more resentment and retaliation. The general feeling between the boys and masters was one of distrust and enmity – not surprising when the cane was always on the go.

Among the objects of the boys' dislike was the gate sergeant, Peviar, who was apt to be over conscientious in his duties and between him and the school there existed a bitter and perennial feud. One evening in October, an attack of a particularly vicious nature was made with stones being hurled at Peviar's gatehouse. The victim reported the matter and the whole school were confined to classrooms during free time for the foreseeable future.

The punishment so incensed the boys that for four days they refused to work, broke out in the evenings whenever possible, smashed windows and pelted masters who attempted to keep order. The master decided wholesale punishment was futile and rescinded the order but expelled five boys found to have led the attack.

November 5th was approaching. The boys decided to raise their spirits with a fireworks display, which was strictly against the rules but they organised a collection and purchased a large amount of squibs, crackers and rockets.

On Guy Fawkes Day, as soon as it was dark, a rocket shot up from the centre of court and the rebellion had begun. For the whole evening the court was ablaze, authority was paralysed. Fireworks were carried into classrooms, let off under desks and thrown into fires. All night the noise continued – the college reeked of gunpowder for days.

Mr Wilkinson expelled the pupils judged to be most guilty. One of the victims was popular Augustus Twyford, who'd been treasurer of the firework fund and his selection seemed to the boys to be unfair.

As Augustus set off in a horse and fly on his way home, David joined in with the entire school as they broke out of the gates and followed him up the High Street, shouting and cheering, with townsfolk joining in the general uproar. The feelings of resentment ran so high that many boys were in tears, including David who was incensed at seeing his friend and protector leaving in such an unjust and dishonourable fashion.

When the noisy mob returned to college, they rushed to the master's room and smashed every pane of glass. The bell rang for classes but when the masters arrived, uproar greeted them and their appeals for calm were drowned out by shouting, slamming of desks and stamping of feet. Anarchy reigned, Peviar was knocked down and an outside building set on fire.

The next morning the master called together members of the Senior School, addressing them in his most sonorous voice.

'In recent days, we have witnessed some disgraceful behaviour from you boys that cannot be tolerated,' he said. 'However, I have listened to your grievances and concluded you may have been somewhat unfairly treated in the past.' Cries of 'hear, hear' were heard.

'I've decided that from tomorrow,' the master continued, 'the constraints placed on your free time will be lifted.' Loud cheers. 'In addition, all masters have been advised that use of the cane should be restricted to misdemeanours of only the most serious kind.' Even louder cheers.

'However, these concessions are conditional on a marked improvement in your behaviour. In addition, one shilling will be deducted from the pocket money of each one of you to pay for the damage caused.' A hum of disappointment echoed round the hall.

'I shall also expect a letter of apology to Mr Peviar on my desk by midday tomorrow. That is all, you are dismissed.' The boys returned to their classrooms feeling relieved and somewhat vindicated for the chaos they had caused.

Mr Wilkinson resigned at the end of the school year and returned to the quiet life of a country clergyman. His successor was the Reverend George Edward Lych Cotton who arrived from Rugby School where he'd worked with the legendary school reformer Dr Thomas Arnold.

Reverend Lych Cotton was a reserved character, satirical and grim in his manner but he possessed kindliness and a dry sense of humour which was much appreciated by the boys. He set about tackling discipline and school reform, investing the sixth form with powers and responsibilities that encouraged them to play an important part in the regeneration of the school.

The boys were persuaded to work for the love of learning, rather than from the dread of punishment. Fagging was legalised and limited, while prefects held courts for the judgement of school offences. A house system was inaugurated, organised games introduced and libraries established.

David and his fellow prefects were at first zealous, if not always wise, in the exercise of their new duties but, with experience over time, they learned how to earn the respect of the rest of the school and soon an atmosphere of loyalty and patriotism began which had never before existed.

David's last year at Marlborough College ended in June 1853 and soon he was to leave behind his vicarage home in Easton Royal to start a new life in London.

Chapter 10

During the six years between his marriage in 1846 and his return to the Cabinet, Sidney could not have been happier, his health was robust and the Herbert children were being born. The easing of his parliamentary duties enabled him to spend more time at Wilton and enjoy the rural pursuits on his estates.

In the autumn of 1848, while writing to Florence to update her with David's progress at Marlborough, Sidney added:

'The temptation to neglect public duties becomes very strong when one is so happy at home. Every day I realise how short life is and how miserably small the amount of usefulness any one man can produce, despite the best intentions. But in everything Liz is a comfort and assistance. I am so happy you and she are friends and we can once again play a part in each other's lives.'

Sidney's easy manner and modesty made him popular with his tenants – he remembered their names and took great efforts to keep in touch with events in their personal lives. House servants became virtually members of his family and those who were sick or retired were well looked after. The estate's increased income was reinvested to improve the tenants' living conditions as well as building new houses, roads and a church at Wilton.

The Herberts invited Florence to dinner at their London home in Belgrave Square, introducing her to their large circle of friends and on these occasions she was often accompanied by Richard Monkton Milnes.

Sidney was happy to see the couple together, he was confident that behind Richard's eccentric front he possessed an immense amount of kindness and humanity. The two men had started in politics at the same time and knew each other well. Richard's parliamentary speeches were generally a sign for the House to empty – flowery and contradictory, they caused much mirth amongst those who stayed to listen, with Richard himself having the good grace to join in the laughter.

Richard was delighted to escort Florence in the company of the Herberts; he'd always admired Sidney as a politician and was particularly envious of his popularity with Sir Robert Peel. Richard found Liz to be charming. She listened attentively to his endless chatter and laughed at his jokes but he did not consider her as witty and intelligent as either Caroline Norton or Florence.

With his sensitive understanding of human nature, Richard detected an undercurrent of emotion running between Florence and Sidney which he did not fully comprehend. He knew they'd been acquainted for years and regularly corresponded but there was something about the way they reacted and looked at each other on occasions which seemed to indicate a deeper connection. Richard was moved to write a poem he called *Shadows* to describe his observations of the couple.

Florence was still confused about her feelings for Richard and Parthe complicated her thoughts even more by remarking, 'Before you marry Richard, you'll have to tell him about the baby. Surely you couldn't live with such a lie?'

Although she was annoyed with her sister for her interference, Florence knew she was probably right. Was Richard's love strong enough to survive her shocking revelations? If she accepted him, it was a risk she would have to take.

Whilst at Embley, Florence kept herself busy by nursing the poor in the nearby village of Wellow. Fanny and Parthe were convinced she would bring home some dreadful illness to kill them all and her mother remarked, 'Why can't you take up teaching? – a much more suitable position for a woman of your learning and intelligence.'

To appease them she'd tried working in the school but decided she was not suited to the classroom; her heart was set on nursing. The seventh day of each month was devoted to assessing her life – the day she'd heard of her pregnancy all those years ago, the day of her divine experience. Still she prayed and waited for the revelation of her way to redemption.

In June 1849, Richard came to stay – he could not be put off any longer, now aged nearly forty he wanted to be married and start a family.

One evening, Florence and Richard were alone in the drawing room drinking coffee after dinner, Parthe and Fanny decided to retire early and WEN was in the library.

Richard leaned over, held her hands between his and, looking at her with infinite tenderness, said, 'Florence, my dear, we've known each other now for a long time and I think you understand how much I love you. Would you do me the great honour of becoming my wife?'

Here was the moment she'd dreaded, probably her last chance, how should she respond? She released her hands, avoided his gaze and began playing with her coffee spoon. Richard rose and walked to the mantelpiece where he rested his arm, waiting for her reply. The clock ticked, the fire crackled and so they remained for some minutes, close to each other but far apart in silence.

Florence stood up at last and looked at him, her fingers picking at the embroidery on her skirt. Trying to speak with perfect firmness, she said, 'Richard, you are very dear to me but my destiny is to devote my life to the service of others. I understand the value of what I refuse but I must tell you the simple truth. I shall never marry, not anybody at all, I can never have a life like other women. You are free now to choose someone else.'

At first he was silent, only his face expressed his extreme surprise and disappointment. Then he said, 'Surely I could help you achieve your destiny. What do we live for if not to make life easier for each other?'

Florence was not to change her mind. 'I do appreciate your

offer but although your intentions are honourable, I doubt very much they could be fulfilled. If we were to marry, I would be bound to domesticity and child rearing as any good wife must, but this is not how I wish to spend my life. Please do not think of me as ungrateful or proud.'

Richard became unusually quiet. He placed his head in his hands, gazing at the fire for a moment before he looked up and said, 'Florence, I shall never love anyone as I love you. I imagined our relationship was a passionate attachment on both sides. But now I see there are two different people in our love affair, the one who loves and the one who condescends to be so treated. I shall leave Embley early tomorrow morning and will not bother you again. Please pass my respects to your parents.'

He walked out of the room looking pale and miserable, leaving Florence alone. Her chin and lips trembled, the tears welled up and she began to sob. She had refused him for a destiny it seemed impossible to achieve – everything looked hopeless. She sat down by the fire, staring into the embers as if to read the future in them.

The spaniel Venus came in from her evening walk wagging her tail, bringing in the scent of fresh air. She pushed her head under Florence's hand then promptly curled up at her feet, sinking into blissful repose. Florence leant down to stroke the warm soft creature whispering, 'Oh dear little dog – how I wish my life was as simple as yours.'

When Florence told her parents the next day what had happened they were horrified. How could she turn down such a wonderful opportunity to overcome the misfortunes of the past? In Fanny's eyes, Richard had been the perfect match and now it was too late; to reject a proposal as she approached thirty was probably Florence's last chance of matrimony. Fanny was furious with her daughter and constantly reproached her for her stupidity, crying, 'Now you will end up as an old maid and break your mother's heart.'

Florence withdrew into herself to avoid confrontation. Mother and daughter were caught in a contest of wills in which love and kindness were often forgotten.

Florence was concerned too that she had lost her place in her father's favour when he accused her of forever trying to be different from other people. No real estrangement existed between them, yet there were obstacles in the way that neither of them seemed able to resolve.

WEN was not a person to show his feelings but he seemed now to have a permanent sadness about him. The Nightingales had been married for thirty years but his wife still retained the facility for saying things which drove him in the opposite direction to the one she desired. The differences between them were accentuated by time and they understood each other no better now than they had when they were first married. Family life was not as WEN had expected, he felt awkward in the society nurtured by his wife and kept out of it as much as he was allowed.

Disappointments with life made Fanny more extravagant, more unreasonable and voluble but she and Parthe agreed on every subject. Florence seemed absorbed in her own world, so silence and solitude became WEN's lot. Excuses were made to spend days away visiting the estates at Lea Hurst or his London club where he was well out of the reach of women. He avoided arguments at home by cutting short unpleasant discussions with a sarcastic remark, or by leaving the room.

Fanny would be heard complaining of her husband's frequent absences but was not always satisfied by his presence either. Florence wished that if her father could only show some authority they might be able to regain their old intimacy and once again walk, talk and laugh together.

Some months later, Richard and Florence met at a party in London. Florence was unsure she'd made the right decision and wanted to give him a chance to renew their relationship, but he hardly spoke and avoided her company. Richard had moved on to new challenges and a few months later Florence heard he was engaged to the Honourable Annabel Crewe of Madeley Manor.

Florence couldn't blame him but she wished it didn't hurt so much. She resolved once more to give up any happiness marriage might have given her and concentrate on doing what she could for others – the idea that something positive might be within her reach haunted her life like a passion.

Seeing her unhappiness, the Bracebridges persuaded Fanny to allow Florence to accompany them on a trip to Greece and Egypt. Florence tolerated the journey, behaved graciously and wrote letters home describing their travels. She became attached to a small owl she'd rescued from some boys at the Parthenon, christened it Athena and carried it around in her pocket for the rest of the holiday.

Florence passed the time by recording her thoughts in a small black notebook, reproving herself for her sinful past and what she perceived of as her lack of worth. Her thoughts were tortured by how happy the Herberts seemed together but now Sidney was back in her life, she was not going to let him go again – he must have a responsibility to help with her search for atonement. While she considered Liz was frivolous and possessed no depth, Florence was prepared to tolerate her friendship if doing so would keep Sidney close.

At the end of the trip, with the help of the Bracebridges but without her parents' knowledge, she visited the hospital at Kaiserswerth in Germany and was invited by Pastor Theodor Fliedner, the leader of a small Protestant group, to spend a short time there.

The town's main business of making velvet had failed some years before and the pastor had set out to raise funds for his impoverished flock. His apostolic journey had taken him to London where he'd met Elizabeth Fry, whose work among the prisoners of Newgate inspired him to return home to found the first German organisation for improving conditions in prisons. On realising that the women leaving prison had nowhere to go and no means of support, he and his wife encouraged them to lead new Christian lives by training them to nurse. The redundant velvet factory was turned into a hospital while a summerhouse became living quarters.

Florence returned home feeling exhilarated to have at last discovered a respectable way to learn nursing but her happiness lasted only a few hours. When Fanny found out where she'd been she was furious, the visit to Kaiserswerth was shameful, a disgrace and not to be spoken about. The old resentments broke out, the old accusations were repeated.

Parthe's possessiveness became worse and she developed a childish need to be looked after. The threat that Florence might leave home for good drove her frantic and she used her close relationship with her mother to demand her sister should spend more time looking after her.

'Florence is the one who's disgraced this family,' Parthe complained, 'and yet she's allowed to take expensive trips for months on end leaving me behind on my own. Now my health has suffered and if she wants to nurse someone let it be her own sister.'

'Parthe is right, Florence,' said Fanny. 'You've had your own way, now you must do your duty, stay at home for the next six months and engage in pursuits proper to your upbringing and station. It'll do you good to have someone else to think about for a change.'

Florence was broken once again and Parthe triumphed. The sisters spent time sketching, playing the piano and singing, wandering in the garden talking of art and poetry. In the evenings they played cribbage and read aloud, or Florence sat stitching at some piece of everlasting needlework, watching the hands of the mantel clock until they reached the time when she could safely go to bed.

After a few months Florence was in despair, she seemed to constantly irritate and upset Parthe and knew her mother was disappointed in her, but still she could not be content with the kind of life which seemed to satisfy so many others. She was convinced that her service to God must involve more than being a mere domestic and social convenience.

One evening, after a particularly trying day, she walked out onto the terrace where Parthe was sitting at an embroidery frame working on a cover for her mother's easy chair. Her sister rose and put out her arms towards her.

'Oh Flo, I'm always so glad to have you with me. The house is not the same when you're away. Have I been annoying you – are you cross with me? I'm so sorry.' Parthe stood twisting together her ringless fingers, looking anxiously at her sister. 'Of course you have your faults, everyone has, but I think I love you better because of them.'

Florence felt ashamed of her own lack of tolerance. 'My dear sister, I'm sorry too,' she said and they hugged with happy relief. 'Come for a stroll with me in the garden.'

Florence pressed her sister's hand as they walked side by side. 'What do you want to do with your life, dearest Pop?'

Parthe bent down to pick a pink carnation, smelt its sweet perfume then began to pull the flower to pieces, petal by petal. 'Oh Flo, I know I'm not ambitious, I wish to marry for love and be contented and happy. But it's hard these days for a girl without money to attract a man.'

'True love for a good woman is a great thing,' said Florence. 'I can never be like you but sometimes I envy your simplicity of outlook and a special someone will come along for you soon.'

Despite being like chalk and cheese, the sisters were genuinely fond of each other and returned to the house from their walk, rosy and good humoured.

At the age of thirty Parthe was still an attractive woman, her toilette glass showed she was in the prime of life but her spirits were weary with waiting. She lost confidence in her social graces, sitting silently through dinner parties unable to think of anything amusing to say. Her little nervous laugh became shriller and her frequent poor health gave good reason to decline invitations. Somehow the men she considered desirable never seemed to think the same about her and she dreaded a future alone.

Florence's allegiance to Parthe was renewed by their outburst of affection; she knew she could be uncharitable in her judgement at times but vowed to try and be more tolerant in future. Still she continued to pray for a sign to reveal her way to atonement but none came.

Chapter 11

At the start of 1851, Florence's attitude to life began to change. Buoyed by support from Sidney, she started to see herself as the victim and not the criminal, determined now to find a way to persuade her family to condone her ambitions.

Public opinion had moved on, interest in hospitals was becoming a political and social issue. Towns were more heavily populated, new hospitals were needed to cope with the increase in disease caused by overcrowding and poor living conditions. Anaesthetics were improving the success of surgical procedures and emphasis was being placed on diet, cleanliness and fresh air. Florence recognised the time had come to introduce professional standards of nursing to complement these changes and she desperately wanted to be involved.

Florence's beloved spaniel Venus died in the spring. Elderly now, the little dog had ventured out alone for an early morning stroll. Some hours later, a gardener had found her small, still body lying in the orchard bathed in dappled sunshine, surrounded by clumps of nodding yellow daffodils with birds singing in the canopy of branches above.

Florence choked back her sobs as she wrapped her faithful friend in a favourite blanket and laid her to rest in a grave prepared in a shady corner of the pets' cemetery at Embley. The granite headstone read: 'Here lies our dearest Venus – she loved and was loved.'

When her promised six months of caring for Parthe finally ended, Florence was invited by Sidney to stay at Wilton to nurse Liz through the final stages of a difficult pregnancy with her third child. Also staying to help with the birth was Elizabeth Blackwell, an English woman who'd made history when she became the first woman to qualify and register as a doctor in the United States.

One evening when Liz was sleeping, the two women relaxed and started to talk.

'Elizabeth,' said Florence, 'I really admire and envy what you've achieved. My ambitions to be a nurse seem to be quite impossible with an unsupportive family like mine.'

'Now there I was lucky as my parents encouraged me to undertake medical training,' Elizabeth replied. 'My problem came when all the schools I applied to rejected me and it was only a matter of luck I was admitted to the Geneva Medical College in New York. When the students were asked if a woman should be allowed to join their ranks, they thought it was a joke and approved the idea but when I arrived they realised the joke was on them.'

'How wonderful,' Florence laughed.

'Of course, one of my reasons to become a doctor was to earn a good living and stay free of dependence on a man,' said Elizabeth. 'Marriage can be so constricting on a woman's life, although I do regret not experiencing the passion of love.'

'Don't you think it's possible that a special friendship with a man, outside the complication of marriage, could give both the joy and pain of love whilst also allowing a woman to follow her own pursuits?' asked Florence.

'I'm sure you may be right,' agreed Elizabeth, 'but how many of us would ever be able to achieve such a thing?'

Both women sat silent for a moment lost in their own thoughts until the doctor continued:

'After graduation I worked in clinics in London and Paris. No hospital would employ me so I enrolled at La Maternité, France's leading school for midwives. Sadly, while there I contracted purulent ophthalmia from a young patient and lost the sight of one eye which meant giving up plans of becoming a surgeon.'

'What a terrible blow, after all you'd been through,' said Florence.

'Life can be cruel but we must do our best with the talents and opportunities we are given,' said Elizabeth. 'You must not give up on your ambitions.'

Lying in bed that night, Elizabeth smiled as she remembered her conversation with Florence.

Sidney Herbert had returned to Wilton from London earlier that day and joined the two of them for dinner. Although Elizabeth may now only have one good eye, she was perfectly capable of observing the behaviour of the couple together and was in no doubt about the identity of the "special friend" to whom Florence had alluded.

The two women became close and Elizabeth visited Embley before returning to America, having given Florence new hope that her difficulties could be overcome. She once again approached her mother requesting more time at Kaiserswerth and now Fanny could no longer claim that plans approved by people like Miss Blackwell and the Bracebridges were shameful and with poor grace she gave way.

In the summer, Parthe was unwell and advised to take a three-month cure at Karlsbad; Florence could accompany them, spend time at Kaiserswerth and they would return home together. Her mother wanted the trip to be kept secret and Florence was forbidden to write to any of the family to tell them where she was staying.

Florence was determined to make the most of her time with Pastor Fliedner. She slept in a room at the orphanage, rose at 5.00 a.m. and took breakfast in the dining hall; during the day she helped with the children and worked in the hospital.

Sidney and Liz visited on their way back from a trip through Europe. 'How are you enjoying the life here?' Sidney asked.

'It's not easy,' replied Florence. 'Conditions are frugal but the devotion of the nurses is exemplary. I'm learning basic medicine by assisting experienced sisters and questioning the doctors – yesterday they allowed me to observe an amputation operation.'

Liz broke the news that Richard Monkton Milnes had married Annabel Crewe. After a brief twinge of regret, Florence breathed a sigh of relief and placed that part of her life behind her. She wrote a beseeching letter to her mother in Karlsbad, putting her point of view once again for continuing nursing, saying she could not bear to grieve the family anymore and asked for her blessing, but she received no response.

On their return to England, Fanny and Parthe hardly spoke to Florence as if she had committed some terrible crime. Parthe's health had not been improved by the cure, which she blamed on her anxiety about her sister being at Kaiserswerth, her moods grew worse and she buzzed round Florence like an irritating gnat always ready to find fault. She drove herself into hysterical frenzies declaring she was dying, her sister's behaviour was killing her and she complained of suffering agonies from mysterious pains.

The doctor diagnosed rheumatic headaches, nervousness and instability, suggesting Parthe's health would improve if she no longer lived with Florence, who in turn was held prisoner by her duty as a sister and daughter. In spite of the doctor's advice, Fanny insisted Florence should remain at home and give reassurances that she would not leave. All the old arguments revived – Parthe's health, Florence's heartlessness, Parthe's devotion, Florence's ingratitude.

WEN developed a painful eye inflammation and arranged for a course of cold water treatment at Umberslade Hall in Warwickshire but would only go if Florence accompanied him. WEN saw the treatment as an excuse to escape temporarily from the atmosphere at Embley; Florence was always his favourite and now he looked forward to spending some time alone with her. Florence's heart danced at the idea of a whole week of perfect freedom in conversation with her father and of old times revived.

At Umberslade Hall the two of them played battledore and shuttlecock, took walks in the park and had the most delightful time together. Florence spent her days writing up reports on Kaiserswerth while her father was undergoing his treatment. At night they dined with other patients and later, in the privacy of her father's room, she entertained him with anecdotes of her day, mimicking the people she'd met.

On the last night of their stay, when they both dreaded returning home, Florence took the opportunity to confide her frustrations.

'Papa, you must remember me telling you of my vision saying I should find a way to seek redemption for my sins?'

'How could I forget?' her father sighed.

'Well, I know now the solution is to devote my life to nursing but it seems impossible for me to achieve. If you'll not give me some encouragement I'm sure I'll get worse instead of better. Please, Papa, I'm dependent on you not to deprive me of the only thing to make my life worth living.'

WEN took out his snuff box and gratified each nostril with deliberate impartiality, while observing his daughter over the gold rims of his spectacles.

'Florence, my dear, it appears strange to me that you wish to seek duties outside the home when so many others usually try to avoid them. All this talk of redemption seems very unnecessary. Recently I asked a member of my club, a physician at Brighton hospital, if a young gentlewoman could become a hospital nurse and he answered firmly in the negative. So tell me, where are the opportunities for a woman of your class and with your vocation?'

'That's what I'm trying to find out. Women like me need help to go into the world and use their skills – independence, money and worthiness are what many are seeking. If only Mama was more understanding and didn't still regard me as a child, controlling my movements and restricting my friendships.'

WEN nodded in agreement. He realised now Fanny's treatment of her younger daughter was beginning to look like mania – was Florence's life to be destroyed because of his wife's obsession?

'Florence, you have a man's brain, you are able to think and I hate to see you so unhappy. You're a grown woman, your determination is obvious and I want to help you in any way I can. Let's pray a way will soon be revealed for you to achieve your ambitions.'

'I hope so too, Papa, but I'm not sure prayers will help – I used to pray so much but it did no good. Now I hardly ever pray but knowing you're on my side means the world to me.'

'My darling daughter, I don't really understand you but I love you dearly all the same.' Father and daughter hugged, relishing the return of the old familiar affection between them.

On the pretext of showing an interest in Catholicism, Florence was introduced by the Herberts to Henry Manning, a priest well-known for his work with the poor of the East End of London and a colleague of Sidney's at Oxford. Having soon discovered she was not a suitable convert but her interest was in medicine, Manning suggested he could arrange for her to work in a Catholic hospital where the nurses were nuns.

Once more Fanny refused permission but she was now persuaded by WEN that this negative behaviour was threatening to ruin her daughter's life. With the world against her, Fanny had to soften her views and concede that Florence couldn't stay at home for ever, although she was still hoping she would marry.

Making the most of her mother's change in attitude, Florence arranged to visit Mary Clarke in Paris and spent a month during the summer studying the hospitals and institutions there. She accumulated an enormous quantity of reports and statistics illustrating hospital administration, as well as nursing arrangements throughout Europe.

By coincidence, Sidney too was in Paris at that time, summoned to the bedside of his half-brother Robert who'd suffered a dangerous attack of lung inflammation.

During his convalescence and shaken by the closeness of death, Robert seemed to have a change of heart, telling Sidney he might after all return to England and take up his proper place in Wilton as the Earl of Pembroke. When his good health returned, Robert changed his mind once again and decided to remain in Paris, much to Sidney's relief at being able to stay in his beloved Wiltshire home.

On 14th September 1852, Arthur Wellesley, 1st Duke of Wellington died at Walmer Castle. Sidney had admired his achievements more on the battleground than as a politician. The Iron Duke had obstinately attempted to maintain the status quo against an increasing tide of popular reform, resulting in his house and carriage on occasions being stoned by irate protesters. Now he was dead and all was forgiven.

Queen Victoria declared he was the greatest man the country had ever produced and Prince Albert helped to plan his state funeral to be the most extraordinary street procession ever seen. Sidney attended the service at St Paul's Cathedral, which was festooned in black crepe and sat with other distinguished guests on special tiered seating erected for the occasion.

Undeterred by November's stormy rain and piercing wind, over one million people lined the route of the Duke's funeral cortege. By 3.00 p.m. the service was complete and the coffin descended into the burial crypt accompanied by the *Dead March in Saul* and every parish church in England started tolling its bells.

Early the next year the new leader of the Peelites, Lord Aberdeen, formed a coalition government that against all predictions became united and strong, improving relations between the Whig party and the more liberal Conservatives. Sidney returned to office as Secretary at War, hopeful now that after Wellington's death army reforms would be more likely to be achieved.

In Sidney's view it was time to introduce a more egalitarian system. Officer training was inadequate, career structures hardly existed and commissions were purchased with princely sums only in reach of the wealthy. Snobbery existed between aristocratic infantry and cavalry officers towards the artillery and engineers, who learnt their trade and whose promotion depended on seniority and ability.

The staff of Sidney's office did not include a single soldier but was composed of ex-colonials totally ignorant of military matters. The work bored him, a monotonous routine coping with a dreary mass of trivial details and statistics. Opportunities for coming into close touch with the soldier's life were few and those for initiating large schemes for reform even fewer.

'I wonder how anyone can engage in public life,' Sidney wrote to his mother, *'yet the willingness of men of fortune and station to undertake the labour, the cares and face the abuse is what maintains this nation. Sometimes when I look at my little son George I think "when you grow up if you want something to do, sweep a crossing but don't go into Parliament".'*

Chapter 12

One night in early January 1853, the Herberts went to dine in London with Lord Charles and Lady Charlotte Canning. Charles and Sidney had been acquainted at Oxford and served together in Peel's government.

The Cannings were married when Charlotte was eighteen and for her the marriage had brought humiliation and disappointment without the consolation of children. Charles appeared to be the model husband but he possessed a chilly remoteness and was flagrantly unfaithful to his wife. As a distraction from her miserable marriage, Charlotte undertook lady in waiting duties to Queen Victoria for six weeks of the year and devoted her free time to charitable deeds.

During dinner, Lady Canning said to Sidney, 'I'm chairman of a committee involved in running a small charitable institution caring for sick gentlewoman. We're looking for a superintendent to help us run the place and sort out the finances, which seem lately to have become quite a muddle. I wondered if you might know of anyone suitable?'

'What kind of skills are you looking for, Lady Canning?' asked Sidney.

'The ideal person would have to be of strong character, must be well organised and with an interest in caring for the sick,' she replied.

'Do you think the committee might consider a woman?' Sidney enquired.

'If you know of a suitable woman, I am sure we should be happy to meet her.'

'In that case, I think I may know of someone,' said Sidney.

He went on to describe Florence, her desire to serve others and her passion for nursing. Lady Canning thought she sounded a good possibility and asked Liz to write to Florence giving her details of the vacancy.

When she received Liz's letter, Florence had just made plans to visit Paris again with her cousin Hilary to observe nursing practices in the hospitals, but the position at the institute sounded promising. Before she left for France, Florence wrote to Lady Canning expressing her interest and a correspondence began between them.

Florence's visit to Paris was cut short when she returned to nurse grandmother Shore who, at the end of March, slipped into the deep sleep of death with her son and granddaughter by her side.

A month later Florence was invited to attend an interview at the institute. Lady Canning was taken aback at how young Florence looked when she entered the room although, now aged nearly thirty three, she was only four years younger than herself.

'Good morning Miss Nightingale, thank you for coming to see us. Would you please sit down?'

Florence sat on an upright chair placed in the centre of a semi-circle, from where she was assessed by half a dozen formidable Ladies of the Committee. She arranged the skirts of her best black woollen day dress, straightened her jacket bodice, placed her hands in her lap then looked up, her grey eyes coolly examining their expectant faces.

'Would you please start by telling us something of your background and experience?' Lady Canning asked. Florence explained her ambitions to nurse, her research, the training at Kaiserwerth and her experiences of caring for the cottagers at Wellow and The Hollow.

When she'd finished, Lady Canning continued, 'Now I think you're familiar with the duties of superintendent, so please give us reasons why you would be a good candidate.'

Florence answered in a clear strong voice. 'Lady Canning, ladies

– my understanding is you require a person with nursing knowledge to be dedicated to your patients, to run the operations of the institute efficiently and ensure budgets are maintained. All these requirements fall within the scope of my abilities.'

She paused for a moment and looked round the room. 'I want nothing more than to devote my life to the service of others. I'm well organised and understand the intricacies of balancing books. If you choose me I will put into effect ideas to improve the lives of the patients – reallocating menial tasks to allow nurses to spend more time tending the sick and as a result make this a finer institution.'

Florence's sincerity impressed Lady Canning. 'You seem very young to take on such responsibilities,' she said. 'If we were to offer you the position, would you be prepared to employ someone older and more experienced to become your personal attendant?'

'Yes certainly. I know a Mrs Margaret Smith who recently retired as matron of a union workhouse and is a trustworthy and efficient lady.'

Lady Canning replied, 'Mrs Smith sounds satisfactory but make sure she understands she will receive no remuneration and I'm afraid that also applies to yourself. Do you have any questions?'

Florence asked, 'I will need to live on the premises of the institute to give of my best – would this be in order?'

'Yes, I am sure that could be arranged.'

Florence continued, 'In addition, may I have your word that I would be allowed to carry out my duties in the way in which I choose to do so?'

Lady Canning paused as an audible whisper ran round the committee. 'Miss Nightingale, this position is initially to last for one year during which time your performance will be closely observed. As long as the expectations of the committee are satisfactorily met, there will be no interference in your preferred manner of working. Does that sound fair?'

'Yes, quite fair,' agreed Florence.

Lady Canning concluded. 'Excellent, the committee will now spend some time discussing your application and I shall write to you within the next few days.' Florence thanked the group for their consideration and left the room.

The concerns of the Ladies of the Committee centred on her social position – was it peculiar for a young society lady to apply for such a post? Should a lady of her standing be allowed to nurse ladies with more humble backgrounds? Was it nice for a lady to be present at medical examinations and, worse still, during operations? Would she be prepared to take orders?

Lady Canning was adamant Florence was the right person – despite her youth and lack of experience she was intelligent, dedicated to nursing and deserved a chance. Finally, all the ladies agreed Florence should be appointed and Lady Canning wrote offering her the role of Superintendent of the Institute for the Care of Sick Gentlewomen in Distressed Circumstances. She was to commence later that year when new premises had been found.

Florence had assured her parents she would not accept the position without their permission and when news of the offer was broken to them, the familiar scenes took place. Parthe became hysterical, collapsed and had to be put to bed. Fanny cried in despair, 'Is a life away from those who love you the only one you'll allow yourself?'

WEN retreated from the mayhem at the Burlington to the Athenaeum Club to contemplate the situation in peace. He finally concluded Parthe's behaviour should no longer be allowed to control her sister's life and decided to enable Florence to leave home by providing her with a personal allowance of five hundred pounds per annum.

Florence was delighted and instantly replied to Lady Canning's letter.

'I beg to thank you for the kind and considerate manner in which you have made known to me the offer of the Ladies of the

Committee. I shall be happy to accept that offer as proposed.

May I beg to repeat that should I be unable to affect the good which I have in view, I shall wish to feel at liberty to retire at the end of twelve months. I have communicated with Mrs Smith who will be glad to accept the office of Matron and declines any salary but I must take upon myself all her expenses as decided by the Ladies of the Committee.'

With her new financial freedom Florence took temporary rooms in Pall Mall, away from her resentful family and in August 1853 moved into the residence of the institute at No. 1 Harley Street, leaving home for ever. Fanny still refused to give her blessing to what she considered to be an impossible undertaking and regarded as no better than being in service.

Florence was in her element – her abilities exceeded the expectations of the Ladies of the Committee but the task of dealing with sick and querulous women, embittered by the unfortunate circumstances of their lives, was not an easy one.

She became devoted to her patients and did an immense amount of practical nursing, while her main responsibility was to make sure everything ran smoothly and the books balanced. When Florence arrived the accounts were in confusion, which had made her nervous. She began controlling the finances by changing from monthly to weekly bills, grocery contracts were agreed, resulting in wholesale prices, pharmacy expenses reduced by having drugs dispensed on the premises.

Life was hard – there were medical failures and she faced suspicion and accusations of inefficiency, but gradually she came to understand that the best way of achieving results was to convince the committee and medical staff that her ideas were actually their own.

After a few months, she invited her cousin Hilary to tea. 'So dear Florence, how are you enjoying being a working woman?' she asked.

'Oh Hilary, I'm like a pig in a puddle – so happy to be doing something useful at last. I've almost more to think about than I know how to manage.'

'And how about the dreaded Ladies of the Committee?'

'Oh you know, talk, talk, talk and nobody ever says anything. We have our differences – Lady Canning is very understanding and Liz Herbert has joined to support my views so that's been a great help.'

'What kinds of patients are you dealing with?' asked Hilary.

'Most are governesses with no independent means. The poor things have often lost their jobs through illness and need to be brought back to health quickly so they can return to work. Patients are allowed to stay here for only two months, unless of course they're dying, otherwise they'd be happy to take up valuable beds even though fit enough to leave. Would you like to look round and meet some of them?'

'I'd be delighted,' Hilary replied.

Florence led her cousin down the corridors of the large house, looking in on patients she knew would be well enough to cope with a visitor.

'You should have seen the furniture when I arrived – filthy, damp and broken, the bed linen not even fit for dogs. So I threw it all out and encouraged the ladies and their charitable friends to donate replacements.'

Hilary was touched by the way the patients reacted to Florence – one lady told her, 'Miss Nightingale is a wonderful woman, so kind and helpful. I'm leaving tomorrow and she's found me a new position. I'll always be grateful to her.'

Later Hilary said, 'I'm so proud of you Florence – the patients obviously love you.'

'Well I understand their loneliness and financial difficulties. I'm happy to help but their devotion can be quite tiresome. Now let's go back to my room and eat cake.'

Fanny and Parthe continued to disapprove although, at

Florence's request, weekly hampers of provisions and flowers were sent for the patients from Embley.

During a brief visit to London, Fanny invited Florence to take tea with her in the Burlington. The two women chatted awhile about how things were at Embley, then her mother said, 'Now my dear, I hope you're not working too hard in that nursing home, you look a little tired.'

Florence smiled. 'No, Mama – I'm quite well, thank you. In fact I feel better than I've done for years and I'm enjoying spending my time doing something worthwhile.'

'Very commendable I'm sure.' Her mother sniffed and turned her head, patting her hair with placid indifference. 'I'm in town to buy a new outfit for Diana Worthington's wedding – you remember her, sweet little thing with golden curls and the bluest eyes? Well, she's marrying Sir George Morley at Ingleby Manor. Should be a great occasion but I can't help wishing it was your wedding I was looking forward to.'

She looked expectantly at Florence. 'Is there no one on the horizon? Some handsome physician perhaps? You must be awfully lonely.'

Florence was exasperated. 'Mama, I'm not in the least interested in marriage. I just wish women's lives were more rewarding to put men off from asking such a sacrifice. It's true I'm alone and nobody knows that better than I do – but would marriage diminish that solitude?'

Fanny shrugged her shoulders while her daughter continued. 'Certainly none of the marriages I'm familiar with. I've seen husbands of friends curl their lips with a curious smile at how little their wives understand them. Most men know their wives as well as they know Abraham and it seems to me that appearances have very little to do with real contentment. Can't you see I'm not destined to marry?'

'All I can see,' her mother replied, 'is that you take a too gloomy view of things. What happened all those years ago was a terrible mistake but it's over now, in the past. Don't let your future happiness be ruined because of it.'

'I'll do my best. Goodbye Mama, I must go now.' Florence kissed her cheek and left the room trying not to show her frustration at how little her mother still understood her.

Watching her daughter leave, Fanny sighed and thought, 'Florence never behaved like other normal women and now I suppose she never will.'

Florence made a friend in Dr Bowman, one of the best known surgeons of the day and assisted him as he performed a difficult cancer operation using the new anaesthetic chloroform. When the patient was settled, Florence and Dr Bowman had tea together.

'You know, Miss Nightingale.' the doctor said, 'that was excellent work you did today. Your talents are wasted at the institute, you should be in a hospital.'

'Well, that is my dream but how could it ever happen?' Florence asked.

'As a senior surgeon at King's College Hospital, I'm sure I could convince the board to appoint you as a superintendent of nurses – then you would have the scope of training your own staff.'

Florence was excited. 'That would be marvellous. Thank you so much, Dr Bowman.'

Rumours reached Embley of her intentions and once more there were accusations and reproaches. How could she contemplate working in such disgusting surroundings with immoral companions and unmentionable diseases? Why could she not be a respectable teacher instead? But Florence had become a confident and independent woman, turning a deaf ear to the protests of her family and soon the dissenting voices faded and were heard no more.

Within a year Florence had achieved success, the institute was running smoothly and the committee was satisfied. Now she was restless – while she was moving forward, her path to worthiness had still to be accomplished. She began visiting hospitals and collecting facts to establish a case for reforming conditions, but she knew that before any scheme could be started, a training school must be set up to produce capable, respectable and qualified nurses.

Sidney's responsibilities at the War Office included overseeing the work of military hospitals and he wrote frequently to Florence, asking for advice on nurses' pay and conditions.

In one letter she replied: *'I'm sorry to tell you senior hospital appointments are often made as the result of bribery or private negotiation - any hospital official supporting unpopular reforms could find his own job in danger. I fear our task will be long and almost impossible to achieve.'*

Chapter 13

Tragedy struck the Llewellyn family in 1853 when their eldest son John contracted tuberculosis while studying at Queen's College, Oxford and died aged twenty-two years. He was buried in the churchyard of his home village with his father officiating at the funeral and the little church was crowded with sympathetic villagers wishing to pay their respects. David watched his brother's coffin being lowered into its grave with his despairing parents, brother and sister standing beside him.

As time went on, life for the Llewellyns gradually returned to the familiar way of things. Arthur was at Queen's studying for a BA degree before taking holy orders, with plans to return and assist his father in Easton Royal. His sister Sarah, now thirteen years old, was a pupil at the National School in the village, an obedient home-loving girl and a great help to her mother with parish duties. At nearly seventeen, it was time for David to make decisions about his own future.

David was now a serious young man, tall and slim with Florence's pale oval face, chestnut brown hair and grey penetrating eyes. Although his studies at Marlborough College had reached the standard required, he was not keen to become a clergyman or attend university. His parents were kind and caring but not able to advise or financially support his ambitions which lay beyond the confines of a sleepy village in Wiltshire.

David possessed an enquiring mind, was willing to work hard and keen to use whatever skills he could learn to make a difference to others – maybe Mr Herbert would be prepared to help him?

One morning he asked his mother, 'How did such an aristocratic and influential person come to be my godfather?'

Mrs Llewellyn thought for a moment. 'At the time when you were born, life was difficult,' she said. 'Your father was poorly paid and the work insecure, we had no permanent home. When we lived near Chilmark, your father assisted Reverend Lear who understood how things were for us – he was friendly with the Pembroke family and knew Mr Herbert to be a kind, altruistic gentleman. When Reverend Lear asked him for help on our behalf, luckily he agreed.'

David nodded, 'That was very good of him.'

His mother continued, 'Mr Herbert offered to become your godfather and agreed to pay to educate all three of you boys. His recommendation to the Marquis of Ailesbury led to us moving here for a better life and we shall always be grateful for his kindness and generosity.'

Encouraged by his mother's words, David decided to write to Mr Herbert and ask for guidance.

After obtaining Florence's approval, Sidney proposed David should become involved in the world of medicine, which also seemed to the boy the right way forward. Many of his friends had suffered serious sickness and the recent death of his brother made him realise the importance of learning how to treat and cure these terrible illnesses.

On hearing his decision, Sidney wrote: '*My dear David – I am delighted you are keen to undertake a medical training. You now need to choose which specialism suits you best. Physicians are considered to be the most knowledgeable – an elite group of university educated academics with the monopoly over the practice of 'physic' or internal medicine.*

Surgeons are regarded as craftsmen whose work demands speed, dexterity and physical strength, as well as knowledge attained through apprenticeship. Apothecaries are legally allowed to prescribe medication but are only paid for drugs dispensed, not advice offered.

I suggest you may like to consider undertaking an apprenticeship in surgical practice with my friend, Dr Richard Hassall, who lives in Richmond. Dr Hassall's father Thomas was for many years the doctor of my grandmother, the Countess of Pembroke. In fact he attended my own dear mother when I was born unexpectedly early at my grandmother's house, Pembroke Lodge.

Since the recent death of his father, Dr Hassall is now running the practice and looking to take on an apprentice. I should be happy to recommend you for the post if you think this would be agreeable. Please reassure your parents I would of course bear any expenses involved in the training. I look forward to hearing your decision and remain your loving godfather Sidney Herbert.'

David saw this offer as a golden opportunity to leave home, live in London and learn skills to assist him through the adventures of the rest of his life.

Understanding his parents might not be totally supportive he tentatively explained Mr Herbert's suggestion. His mother was at first unhappy, medical students had a reputation for idleness, drunkenness and debauchery. She was worried how he would survive in London which she'd heard could be an unfriendly and dangerous city, full of thieves and cut-throats. She was still grieving for one son and the loss of another was inconceivable.

David assured his mother that Mr Herbert had found him a safe place for his apprenticeship, he would be careful to take care of himself and avoid trouble. The Reverend Llewellyn had confidence any arrangements made would be appropriate for his son who was a sensible, intelligent boy and deserved a chance to succeed. Finally, they both agreed that David should visit Dr Hassall and if he was considered to be a suitable apprentice, they would support his plans to enter the world of medicine.

Sidney arranged for the Herberts' coach with armorial bearings and four splendid horses to transport David to meet Dr Hassall in Richmond. The day was warm for September and the collar of David's Sunday shirt felt too small, his woollen suit was tight and hot. The hustle and bustle as they approached London fascinated him – he'd never before travelled farther than the few miles to Devizes market. Finally the coach drove through a pair of wrought iron gates, rattled down a gravel drive and pulled up by the open front door of a grand Georgian house.

The butler ushered David into a spacious entrance hall and offered him a cool glass of lemonade served on a silver tray. While visiting the cloakroom facilities, David ran one finger round the inside of his collar and observed himself in the mirror. With shaking hands he flattened his hair, lovingly cut and washed by his mother the night before, then pulled a face as he noticed an angry red blemish on his chin and a line of down on his upper lip.

Back in the hall, David sat on an upholstered chair and waited. The ticking of the clock matched his quickened heartbeat, paintings of Hassall ancestors gazed down on him. One day he too would own a big house – he must overcome his nerves and make a good impression.

Soon David was shown into Dr Hassall's consulting surgery. Cabinets of neatly labelled drawers lined the room with shelves above holding rows of bottles of different shapes and colours. Prints of anatomical drawings hung on the walls and a human size skeleton stood in one corner near a deal bookcase holding volumes of medical dictionaries. The sweet pungent smell of chemicals reminded David of the school laboratory.

Dr Hassall rose from behind his large, cluttered, leather-topped desk and held out a welcoming hand, there was in his appearance an air of good nature which gave David a reassuring confidence.

The doctor was a smartly dressed, middle-aged man of medium height with a slight athletic frame. The majority of the flesh on his face was obscured by a large drooping moustache mingled with a pair of fine whiskers and the intensely blue eyes, through which he observed David, were inquisitive but kind. 'How good to meet you David, please sit down,' he said.

'Thank you, sir.' David obediently sat on the only available chair, while Dr Hassall slumped back on his own seat with his feet resting on a stack of medical journals piled up on the floor beside him.

'Now,' the doctor declared, 'I understand from Mr Herbert you wish to be a medical man. Can you explain to me why?'

David had anticipated this question. 'Yes sir – I want to make a difference in the world by helping other people.'

A smile flickered across the doctor's face. 'Very commendable,' he said. 'What do you think you learnt at Marlborough to help you study medicine?

'Well sir, perhaps Latin and science?' David offered.

'That's excellent. A liberal education is important. Medical science is advancing all the time and we still have a great deal to discover.'

Dr Hassall leant forward in his chair. 'I would teach you as an apprentice as much as I can about everyday practice but most important of all is the ability to get on with people. If you speak, dress and behave like a gentleman you will be judged a man worthy of trust. Most patients have no faith in medical qualifications, preferring to select their medical man on the basis of his social skills or good looks.'

David looked shocked at this revelation as the doctor continued, 'Well maybe I exaggerate but tact and discretion with the ability to act decisively and inspire confidence – those are the qualities required. Our relationships with our patients can sometimes be described as the blind leading the blind, but as long as Mrs Bloggs trusts you and likes you enough to invite you to dinner and so on, everything will be fine. Medicine is a very serious profession to undertake – people's lives depend on us. You must be sure you will be able to face that responsibility. Any questions?'

'Sir, how long would be my training?' asked the boy.

'Three years with me then another two at medical school, so five years in all,' replied Dr Hassall.

'Sounds like a long time, sir.'

'Maybe it does but if you want a successful medical career that is the only way to go. The Society of Apothecaries is the main examining body and if you pass the course you will be issued with a licence to set up in medical practice – then it's all up to you.'

'And sir, could I ask what would be my duties here?' David asked.

'At first you would keep the drug store stocked up, tidy the surgery, put patients at their ease and assist as I perform operations,' Dr Hassall answered. 'Then when you were ready, we'd progress to more responsible tasks. Does that seem in order?' David nodded.

'Good,' continued the doctor. 'Now let me show you round.'

Dr Hassall rose and motioned the young man to follow him out of the surgery. The doctor's wife appeared from the drawing room and was introduced to David who liked her at once, her face was kind and friendly and she smelled of lavender. The Hassall's two sons were away at school and she missed their companionship – she would enjoy having a young man living in the house again.

Mrs Hassall took David upstairs and showed him a room containing a wooden bed, wardrobe, chest of drawers, a desk with a chair and a large window overlooking the garden.

'How would this room suit you, David?' she asked.

David replied that he had always shared in the past and a bedroom of his own would be luxury. A light luncheon had been prepared to be served in the dining room, so the three sat down to eat and become acquainted.

After coffee, the doctor excused himself to visit a patient and left saying he looked forward to their next meeting. David's coach was summoned to the front door and Mrs Hassall waved him off with a smile. The journey home was spent dreaming of what it would be like to be a doctor and live like the Hassalls, now he was eager to start his apprenticeship.

Dr Hassall had been impressed by the boy and was happy to take him on. Over luncheon David had explained how much he appreciated Mr Herbert's support and the doctor recognised that the boy's obligation to his godfather would ensure he worked hard to make him proud of his achievements.

Sidney agreed to pay six hundred guineas to cover the cost of the apprenticeship, to include tuition with bed and board at the Hassall's house for the first three years, followed by two years of medical school costs for living expenses, books and equipment, lectures, hospital practice and examination fees. In addition, he arranged for David to receive an annual allowance of fifty pounds for personal expenses.

The practicalities of the apprenticeship were concluded and a date proposed for him to commence. Now David bound himself to his master with the promises that, *'his Master he would faithfully serve, his secrets keep, his lawful commands everywhere gladly do'.*

So it was in November 1853 that David Herbert Llewellyn moved into Dr Hassall's house in Richmond and began the first part of his apprenticeship to become a medical practitioner. At first some of the operations he witnessed repulsed him – boils lanced, teeth extracted, hideous skin disorders calmed, tumours removed and broken bones re-set. As time went on he became used to the unpleasant sights and sounds as a genuine interest and understanding of his work overcame his initial disgust.

David accompanied Dr Hassall on visits to patients, learning not only the etiquette required but also how different were the lifestyles of the urban upper and middle classes from the humble farming community familiar to him in Wiltshire.

Remembering Dr Hassall's words that being a gentleman of trust and sociability were the most important requisites for a successful doctor, David was determined to do his best to become such a person. He found the prospect daunting and when Dr Hassall was invited to take luncheon or dinner in the homes of his patients, David was happy to be sent downstairs and entertained in the servants' quarters where he felt more at ease.

Following the Christmas recess, Sidney wrote to David suggesting he might like to see the new Palace of Westminster, still under reconstruction after the devastating fire of 1834. The last time they'd met had been during his last year at Marlborough when Sidney had visited him at school accompanied by his sister, Mary Caroline.

Now they were to be alone together for the first time. The journey from Richmond to Westminster took longer than anticipated and when he arrived late, David hurried from the hansom cab flushed and anxious that Mr Herbert might think badly of him, but he need not have worried.

As he was shown into the Central Lobby, Mr Herbert was there to greet him, holding out his hand and smiling warmly. 'Good morning David, how good to see you.'

'Good morning, sir – I'm sorry to have kept you waiting.'

'Oh think nothing of it. I know how unreliable journey times can be. Now I'm sure you'd like a look round – where shall we start?' The shy, tongue-tied schoolboy Sidney remembered had become a young man and, as they talked, he felt a surge of pride in his son.

David had grown taller and carried himself with an air of assurance and grace only age could bring. He looked every bit the man about town with legs encased in a pair of brown slim trousers accompanied by a long black jacket, a checked waistcoat and a red cravat. His pale face showed the beginnings of a pair of side whiskers and a small moustache, his dark hair curled on the high collar of a crisp, white shirt.

The Central Lobby was an impressive lofty stone octagon with an intricately tiled floor and mosaic covered vault, with corridors leading off in different directions. As they walked round the palace, Sidney pointed out the beautiful interiors, the carvings, gilt work, panelling and furniture. 'Charles Barry was the architect responsible for the design, assisted by Augustus Pugin, an expert on the Gothic style. It's all costing a great deal but well worth it in my view.'

'How did the fire start, sir?' asked David.

'The Clerk of Works needed to burn a pile of redundant wooden tally sticks, deciding two stoves in the basement would safely do the job. Later that evening a doorman shouted the panelling was on fire and in no time the flames had spread.'

'That must have been quite a sight.'

'Indeed, thousands of people arrived to watch. Most of the structure was destroyed but luckily the wind changed direction and Westminster Hall was saved. A great deal has been rebuilt but there is still much to do.'

Sidney showed him the new Chambers of the Commons. 'We just moved in here recently – much less cramped than the White Chamber where we'd been since the fire.' David marvelled at the great size and magnificent roof of Westminster Hall, the paintings in the Royal Gallery and the architecture of St Stephen's Chapel.

With the tour complete, they sat down in Bellamy's Kitchen for a light luncheon of cold meat, bread, beer and cheese. The place was busy with people coming and going, many of them greeting Sidney with a friendly word. David was proud of how popular his godfather appeared to be and how graciously he responded to each acquaintance.

'And how are you enjoying life with Dr Hassall?' Sidney asked.

'Well sir, some of the things I deal with are quite gruesome but I'm getting used to the work. The Hassalls are kind to me – I'm really quite happy with them.'

Sidney smiled, 'That's good. I can't stand the sight of blood so I admire what you're doing. And how are your parents?'

'My father suffered a bad bout of influenza and seems to have recovered. But sir, I think they're still grieving over John.' David looked down at the floor.

'I'm so sorry for your loss,' Sidney said.

'They were glad to receive your letter, Mr Herbert.' After a short silence David raised his head, his grey, intelligent eyes fixed on his godfather and at that moment he looked so much like Florence, Sidney was caught off guard and unable to speak.

'Tell me sir, what's happening in parliament these days?' his son asked.

Sidney regained his composure and answered, 'Not a very happy situation, I'm afraid. Russia and France are at odds over custody of the Holy Places in Jerusalem. We're trying to resolve their differences but Louis Napoleon wishes us to be in a closer relationship with France and we're morally bound to give assistance to Turkey.'

'That all sounds serious, sir.'

'Yes, David, I think you may be right.' Sidney sighed, fearing his life was soon to become much more complicated.

'The trouble is,' he continued, 'the army is totally unprepared for major conflicts, the navy has always been our main form of defence. The government has been reluctant to invest in what they believed to be an outdated institution. I've only just managed to persuade them to finance the manufacture of a new improved rifled musket to replace the obsolete Brown Bess.'

'You know, sir, some of my friends in Easton Royal enlisted when they lost their jobs on the farms,' David said. 'I heard their barracks were horrible places, crowded and dirty. The lads were hungry and badly treated, often flogged for minor misdeeds. But once they'd accepted the Queen's shilling that was their life for at least the next twenty-one years.'

Sidney nodded, 'There's a lot to be done to improve conditions for the troops and I shall do my best to persuade the government of the need to do so. We've recently established an experimental camp at Cobham to undertake training, let's hope we're not too late.'

The time arrived for David to return to Richmond. The two men shook hands and parted, sharing warm feelings of affection and the promise they would meet again soon. Within a few weeks, Sidney's fears were realised when rumours of war began to rumble through the corridors of parliament.

In April 1854 Russia invaded the Ottoman Empire. The view was generally held that the possession of Constantinople by Russia, with free entry for her fleets into the Mediterranean, would constitute a menace to Europe. A similar danger could arise if Russia possessed, by treaty, virtual control of Turkey, leaving Britain's main route to India under threat.

Prime Minister Lord Aberdeen and others, including Sidney, considered Emperor Nicholas would be unwilling to incur the hostility of Europe. Another section of the Cabinet expressed different ideas, believing a descent on Constantinople to be fully planned and imminent, a view echoed by the British public and the press.

The irrational impatience of the nation was not to be restrained and, before peaceful negotiations could be completed, war was declared and by September the allied armies of France and Britain had landed in the Crimea.

Chapter 14

At the outset of the Crimean War, Sidney's political position was delicate, his mother was half Russian and the Palace at Yalta, an important strategic building for the army, belonged to his uncle Prince Woronzow. Suspicion of Sidney's motives was inevitable and he needed to quickly show where his loyalties lay.

His friend, Henry Pelham-Clinton, was now Secretary of State for War with responsibility to oversee operations in the Crimea but seemed totally out of his depth. It was Henry's misfortune to be placed at the head of a weak and corrupt system, with a brief to improve efficiency but without sufficient authority or opportunity to do so.

Henry was not a happy man, his personal life was fraught with difficulties. Lady Susan, his wife of twenty years, had left him and their five children to conduct a well-publicised affair with Lord Horatio Walpole, resulting in an illegitimate child and subsequent divorce.

On the death of his father the following year, Henry succeeded to the title of fifth Duke of Newcastle-under-Lyme, inheriting estates burdened with debt. The situation was not helped by his eldest son who spent his time gambling and losing money he could not afford.

Sidney offered to help Henry by taking on numerous tasks which were not in his own remit and, in addition, lent him a considerable sum of money to help ease the worry of his present impoverishment.

Preparations for war were chaotic. To provide an army of twenty five thousand men meant almost the entire effective establishment would need to be sent out. Armaments and training were deficient and large field exercises virtually untaught – not an ideal situation for the conditions about to be faced.

Staff working at the commissariat responsible for supplies and transport proved unequal to the demands of the campaign. The availability of tinned food simplified provisions but fresh meat, fruit and vegetables were often rotten by the time they arrived at their destination. Clothing and boots sent for the troops were more suited to tropical climates than the fierce Russian winters.

During the summer a cholera epidemic swept through London. The mortality rate was high, hospitals were overcrowded, some nurses died and others ran away. Florence worked as a volunteer at the Middlesex Hospital to superintend the nursing of cholera patients. Many were women from the red light districts, filthy, drunk and crazed with terror and pain.

Florence was intimidating to the other staff – she did not suffer fools gladly and made no friends. The welfare of her patients was her only concern but beneath her gentle manner on the wards there was the hardness of steel.

With improved methods of communication, people at home were able to follow the progress of the Crimean campaign within a time gap of only a few days. War correspondents sent back reports on strategy and tactics, mixing with the soldiers in camp and trench to bring home the horrors of war to the British public.

William Howard Russell, a *Times* newspaper war correspondent, wrote letters from Scutari describing the terrible conditions he encountered.

He pleaded: '*Are there no devoted women among us able and willing to go forth and minister to the sick and suffering soldiers of the East in the hospitals of Scutari? Are none of the daughters of England at this extreme hour of need ready for such a work of mercy? France has sent forth her Sisters of Mercy unsparingly and they are even now at the bedsides of the wounded and dying giving what woman's hand alone can give of comfort and relief.*'

Florence read Russell's report and knew this was her long-awaited opportunity. The vivid recollection of her shock and disbelief at hearing the doctor's pronouncement of her pregnancy all those years ago still haunted her. Clear memories of the trauma of childbirth and the vision of her son's face remained, but her divine experience with God had given hope for her sins to be forgiven. Now at last the struggles and sacrifices required to complete her path to redemption had been revealed.

Her decision was a foregone conclusion; all her adult life had been a preparation for the work she was about to undertake. She was highly trained and disciplined, not only intellectually but also in practical nursing, the certain knowledge of what now must be done seemed to Florence like the letting in of sunlight on her dark existence.

Without consulting Sidney, she made plans to recruit nurses with approval from her friend Lord Palmerston and obtained a letter of introduction to the Chief Medical Officer at Scutari. Florence called at the Herberts' house in Belgrave Square to discuss her plans but they were away in Bournemouth.

So she wrote to them instead but her letter crossed in the post with one from Sidney, formally inviting her to take charge of introducing female nurses into the hospitals of the British Army in Scutari. He had recognised there was only one person who would be capable of managing such a scheme.

By sending Florence and her nurses, Sidney knew he was risking his personal and political reputation if the mission failed but he had every confidence in her determination, courage and ability. Whatever the cost, he owed her his support to atone for past demeanours and knew very well how much this opportunity would mean to her.

Sidney promised to secure the fullest assistance from the medical staff in the Crimea and gave Florence unlimited power and government backing for whatever was required for the success of her mission. Her position would ensure the respect and co-operation of everyone concerned, she would be well looked after on her journey and her orders obeyed without question.

Florence gladly accepted the terms of the offer, here was her ideal opportunity to advance the cause of nursing, if she could only make this mission a success the image of female nurses would change forever. Supported by Henry Pelham-Clinton, Sidney placed her application before the Cabinet and the next day it was unanimously approved.

The challenge was thrilling; Florence's appointment was announced in *The Times* and caused a sensation. No woman had ever been placed in such an important role before and the question was asked, *'Who is this Miss Nightingale?'*

The Examiner published a short biography which brought disapproving comments from those who considered female nurses would not survive in war conditions and that it was improper for young ladies to nurse male patients. *The Times* ran a leading article appealing for donations to help the war effort and within a week the Fund for the Relief of the Sick and Wounded had raised more than £5,000, which later rose to £12,000.

The Nightingales were divided in their response. Although unhappy Florence was being sent to a war area, they congratulated themselves on the achievement of their daughter. Despite having driven her mad with their objections in the past, the family hurried from Embley to London and joined in the excitement.

In their haste, Athena the owl was left shut in an attic and found dead by one of the maids. The little body was sent to Florence who burst into tears and said, 'Poor little beastie – it was odd how much I loved you.' Before her departure to Scutari she arranged for the tiny corpse to be sent to a taxidermist for preservation.

The correspondence generated by the *Times* article was overwhelming but Florence knew well how much depended on those nurses she took with her. Many who applied were quite unfitted for the work and unaware of the hardships to be faced or the horrors to be witnessed.

The maximum number of nurses in the party was agreed at forty. With the help of Liz Herbert and Lady Canning, everyone was interviewed who looked the slightest bit promising and thirty eight were recruited. Each nurse signed a contract agreeing to Florence's orders. A uniform dress would be provided, alcohol was strictly forbidden and misconduct with the troops would be punished by instant dismissal.

Fourteen nurses with hospital experience were selected, the remaining twenty four being members of religious institutions. Florence stipulated the party should be non-sectarian to ensure maximum support for the mission from the general public.

Florence went to say goodbye to Sidney and was shown into his dark wainscoted office in Westminster. 'Thank you for giving me this wonderful opportunity, dear Sidney. We're almost ready to go now,' she said.

Sidney had risen from his seat and stepped forward, not concealing his pleasure at seeing her. 'I hear you've had a busy time with interviews,' he said.

'Let's hope we've made the right choices,' replied Florence.

'I'm sure if you'd accepted all who volunteered, we'd not only have many indifferent nurses but also many hysterical patients.'

Florence smiled. 'You are quite right, my dear.'

Sidney was once again moved by the firm, calm sweetness of her smiling lips, grey steadfast eyes and the grace of her tall slender figure. 'Florence, you deserve now to show what you can do. You have the love and best wishes of the whole country behind you – it'll not be easy but if anyone can succeed it has to be you.'

She was comforted by his words. 'Your faith in me is overwhelming. I'll try not to let you down.'

'You must write often – I'll do what I can to help. May God bless you, my dear, and bring you home safe and sound.' Sidney put his arms round her and held her close. Florence's pulse quickened at the glorious, intoxicating, familiar feel and smell of him as they stood together for a few moments in silence.

'Please be sure to let me know of David's progress with Dr Hassall,' she said at last with a slight tremble in her voice. 'I'm so happy that the two of you can meet together more often now.'

'David is a splendid young man – it's a pleasure to spend time with him,' replied Sidney.

Tears rose into Florence's grey eyes too fast to be hidden. She quickly composed herself and said in what she hoped was an offhand way, 'I expect I'll drive you mad with my moaning but let's pray for all our sakes the war will soon be over. Goodbye, my dearest Sidney.'

He smiled and kissed her on both cheeks. The couple parted, united in their dread of what was to come and unsure of when they would meet again.

On the day of Florence's departure, her family was there to see her off. Her father said, 'I'm so happy the Bracebridges have agreed to accompany you, otherwise I'd never have allowed you to go – you'll need to be among friends if you are to succeed.'

Her mother added, 'Do be careful Florence, foreigners do not respect women like English gentlemen do.'

Parthe said, 'My dear sister, I'm so frightened for you,' and burst into tears.

Florence tried to reassure them. 'I want to go, I'm not afraid – I hope you understand this is what I was meant to do.'

Her father hugged her and replied, 'I shall never understand but I'll always be proud of you – God speed my darling, brave daughter.'

On the evening of 21st October 1854, the *Angel Band* set out under the cover of darkness escorted by the Chaplain Sidney Osborne, Charles and Selina Bracebridge and a courier.

Florence hated fuss of any kind and was anxious not to make their departure a public affair. She was thirty-four years old and the challenge ahead held terrors for her inexperience but, terrible or not, this was the final sanction of what she had wanted for so long. Their journey began via Boulogne, then Paris to Marseilles where they caught a fast mail boat to Constantinople.

Florence took with her three letters – one a message of support from Henry Manning, one from her mother giving her blessing at last and one from Richard Monckton Milnes which read *'So you are going to the East – you can undertake that when you could not undertake me.'* Concealed in her luggage was a small black velvet box containing a turquoise and pearl heart-shaped pendant on a fine gold chain.

On 4th November, after a terrible journey, they arrived at their destination of Scutari in Turkey. The two hospitals, the General and the Barrack were hellholes. There were no washing facilities and no clean linen; shirts were stripped from the dead and torn up for bandages.

The injured lay in their uniforms, stiff with dried blood and covered in filth. The air was rank from the stink of blocked drains and overflowing privies. There were no containers for water, no soap, towels or cloths, no hospital clothes. Vermin crawled over the floors and walls, food, drugs and medical supplies were running short.

Dr John Hall, Chief Medical Officer of the British Expeditionary Army, was in charge of the hospitals in the Crimea and Scutari. After forty-two years' service and with his previous posting in India, Dr Hall had looked forward to a comfortable position at home before retirement and was not best pleased with this new responsibility. In October he had sent a report to Lord Raglan stating the whole hospital establishment was running well and nothing was lacking, which was blatantly untrue.

Dr Hall was a strict disciplinarian and terrified the doctors serving under him. The news of Florence's appointment he had received with disgust – in his view female nurses working in military hospitals would be disruptive to medical discipline and the recovery of the patients. He was, however, aware of her close relationships with Sidney and other members of the Cabinet, so was obliged to accept her position but set out to make her life as difficult as possible.

When Florence and her party arrived at the Barrack Hospital, they were welcomed with every appearance of flattering attention and escorted into the building with compliments and expressions of good will, but when they saw the quarters their spirits sank.

The hospital was a quadrangle, each wing nearly a quarter of a mile long, built in tiers of corridors and galleries one above the other. Six small rooms, including a kitchen and toilet, had been allocated to a group of forty persons. The rooms were damp, filthy and unfurnished except for a couple of beds and a few chairs. There was no bedding, tables or food.

While the nurses were unpacking, Florence managed to find some tin basins containing black tea which they subsequently used for washing, eating and drinking. Water was restricted to one pint per day per person, obtained by queuing up at a fountain in one of the corridors. They slept on wooden raised platforms erected round rooms alive with fleas and where rats scurried noisily at night.

After a few days, Florence went to see Dr Hall and suffered his sharp eyes pricking her all over as she stood in front of him.

'I was wondering when our nurses could start their work attending the sick,' she asked.

Dr Hall stiffened, his whiskers bristled. 'No female has ever been allowed to nurse in the British Army and that is that – do I make myself clear? Women attending common soldiers is just not done.'

Florence looked at him with candid boldness and asked, 'Are the sick being looked after in any way or are they just brought here to die?'

'We have perfectly adequate arrangements to cope with our injured and I will thank you not to interfere,' he snapped.

She did not answer immediately, indignant words rose to her lips but she drove them back. At length, her eyes flashing with anger, she said, 'Well perhaps we could at least clean the floors of the wards and open the windows?'

'I suppose that would be in order,' Dr Hall reluctantly conceded and Florence left his room with her heart sinking. She faced far more serious challenges here than she'd experienced at the institute, she would need to keep her wits about her and not lose sight of the reasons for her mission.

Florence was ignored by the doctors who were under the influence of Dr Hall's supervision, only one allowed her to use her nurses and supplies. She soon came to realise that amongst the medical staff there existed knowledge without authority and authority without knowledge. Patients were looked after by male hospital orderlies who were hopelessly untrained. The work of attending the sick was forced on them, most of them disliked what they were doing and their numbers were totally inadequate.

No official orders were issued on how the nurses should be employed and Florence knew she could not accomplish anything without winning the confidence of the doctors. Dr Hall refused to accept the civilian funds available to support the troops, even when it was obvious supplies were desperately short.

Florence sent Sidney constant reports on the conditions they were enduring but, although sympathetic, he had no power to help her situation. She wrote: *'Dr Hall is neither a gentleman nor a man of education. He is bereft of feelings with only the object of keeping himself free of blame.'*

For the first few weeks she stood by in silence, rigidly obeying regulations, while the skills of her nurses were wasted. No nurse was allowed to enter the wards without permission from a doctor, they had to stand by and watch the troops suffer but do nothing until officially instructed. The nurses, unaware of Florence's strategy, formed the opinion she was indifferent to the needs of the patients.

'Why can't they give us decent quarters?' they complained. 'Get us in the wards or let's all go home. We've not come here to be skivvies.'

She explained they must be patient, silent and dedicated as nurses should be, insisting on discipline in the midst of chaos.

Florence appeared each day in a black merino wool dress trimmed with black velvet, white linen collar and cuffs. Her golden brown hair was wound into a thick coil at the back of her head, parted down the middle in a pin straight line, covered with a white cap and a black handkerchief.

The nurses' uniform was not designed to make the wearer look attractive. Over a grey tweed dress was worn a matching worsted jacket with a short woollen cloak and a plain white cap. The ensemble was completed by a white Holland sash embroidered in red with the words "Scutari Hospital".

One nurse complained, 'There's the caps, ma'am. If I'd known about the caps, ma'am, great as was my desire to come out to nurse in Scutari, I wouldn't have come, ma'am.'

There were no kettles or saucepans, the only fuel was green wood. The tea was undrinkable, made in coppers in which meat had been boiled and not thoroughly cleaned. The food was almost inedible for healthy men, the suffering increased for those with cholera and dysentery.

Florence began to cook the supplies she had brought on her own portable stoves. With the doctors' permission she provided beef-tea, chicken broth, jellies, arrowroot and port wine. Within a week the kitchen in her own quarters became dedicated for special diets but no patient was allowed nourishment from her without the written instructions of a doctor.

The destruction of the British Army began – medical resources were not able to cope with the flood of sick and wounded that started to arrive. Day after day the sick poured in until the two hospitals were filled.

Florence wrote to tell Sidney that at the Barrack they were tending to 1,175 sick including 120 with cholera, and 650 severely wounded were accommodated in the General Hospital:

'The gateway to the hospital should have a sign saying "Abandon hope all ye who enter here". In our corridors I think we have an average of three limbs per man. Operations are performed in the wards – no time to move them.

One poor fellow exhausted with haemorrhage has had his leg amputated as a last hope and died ten minutes after the surgeons left him. Almost before the breath has left his body it is sewn up in its blanket and carried away to be buried later that day. We have no room for corpses in the wards.

The next poor fellow has two stumps for arms, the next case has one eye put out and paralysis of the iris in the other – he can neither see nor understand. All who can walk come to us for tobacco but I tell them we have not a bit to put in their mouths. These poor fellows have not had a clean shirt nor been washed for months and the state in which they arrive is literally crawling.'

There were now four miles of beds in the Barrack Hospital laid out less than eighteen inches apart. The corridors were filled with men lying on bare boards, the filth became indescribable and the stench could be smelt from outside the hospital walls. The situation was desperate.

A hurricane destroyed the field hospitals and every vessel in Balaclava Harbour was sunk, including the *Prince*, a large British ship which had arrived the previous day loaded with stores and winter clothing.

Winter began in earnest with storms of sleet and wind that cut like a knife. Dysentery, diarrhoea and rheumatic fever increased and soon hospital administration had collapsed. In the misery and confusion, the harassed doctors came to realise there was only one person who could take action, who had the money and the authority to spend it.

Chapter 15

At last the doctors turned to Florence for help – she had the Times Fund at her disposal as well as government sources, thanks to Sidney's intervention. Every day she ascertained what supplies were lacking, the goods were purchased in Constantinople, put in her store and issued on receipt of a requisition completed by a medical officer.

Gradually the doctors ceased to be suspicious and accepted the importance of her role. Although their change of heart gave Florence great satisfaction, she never registered her emotion by looks or words or by any change in her demeanour.

Her position was strengthened by Queen Victoria who sent messages to the sick men: *'No one takes a warmer interest, feels more for your suffering or admires your courage and heroism more than your Queen. Day and night she thinks of her beloved troops.'*

The wives of the soldiers were of serious concern to Florence. After following their husbands through the horrors of the campaign, they were now separated from them, quartered in a damp hospital basement where many babies were born.

Florence used her influence and funds to requisition a house to be cleaned and furnished for them. Widows were sent home and the wives who remained were employed earning money in the laundry, boilers were installed and lavatories scrubbed.

Soon Florence was responsible for all hospital supplies and, with Sidney's authority, she refurbished a wing of the hospital, previously destroyed by fire, to accommodate five hundred sick and wounded. The affair caused a sensation and was an important demonstration of Nightingale power.

Florence's relationship with the nurses worried her a good deal and she confided her doubts in a letter to Sidney.

'My determination to carry out at all costs the impossible task I have taken on sometimes makes me sharp tongued and lays me often open to criticism. I'm apt to speak too strongly of those who don't please me. Just as I'm ready on occasion to override my own feelings, I'm also ready to sometimes override the feelings of others.

I must not lose sight of the fact that one main object of this mission is to prove the value of women as nurses. Sadly it's these nurses who are causing me the greatest difficulties, some of them are working well while others are not fit to take care of themselves.

To convince them of the need for discipline is almost impossible – they have to be banned from the wards after 8 p.m. to discourage intimacy with the men. The religious sisters are apt to be more concerned with the souls of their patients than their bodies and are more fit for heaven than hospital.

I know some of them regard me as callous, determined to increase my own power and caring nothing for the sick – reluctance to accept my authority and obey instructions is constant. Indeed many of the nurses heartedly dislike me and although I'm concerned, my purpose here is not to make friends only to get the job done but it is not a pleasant atmosphere.'

Sidney replied: 'Florence my dear, you must try not to be so hard on yourself, we both knew this tremendous task was never likely to be an easy one.

Allow some time to reach the high standards you set, not just for yourself but also for others whose abilities may not be as great as yours. You are a fighter and I know you will overcome the obstacles you face.

Now here's some good news – Queen Victoria has offered to send bottles of eau de cologne for the troops. I think maybe someone should tell her a little gin would be more popular.'

A few weeks later, Florence experienced a blow which

threatened to disrupt not only her mission but also her relationship with Sidney.

Mrs Bracebridge received a letter from Liz Herbert saying that a party of forty-six Roman Catholic nurses under the leadership of her friend, Mary Stanley, had left London and was due to arrive in Scutari the next day.

Florence had not been consulted or informed. The practice she'd agreed with Sidney as one to be avoided at all costs – the selection of nurses for religious reasons and not for their efficiency as nurses – had been thrust on her by the imposition of Mary Stanley's party. Florence was upset and angry.

She wrote to Sidney complaining bitterly: *'I have toiled my way into the confidence of the medical men. I have by incessant vigilance day and night introduced something like order into the disorderly lives of these women.*

At this point arrives a fresh batch of women raising our number to eighty four. To quarter them here is physically impossible, to employ them is morally impossible. You have sacrificed a cause so near to my heart, you have sacrificed me and you have sacrificed your own word.'

She went on to say she could not continue where conditions were imposed that prevented her from carrying out her responsibilities and suggested he should appoint a new superintendent to replace her.

It was an honest misunderstanding on Sidney's part – he was in poor health and nearly worked to death. Liz was prone to act emotionally without rational thought and was easily led into making unwise decisions. She had been persuaded by Mary Stanley and Henry Manning that a party of Roman Catholic nuns should be sent to help the war effort and improve the status of the Church by receiving some of the glory now heaped on Florence and her nurses.

Florence knew it would be disastrous to send them back, racial and religious issues were involved and a scandal could cause irreparable harm. She suggested a compromise by splitting up the party, some Irish nuns to be employed in the Barrack Hospital and inexperienced nurses sent home. The rest she would try to place in convalescent hospitals due to open in a few weeks.

Florence became dejected, her spirits sank to their lowest ebb – her face was utterly white with fatigue, raised blue welts appeared beneath her eyes. Christmas was here and England seemed far away, she missed Sidney, her family and the comforts of home.

Her room was no larger than a cupboard and the black stove sent out from England wouldn't draw – it was terribly cold and she hated to feel cold. Her breath froze in the air and ink congealed in the well, rats scampered round the walls. Papers were piled round her in heaps on the floor, on the bed, on the chair. A fear of failure gripped her – this mission was proving much harder than her worst predictions.

How could Sidney betray her after all they'd been through together? She was dreading the repercussions amongst her nurses and the storm burst immediately. The nuns resented being sent home, Protestants and Catholics not only quarrelled with each other but amongst themselves like troublesome children.

In the second week of January she at last received a response from Sidney. He accepted full blame, confirmed her authority, implored her not to resign, left everything to her discretion and finally authorised her to send Mary's party home, at his own expense if she felt it necessary. Liz wrote an equally penitent letter.

Florence was moved – the letters were most generous and she was grateful but at the same time she did not regret what she had written.

Matters started to deteriorate – stores were not arriving due to system failures, poor communication or dishonesty but Florence's calmness and ability to get things done meant the doctors came to rely on her completely and the patients adored her.

Day and night for hours on end, she and her nurses toiled amongst the sick and dying, each one putting her own life at risk. The nursing of officers Florence left to others, it was the ordinary soldiers on whom she concentrated her devotion.

Mr McDonald, Administrator of the Times Fund arrived to assess the situation and wrote to the paper: *'She is a ministering angel, without any exaggeration, in these hospitals and as her slender form glides quietly along each corridor every poor fellow's face softens with gratitude at the sight of her. When all the medical officers here have retired for the night, she may be observed alone with a little lamp in her hand, making her solitary rounds.'*

Despite improvements in hygiene and diet, mortality rates from disease in the wards continued to rise. There were no men available to bury the dead and in England there was a great storm of rage, humiliation and despair at the lack of respect for their deceased loved ones.

At the end of January, an inquiry was held into the conditions of the army and the conduct of those departments responsible, constituting a vote of censure on the government, which fell as a result and Sidney went out of office.

He wrote to Florence: *'Although I am no longer directly involved in operations, I can assure you I have no intention of giving up my work for the Army. You must continue to write to me and I will make sure your reports and suggestions are redirected.'*

A Sanitary Commission was sent out to examine the state of the buildings being used as hospitals and camps both in Scutari and the Crimea.

Members of the commission discovered the Barrack Hospital

stood in a sea of decaying filth. The porous plaster of the walls was soaked and poisonous gas blew through the pipes of numerous open privies into the corridors and wards where the sick were lying. The water supply had been contaminated by the carcass of a dead horse. The commission authorised work to flush the sewers, lime wash walls and free rooms from fleas and rats. The result was instant and at last the mortality rates began to fall.

Spring arrived, the roads were passable and rations improved. The emergency was over but Florence became once more obsessed by a sense of failure. She continued to nurse the worst cases but what depressed her most was the burden of the administration work. All requisitions, records, correspondence and reports had to be written by herself, there was no one in authority to support her and a constant stream of demanding people knocked on her door.

By May, when the reception of the sick was under control, Florence decided to visit the Crimea to check out reports of bad conduct by the nurses. Despite Sidney's requests to the War Office, no official notification had been issued giving her authority in the Crimea and her orders were being defied.

The hospitals at Balaclava were dirty, the nurses inefficient and undisciplined. Before she could put her plans into action, Florence collapsed, suffering from Crimea fever and was carried from the ship to the Castle Hospital, where she lay critically ill for more than two weeks.

When the news arrived home that she was out of danger, Queen Victoria announced: *'We are truly thankful to learn that the excellent and valuable person Miss Nightingale is safe.'*

Although desperate to solve the problems at Balaclava, Florence realised she was not well enough and moved back to a house in Scutari with windows opening on to the Bosphorus.

In July when she was recovered, the Bracebridges returned to England and Florence continued her work in the Barrack Hospital, despite a cold reception from the medical authorities who considered they were coping quite successfully without her help.

On 8th September 1855, Sebastopol fell and war in the Crimea was over. The Nightingales worried that Florence needed support, so Aunt Mai volunteered to travel to Scutari and on arrival was shocked to see her niece looking thin and worn.

Back in London, Mr Bracebridge made matters worse for Florence by giving a lecture unfairly attacking the British medical authorities and it was supposed that she had instigated the attack. Dr Hall damaged her reputation further by declaring she was an adventuress and should be treated as such.

She wrote to Sidney, *'There is not an official who would not burn me like Joan of Arc if he could, but they know the War Office cannot turn me out because the country is with me – that is my position.'*

And she was right. A legend had grown up as a result of survivors coming home and telling stories of Florence and the Barrack Hospital.

The public saw Miss Florence Nightingale as a saint who had sacrificed married life to devote herself to nursing. Ships were named after her, songs composed for her and she was placed in the position of a heroine whom no one could afford to ignore. All through the Empire rose a chorus of thanksgiving to Florence who still remained among the sick and dying – the woman who had upheld England's honour in the days of disgrace and neglect, saving countless lives.

The Queen and all her people were eager to know how they could reward Florence. Sidney knew she wanted only the means to carry on her work at home, but nothing could be started until she had completed her task of helping the convalescents in Scutari.

He organised a fundraising committee and in November a public meeting was held *"to give expression to a general feeling that the services of Miss Nightingale in the hospitals of the East demand the grateful recognition of the British people".*

The meeting was crowded and wildly enthusiastic. The Nightingales did not attend – Fanny and Parthe were worried they'd be overcome by emotion and WEN that he might be asked to make a speech. Instead, Fanny held a reception for her influential friends in the sitting room at the Burlington Hotel.

Similar fundraising took place throughout the country and money poured in. The Nightingale Fund was formed to give Florence the means to establish and control *"an institute for the training, sustenance and protection of nurses, paid and unpaid".*

Sidney was anxious for Florence to leave Scutari and wrote asking if she had any plans for using the fund on her return home.

Florence replied: *'I do not feel I can make any plan for what I shall do when I go home, if I go home. People seem to think I have nothing to do but sit here and form plans – what madness! I cannot look forward for one month let alone years and can only go from day to day.*

If the public chooses to recognise my services and my judgement in this matter, they must leave those services and that judgement unfettered. I did not ask for a Fund but if I live, I will take their money to be used in hospital matters as I best may judge.'

Queen Victoria presented a brooch designed by the Prince Consort, a St George's Cross in red enamel surmounted by a diamond crown. The cross bore the word *"Crimea"* encircled with the words *"blessed are the merciful".* On the reverse the inscription read: *"To Miss Florence Nightingale as a mark of esteem and gratitude for her devotion towards the Queen's brave soldiers from Victoria R 1855."*

Florence was not impressed by the praise, popularity or jewels.

Nursing had now become a subsidiary cause – she had set herself a new task, to reform conditions for the British soldier. Florence would look after them, not only while they were ill, but also when they were well.

'Tears come into my eyes,' she wrote to Sidney, *'when I think how in all the scenes of loathsome disease, death and human misery, there arose shining out from the men an innate dignity and chivalry. I do believe that of all those concerned in the fate of these miserable sick, you and I are the only ones who really care for them.'*

Florence had an enthusiastic collaborator in the Military Commandant, and together they improved conditions for the convalescents of the Barrack Hospital. Shops selling drink were closed, men were court-martialled for being drunk and a large recreation room was opened called the Inkerman Coffee House. Requests were sent home for puzzles, games, magazines and books and a second recreation room was created in a wooden hut in the courtyard.

The final report of the commission investigating the army's medical operations, confirmed the Crimean disaster had been unnecessary and was caused by indifference, stupidity and bureaucracy. Sidney was absolved of any blame and the chairman of the committee even went so far as to say of him: *'No man could have been more intent on the honour of this country. He was consistently endeavouring to perform his duty and was always at his post.'*

Sidney's pride in Florence's achievements was overwhelming. He addressed members of the House of Commons saying he had received many letters containing high expressions of praise for the energy, tact and tenderness, as well as the extraordinary self-devotion displayed by Miss Nightingale.

It was now February and Florence had been asked to send

nurses from Scutari to the Crimea but she refused to do so until the War Office had issued a statement of her powers.

Sidney intervened once more and this time a dispatch was sent to the medical and military authorities that read: '*Miss Nightingale is recognised by Her Majesty's Government as the General Superintendent of the Female Nursing Establishment of the military hospitals of the Army. The Principal Medical Officer will communicate with Miss Nightingale upon all subjects connected with the Female Nursing Establishment and will give his directions through that lady.*'

Shortly afterwards, Florence at last received a courteous letter from Dr John Hall inviting her to accompany a party of ten nurses to the hospital of the Land Transport Corps in the Crimea – it was a triumph.

At the end of June, when the hospitals were almost empty, Florence returned to Scutari. On 16th July 1856 the last patient left the Barrack Hospital and after nearly two years her mission was ended. Florence's health had been seriously damaged, she was painfully thin and deeply depressed, afraid of her fame and worried she would disappoint the public's expectations.

A month later Florence and Aunt Mai travelled back incognito in the names of Mrs and Miss Smith, declining the government's offer of a special ship and grand plans to welcome them home. Aunt Mai stayed in Paris and Florence slipped alone into England, closely veiled in black so as not to be recognised.

At eight in the morning, Florence rang the bell of the Convent of the Bermondsey nuns. She spent several hours on her knees in the chapel saying prayers for all those who had died and suffered in the Crimea, thanking God for her survival and for allowing her to complete her long and difficult path to redemption. She was free at last.

Florence took the train north and walked from the station to

Lea Hurst. Mrs Watson, the housekeeper saw her first, burst into tears and ran out to meet her. When word got out she was home, the park round the house filled with crowds eager to welcome back the Queen of Nurses.

Chapter 16

The after-effects of the Crimean war on Florence and Sidney were in one way similar – both were mentally and physically exhausted but in other ways they were quite different.

Florence had been to hell and back, ghosts of the dead haunted her and what she'd seen she would never forget. Her mission now was to implement the lessons learned to ensure the soldiers who had suffered and died had not done so in vain. Action had to be taken while the horrors of war were still fresh in people's minds.

Sidney, on the other hand, wished only to forget the past, his office was piled high with letters and reports sent to him by Florence – he'd spent many hours and used many personal and political contacts to help fulfil her demands. Although he'd done his best, the work did not suit him and he could not cope with the constant pressure she put him under.

For so long now he'd been obligated by his own guilt for seducing an innocent young girl. He loved Florence – no one was more proud of all she'd achieved and he'd been her champion in her search for redemption. Surely now she must release him from his responsibility and allow him to spend more time in peace and quiet at Wilton with his wife and young family?

Sidney went to Karlsbad Spa for a much needed rest, writing to Florence:

'I shall be delighted when this drinking and bathing time is over. Getting up at six in the morning and drinking eight enormous glasses of hot water is dreadful. The treatment lasts two hours with fifteen minutes rest between each glass then followed by one hour's walk. But after dinner and a glass of wine I feel strong and ready for anything.'

On his return, he went off to Ireland for a month's salmon fishing during parliamentary recess. Florence wrote him letter after letter from Lea Hurst, begging him to return and see her but he was not over anxious for a meeting, which drove her to distraction. He wrote encouraging her to rest and recover, then to continue her nursing work in a hospital.

Florence was furious, Sidney had failed her and she was driven by the certainty that delay could be fatal. She was inundated with invitations to appear at public functions and her postbag was enormous, begging letters arrived in shoals. Parthe wrote acknowledgements but Florence replied to none of them. She signed no autographs, granted no interviews and deliberately disappeared from view, being a national heroine was nothing but an embarrassment to her.

Florence returned to London and requested an interview with Lord Panmure, now Secretary at War, who was on holiday in Scotland. He replied suggesting a meeting after the recess.

At the end of August, Sidney returned from Ireland and he and Florence met at the Bracebridges. Sidney told her he was not enthusiastic about her plans for army reform which he considered too ambitious a task and went off to spend the rest of the holidays at Wilton.

Then Florence's luck changed. Early in September 1856, Queen Victoria asked Sir James Clark, the royal physician and an old friend of the Nightingales, to invite Florence to stay with him at his home, Birk Hall, in Scotland. The Queen and the Prince Consort wished to meet this iconic figure of whom they had heard so much and later that month they spent an afternoon together at Balmoral.

Sir James accompanied Florence into the drawing room where the Queen and Prince Albert were waiting.

'Good afternoon, Miss Nightingale – how pleased we are to meet you at last.'

Florence dropped a deep curtsey, 'Thank you, Your Majesty.'

The Queen continued, 'We must congratulate you once again on your marvellous achievements during the Crimea – such an unfortunate war with all that terrible waste of life. But you and your nurses seem to have worked wonders, despite the appalling conditions.'

'We did our best ma'am. Most carried out their duties in an exemplary manner, although regrettably others did not take so well to the harsh surroundings. Thank you for the honour of the award you bestowed on me, which I accepted on behalf of all those who worked tirelessly throughout such difficult times.'

'It was the least we could do in recognition of your wonderful service, Miss Nightingale.'

'We were privileged to serve our country, ma'am and pray attitudes have now changed towards women who wish to train as professional nurses,' Florence replied.

The Prince commented on how he hoped lessons would have been learned by the government departments whose incompetence had caused so much suffering.

Florence said, 'I do so agree, Your Highness. Lack of preparation and poor communication between those with power and those at the sharp end of the action caused a great deal of unnecessary misery. I'm currently working on proposals to strengthen army command structures, as well as to improve conditions in the barracks.'

'That's very commendable,' the Queen said, nodding with approval.

'Well, ma'am, I so admired the soldiers for their conduct, patience and self-denial in the face of unspeakable hardships. Your messages of sympathy and support were deeply felt and much appreciated by them all.'

Florence's charm, enthusiasm and modesty made a profound impression on the royal couple as they listened to her ideas for reform.

When, after nearly an hour, Florence had left, the Queen

remarked, 'What a delightful young woman, so gentle and pleasing – I'd expected her to be rather cold and stiff. She must have been very pretty with those fine dark eyes but now her face is so thin and careworn. Miss Nightingale is only thirty six, two years younger than me but you'd think she was much older. She's certainly suffered a great deal, sacrificing her health and devoting herself to her cause like a saint.'

'I thought she was clever and comprehensive in her views, without the slightest display of religion or humbug,' agreed the Prince. 'Such character in a woman is most rare and extraordinary. I wish her well, although she will need a great deal of strength to make an impression on the mighty machine of government.'

The sincerity of the Queen and Prince Albert in their support for her reforms raised Florence's hopes but it was Lord Panmure she had to convince and he was not an easy man to deal with. Nicknamed "The Bison" for his brawny physique and resolute temperament, she knew to win him over would be a difficult task.

A meeting was eventually arranged and her success exceeded her expectations. Lord Panmure agreed there should be a Royal Commission to investigate army reform and instructions were drawn up according to her suggestions. Florence lost no time in compiling a list of eminent commissioners with civilians, medical and military men equally represented.

When she'd agreed the outline terms of the commission with Lord Panmure, Florence wrote Sidney a long and happy note of her progress. She had done well but it was he who would have to apply the pressure to ensure success, everything depended on him.

Sidney finally agreed to meet her at the Burlington to discuss his involvement. Florence excitedly explained her plans but Sidney was still not convinced. The war was over, it had been discreditable and there was a universal wish to forget the horrors.

'Listen Florence, my dear, are you positive you understand

what you're getting into?' he asked her. 'Panmure dislikes change and finds his job easy by the simple process of never attempting to do anything. I'm far from sure setting up a commission would have any hope of achievement and will require a great deal of work. You know you will be strictly judged after your success in the Crimea?'

Florence was incensed. 'Of course I will be judged, I'm a woman in a man's world but you must help me. What's the use of fame if one may not reap the rewards? Remember your father's words in his diary – army reform means so much to us both. Our work together is unfinished, your support is crucial and you can't let me down now after all we've been through.' She pressed her fingers to her eyelids in the way he knew so well.

'I still think it would be like pushing water uphill to make any progress,' he replied.

'We both know that of the twenty one thousand men lost in the Crimea, two thirds died from disease and inadequate care rather than from wounds in battle,' retorted Florence. 'Every day and every hour, wherever the British army has barracks or hospitals, the system is still murdering men as it murdered them in Scutari.'

The spell cast by her presence and Sidney's own sense of responsibility were once again too powerful for him. By the time he left, he'd reluctantly agreed to accept the chairmanship of the commission but he was far from well, easily depressed and viewed the future with gloom.

It was later that year, in October 1856, when David Herbert Llewellyn's three-year apprenticeship with Dr Hassall in Richmond ended and the time came for him to move on to the second part of his training at medical school.

Out of the eleven hospitals which were now the main centres of medical teaching in London, Dr Hassall recommended David be registered as a student at the Charing Cross Medical School. The isolation of his solitary apprenticeship in Richmond was replaced by the community life of college residence, where he had his own small room with shared washing facilities. Supervision was strict, hours of work and leisure defined, the students' behaviour regulated by rules set down by the staff of the Medical School.

David's fellow students were a motley crew. Mixed motives dictated their choice of profession, diverse attainments marked their pre-medical education and uncertainty clouded their professional future. Neither a dedicated altruism, nor a love of science, provided a common base for choosing to study medicine. Decisions reflected economics, family ties and personal taste but most common was a family medical background.

Many persevered in their course as a matter of duty or because they had nothing better to do. Medical schools by experiment, initiation and necessity, attempted to shape them into a body of professional men, sharing a basic educational experience and a sense of belonging to a group.

David soon settled into college life, his years at Marlborough had taught him how to mix easily with the other students as they socialised in the dining and common rooms. He chose his friends wisely, preferring a few tankards of ale and a game of billiards in the local public house to the wild gin-drinking parties enjoyed by some.

Sidney and David continued to meet up at his club in Pall Mall. Sidney spoke of Florence Nightingale and her nurses and what a difference they'd made to the treatment of soldiers in the hospitals of Scutari and the Crimea. David was impressed by what he'd heard of her bravery and determination against all the odds – she was the heroine of the day.

'Sir, do you think it might be possible for you to introduce me to Miss Nightingale?' he asked his godfather.

Sidney thought it was most unlikely Florence would agree to come face to face with her son, telling David, 'She's rather busy at the moment but I promise I'll do my best.'

David's course of study was over four terms each of six months duration. Lectures were held on chemistry, botany and physiology, together with the principles and practice of medicine. During practical anatomy David learnt to perform dissections on cadavers, an activity by necessity restricted to the winter months. He attended every course, never missed a lecture and by dint of hard work his grades remained in around the middle of the class.

After completing the introductory course and passing his interim examination, he began clinical practice on the wards of the hospital. David worked hard studying late into the night, often falling asleep over his books with his candle still burning.

Florence waited with increasing impatience and frustration for news of progress on her proposed reforms. Early in the year of 1857, she wrote to Lord Panmure who was spending the winter recess in the country: *'Here is that woman bothering you again – just to remind you I am in London, awaiting your decision.'*

When she received no reply, Sidney explained, 'I understand Panmure has gout in both hands and is unable to write.'

Florence retorted, 'Gout is a very convenient thing when there is unpalatable work to be done. It seems that Lord Panmure is more convinced of the necessity of reform than eager to carry it out but I shall never leave him alone until we succeed.'

There was strong opposition in the War Office to the reforms but public opinion was now supporting change and Panmure was finally forced to act. In April, he brought an official draft of the instructions to Florence for her approval before submitting them to the Queen. On 5th May 1857 the Royal Warrant was issued and the following week the commission began to sit.

The strain on Florence now became enormous with the pressure intensified by petty irritations, tensions and emotional conflicts generated by the Nightingale family. Fanny and Parthe revelled in their positions as mother and sister of the famous Miss Florence Nightingale, bathing in her reflected glory.

Parthe told people, 'Even though she is my sister, I don't

hesitate to say she is a remarkable woman.' The two women insisted on remaining with her in London, doing little to help but persuading themselves and others that they were victims of their devotion for another who was dying of overwork.

Florence coached Sidney before every sitting of parliament and spent time teaching the members of the commission what to say at official meetings. Her demands were high, particularly on Sidney as she told him, 'Your influence within the House of Commons is the only means by which we can achieve our aims.'

Sidney's powers were incomparable, if only she could get him to apply them to the work but he was hanging back and complaining about his health – he suffered from fatigue, depression and general malaise. To Florence his complaints were fanciful and she grumbled about them. She told him, 'Your honour is at stake,' and kept an iron grip by exploiting his sensitivity on the subject of his personal obligations.

Sidney finally proposed four commissions – to improve conditions in army barracks and hospitals, to restructure the army medical service, to establish a statistical department and to institute an army medical school. Each would be chaired by himself, each would have executive powers and be financed by the Treasury.

After receiving Panmure's agreement to his proposals, Sidney went off to fish in Ireland, urging Florence also to take a break but she toiled on, still being annoyed by Parthe and Fanny.

In August, Florence collapsed and became dangerously ill with what her doctors diagnosed as a chronic form of brucellosis contracted in the Crimea – her whole body ached with pain and fever. While lying in her bed at the Burlington, she loved to feel the soft summer air stream in through the window and to smell the sweet, light fragrance of newly mown grass rising from the gardens below.

Florence's collapse was the start of her retirement as an invalid and she used her illness as an excuse to keep her family away.

Soon distraction came to Fanny and Parthe in the form of Sir Harry Verney, owner of an historic mansion, Claydon House, in Buckinghamshire. Sir Harry was a wealthy widower with a large family and a great admiration for Florence but when she'd shown no inclination to respond to his advances, he had turned his attention to her sister.

Parthe was not very much in love with Sir Harry but, now at the age of thirty eight, thought she could live with him comfortably and the couple were to be married next June. The prospect of becoming Lady Verney occupied Parthe and the business of organising a wedding delighted and distracted Fanny. At last Florence was left alone.

Chapter 17

When Florence moved into larger accommodation in an annexe of the Burlington Hotel, Aunt Mai and her daughter Blanche's husband, Arthur Clough, came to stay. Arthur worked at the Education Department, but was happy to be Florence's assistant in his spare time – no task was considered by him too mundane and all his duties were carried out with dedication and efficiency.

Florence spent her days lying on the chaise longue, rarely getting up or going out. She was convinced she was dying and started organising her own funeral.

Sidney arrived with a bunch of red roses to cheer her up. 'Good evening, my dear – how have you been feeling today?' He bent down and kissed her cheek.

'As well as can be expected for a dying woman – the flowers are lovely, thank you. What news of Lord Panmure and the reforms?'

'I'm sorry to tell you but he's once more lost his nerve and stalled their progress.'

'Oh wretched man, can't he see what's at stake? Right, it's time now to pull out the big guns. Get the press involved and tell the country the truth about the army's disgraceful living conditions.' Sidney knew she was right. The only way for change was to get the public on their side and put the government under attack.

Florence continued, 'I'll write a pamphlet explaining the facts. We'll have two thousand copies printed at my expense and send them to everyone – the Queen, commanding officers, doctors, members of the Commons and the Lords. I'll send them each a personal letter, that'll shake them up – this so-called fame of mine has to have some advantages.'

Sidney agreed to support the campaign by giving interviews for articles in the newspapers. 'Are you sure you're well enough for all this?' he asked.

'Oh yes, Arthur will help, he's good at paperwork and so willing – he's an angel, not a man.'

Florence's doctor was not happy that she was continuing to work, telling her, 'Excessive mental exertion on the part of a woman is unnatural and could lead to breakdown. Standard treatment for your condition is rest and quiet.' But Florence ignored his advice and was hostile to anyone who tried to prevent her from achieving her plans.

By the end of the year Panmure gave way. Pressure on him in the press and in the House was gaining strength and, in December 1857, the four commissions were granted and set up.

The work now involved to collect information was physically exhausting. Inspections of the barracks meant constant travelling, there was opposition from commanding officers and the commissioners were often left waiting on barrack squares in the cold and wind. After one particularly exasperating visit, Sidney observed to Florence that, 'the Big Wigs were surly'. Florence was frustrated that she was no longer well enough to travel with the men and was incensed when she heard of their inconsiderate treatment – she came to hate red tape and loathed bureaucracy.

As time went on it became evident that the commissioners were succeeding beyond their hopes. The long hours, exhausting journeys and difficult interviews were gradually achieving results but Sidney's health was becoming a serious concern. In February he suffered terrible headaches and was unable to work.

In March he was in bed again and wrote: *'Here I am idling my time in bed, I have been heartily ashamed of myself for the last few days.'* Three days later he wrote: *'I am really not ill, only washy and weak from which I always recover wonderfully.'*

Florence was not the slightest bit sympathetic. What was a headache compared to how she was feeling here on her deathbed?

Working together they were unequalled, her determination and passion for facts together with his incomparable talent as a negotiator were a combination impossible to resist. But because the two were so different, complications inevitably ensued.

Florence never praised or thanked him – she grumbled at him and had no time for pleasantries. Sidney scolded her, telling her she was irritable, exacting and impatient, that she exaggerated and was too fond of justifying herself.

Only the words used at the end of every note he wrote her and those he spoke every time they parted, 'God bless you,' showed the deep affection between them. The bond which united them was so strong it needed no affirmation.

Sidney had not forgotten he'd promised David to ask Florence for a meeting. The time had to be right, she must be calm and in a mood to give the idea proper consideration.

One evening the two of them were alone, relaxing after a particularly successful day and reading the newspapers, when Sidney said, 'Florence, David would like to meet you. Do you think that might be possible?'

Florence looked up. 'Oh Sidney, how could you ask? Every day since that child was born I've thought about him. The pain has at times been unbearable but I gave him away and that's how it has to be,' and she continued to read her paper.

Sidney persisted. 'I'm not asking you to be his mother, just talk to him. Are you not curious to meet your son?'

Florence was annoyed by the question. 'I cannot claim David as my son. Your contact with him has been a great comfort and I'm happy he's doing well, but do you think I could face him and not give away our secret? Poor boy, how could I risk that possibility? There's no chance of me agreeing to meet him, you must forget the whole idea.' She refolded her paper and carried on reading.

Her reaction was just as Sidney had expected. 'I understand what you're saying but surely you're not afraid of him?' he asked, twisting the heavy gold signet ring on his little finger.

Florence remained silent for a full minute. Finally she lowered her newspaper and said, 'No, of course not, only of myself.'

'Medicine has become his life – to meet you is his dream. I've always done my best for you but now I'm asking – forget your own feelings – consider those of our son. Do you want to die wondering why you turned your back on him? Please Florence – just for a few hours, it would mean a great deal to David and to me also.'

Florence was taken aback. Sidney was a warm-hearted man and seldom angry but when his chin quivered as it did now, she knew he was really annoyed. He stood up and crossed the room, standing with his back to her, looking out of the window.

Was she being unreasonable? Should she do this for him? Could she be trusted not to give herself away? She'd been through so much already, surely she could handle talking to her own son? It would be wonderful to meet him. Florence's resolve wavered and she changed her mind.

'Very well Sidney,' she said, her voice was low and calm. 'Please arrange to bring David over next Wednesday evening.'

Sidney turned to face her. 'Thank you Florence – you won't regret it. God bless you.' He kissed her cheek and left her still wondering if she had done the right thing.

On the following Wednesday evening, Sidney and David drove in a gig to the Burlington as arranged, it was early dusk but in Florence's drawing room the blinds were drawn and the lamps lighted. She waited, sitting upright in her chair wearing her best black silk dress and white lace cap, with her fingers drumming on the round table in front of her. As the two men entered the room, her heart beat so violently that for a few moments she was unable to speak.

Sidney walked across the soft carpet towards her with David by his side. 'Miss Nightingale, may I introduce David Herbert Llewellyn, my godson.'

Florence held out her hand. 'Good evening David, I'm pleased you've come. I've heard a great deal about you.' She was relieved that her voice showed no sign of nervousness.

'Good evening, Miss Nightingale, it's such an honour to meet you.' An unmistakeable delight shone from the grey eyes that looked so like her own – could this really be her son?

'Please sit down both of you. I expect you'd like some refreshment.' She rang the bell for the maid who brought a tray of coffee and cake.

Florence took a moment to compose while she busied with the cups, hoping David wouldn't notice her shaking hands. Now she looked up and observed him, wanting to talk but not knowing what to say. So this was her son, she could hardly believe it was true but she must betray no sign of emotion. She glanced at Sidney who smiled and nodded with encouragement.

David was smartly dressed and at almost Sidney's height, taller than she'd expected. His polished shoes shuffled slightly on the carpet, his hands were tightly clasped together. A wave of calm and love swept over Florence as she realised they were both as anxious as each other and at last her face lit up with a tender smile.

'Well David – I understand you are training to be a doctor – such a noble profession,' she said.

'Yes, Miss Nightingale, this is my final year.' His voice was clear and steady. 'When I qualify I hope to eventually have my own practice.'

'Your parents must be very proud of your achievements,' she said.

'They are – but it is Mr Herbert we have to thank.' He looked across the room and smiled at Sidney whose own smile reflected his son's completely.

Florence continued. 'Medicine is certainly at an exciting stage of development and many people are working on amazing advancements. Knowledge of sanitary conditions is much improved and new hospitals will have to be built with these theories in mind.'

'We've learnt about the work of a French Professor, Louis Pasteur. He's discovered infections could be caused by micro-organisms in the air.' David talked enthusiastically of his course and the modules he'd been studying, while Florence asked questions, admiring the knowledgeable and confident manner of his responses.

'Miss Nightingale, I have such respect for your success in the Crimea, it must have been a terrible ordeal.' Florence recounted something of her experiences in Scutari as her son listened with rapt attention.

'It's amazing how you achieved so much working in those dreadful conditions,' he said.

'David, you will learn that life is a series of problems we cannot expect others to solve for us. Anything worth achieving has a price – you must decide where you want to go and find out how to get there. Assume responsibility for yourself, face your challenges and be prepared for the pain involved.'

David nodded. 'I know it will not be easy,' he said.

'The world can be cruel,' Florence continued. 'Your success in medicine will depend on your attention to detail. Be disciplined and always remember to put yourself in the place of your patient.'

Sidney saw Florence was tiring and intervened. 'Well David, I think it's time we left.'

David rose and put out his hand to Florence. 'Miss Nightingale, thank you so much for seeing me. I have enjoyed our meeting more than I can say. I shall always remember your advice and hope your health will soon be fully recovered.'

Florence took his hand and held it for a moment while trying to smooth her face into smiles. 'Goodbye David and good luck with everything you do in life. You have a charming way about you which I'm sure will help a great deal.'

When the two men had left the room, Florence buried her face in her arms and wept.

Chapter 18

The year of 1858 was a year of successes for the reformers. In February, Lord Palmerston's government fell and Panmure was out of office. Three months later Lord Ebrington moved a series of resolutions on the health of the army based on the report of the commission.

Florence spent the summer at the Burlington, leaving only for a short stay at Malvern Spa. She was carried in a chair to the railway station and on to the train, attracting the curiosity of onlookers who already recognised her as a legend.

Sidney knew his health was failing and took the opportunity during the recess to put a few matters in order; he and David had become close and he was concerned his son would be hit hard by his death. After obtaining Florence's approval for his plans, Sidney arranged to meet his old friend Henry Pelham-Clinton for dinner at his club. He ordered a bottle of champagne and the two men sat down to talk.

'Sidney, it's so good to see you but you don't seem well, is everything alright?' Henry asked.

'Listen Henry – I've a favour to ask you. I'm afraid things are not looking too good for me, I probably don't have long to live.'

Henry's face dropped. 'Oh no, that's terrible, I'm so sorry.'

'I have something else to tell you,' Sidney went on. 'Over twenty years ago, I fell in love with a young lady and we had a son together. We weren't able to marry and the boy, called David, was brought up by another family. As his godfather, I've kept in touch with him all his life and now he's in his last year of medical training in London. What I'm asking is would you, dear Henry, consider acting as a confidante to my son if he needs someone when I'm no longer here?'

Henry took a few moments to take in the meaning of Sidney's words. 'Of course, you are my dearest friend and I'll do anything I can to help you – a small repayment for all the kindnesses you've shown me over the years.'

'Well that's good. In exchange I'll include in my will cancellation of the debts you owe me. Let's hope I'll be around for some time yet but I just needed to make sure David would be taken care of by someone trustworthy. Now where's a menu, let's have some dinner.'

Henry was devastated to hear the news of Sidney's illness and surprised by his revelations of David's existence. He was intrigued to find out who'd been the young mother but knew Sidney would never betray her trust. After Sidney's death, he was instructed to write reports to this anonymous lady with news of her son and send them to Sidney's lawyer who would ensure she received them.

Sidney visited his lawyers to explain the arrangements and to draw up his will. His executors were to be Liz's brother and his sister Emma's husband; he left the responsibility for the management of the Wilton estates and properties to them until his eldest son came of age.

Liz would receive all his plate, pictures, prints, books, china, linen, household goods and furniture. Also his wines, liquors and household stores and all other articles whether "of use or ornament" in any of his properties, as well as his carriages, horses, harnesses and stable furniture.

Any servants of ten years' service or more would be given one year's salary as a bonus, £300 was left to the Salisbury Infirmary and £1,000 in trust for the upkeep of the church at Wilton. Among other small legacies to estate workers was a gift of £50 for the Marquis of Ailesbury which Sidney privately agreed with him should be passed on to David.

To Henry Pelham, Duke of Newcastle, was left, for his own use, any sum owing on his Bond.

When Lord Palmerston formed his new government in 1859, he invited Sidney to become Secretary of State for War. Sidney's first reaction was one of despair – he'd grown weary of politics and politicians. He must accept, his duty was clear but he knew he was not equal to the task and wrote to Florence telling her he had accepted the post but also about his doubts.

She replied: *'I quite understand the difficulties you are facing, but you must carry on. Your new position will provide the ideal opportunity to us to help push through our reforms.'*

Liz encouraged Sidney by offering to handle his appointments and help him to deal with the masses of paperwork. Although her husband was caring and generous, Liz had always suspected he had never really loved her and theirs had been a marriage of convenience. She had no idea of Florence's earlier affair with Sidney but was well aware of the closeness and affection between them.

Liz was not jealous of Florence but realised that by working with her was the only way she could share Sidney's life and to do so she was prepared to be the lesser third in the triumvirate. Florence in turn was convinced that Liz did not understand Sidney as well as she did, but tolerated her involvement in their work if that kept Sidney happy.

At the end of his medical studies in March 1859, David Herbert Llewellyn sat his final examinations for qualification. To complete the course, he spent three months as a dresser to John Travers, a Resident Medical Officer at Charing Cross Hospital. The two men became good friends as they worked together each day, providing basic care for medical and surgical patients on the wards.

On the 25th August, David was awarded his Licence of the Society of Apothecaries with silver medals in chemistry and surgery. After five years of study, he at last possessed endorsement of his knowledge and abilities from a recognised medical body. Both Dr Hassall and Sidney were delighted by his achievements.

Dr Hassall wrote to him with congratulations and words of advice.

'You have worked hard and deserve to do well in the grandest profession in the world. The best way to build up a practice is to go out, mix everywhere with influential men and get them to know you. You will make little or no progress by expecting the practice to come to you.

Inspire respect, be friendly, genial and convivial but make sure you preserve the tone of being a gentleman. You have made a good start by choosing the profession for which you feel yourself most fit - some people miss that and repent too late. My best wishes and those of Mrs Hassall go with you.'

Sidney arranged to meet him at his club and greeted David warmly. 'Many congratulations David, you have made me very proud.'

'Thank you sir, but my success is all due to your support and encouragement.' David was worried by how thin and tired his godfather looked. 'But sir, are you unwell?'

Sidney smiled. 'My duties in government are sapping my strength and someday soon I'm hoping to step down and retire to Wilton. My health is not good and I fear will not be repaired unless I spend more time in the country.'

'I'm very sorry to hear that, Mr Herbert.'

'I wanted to tell you that if the worst happens and I'm no longer able to help you through life, I've asked my good friend Henry Pelham-Clinton, the Duke of Newcastle, to look out for you.' Sidney passed David an envelope. 'In here you'll find details of how to contact him should the need arise.' David looked shocked and upset.

Sidney reassured him. 'Please God it may not be for some years yet. Now I have something for you.' Sidney handed him a parcel which David unwrapped, revealing a splendid gold watch and chain.

David was near to tears, he'd never before received such a wonderful present. 'Sir, I'm really grateful not just for this gift but for everything you have done for me throughout my life. I only hope I can repay you by making a success of my career.'

'I'm sure you will,' replied Sidney. 'Now let's talk about you and your future.'

David told him of his plans to move, of Dr Hassall's advice and his determination to set up in his own practice. Sidney watched with pride as his son talked and thought how like Florence he was, not only in his physical appearance but also with his enthusiasm and love for medicine. He hoped he'd done his best for him, although he probably could have done a great deal more. David had become a man with a profession and his life before him; from now on he must take responsibility for his own mistakes and revel in his own triumphs.

At the time of their parting, both men wondered if they would ever meet again.

Sidney's daily life was not an enjoyable one. He spent the early morning catching up on the previous night's affairs and then tackled his own correspondence and parliamentary business. At noon he went to his office to deal with matters of a varied nature. A circulation despatch box arrived, the contents had to be read and noted before the scarlet box was carried by a waiting messenger to the next minister on the list.

Urgent messages came through from colleagues that he could not ignore. Some unexpected important person would ask to see him and though his business might be trivial, it was not wise to refuse. Notes arrived from the Prime Minister, or other senior members of the Cabinet, requesting instant replies.

In the early evening, when Sidney was finally able to leave his office, jaded and weary, he took home another pile of red boxes. After a hasty dinner, he sat down to grapple with their contents until he was so tired he had to leave the task half-finished and seek a few hours of unsatisfying sleep.

While parliament was in session the amount of worry increased. He went earlier to his office, his duty was to attend the House of Commons and in that heated and unwholesome atmosphere he remained until one or two in the morning. On the days parliament did not sit, there would probably be a Cabinet meeting lasting several hours.

A few days of such a life would be sufficient to make most people tired but this routine was repeated for weeks on end with no respite. It was not surprising then that after one year and not in good health, Sidney Herbert began to sink under the strain.

Chapter 19

On leaving Charing Cross Hospital Medical School in 1859 at the age of twenty two, David Herbert Llewellyn commenced his new life as a doctor by moving into a small house in Harrow where his rent included the services of Jane, a young servant girl with a shy but willing nature. He grew a beard and bought a new suit and hat in the latest style, as he knew shabbiness would not inspire confidence.

Now he was ready to launch himself into the world of medical practice. Statistics for students leaving medical school were not encouraging – a small percentage set up leading practices or followed distinguished medical careers, while around half made an adequate living. The rest gave up or failed altogether.

David's question was where to become established. He could not do so where there were practices run by doctors already liked and trusted by their patients – respectable middle-class families were not going to change their doctors without good reason. Potential patients needed to be reassured about the background, morals and character of the man they might consult.

David was confronted by a public whose recognition of the value of a qualified practitioner was less than wholehearted. The image was still of a seller of drugs, rather than a diagnostician and prescriber of treatments; suspicion existed that medical advice was motivated as much by desire of profit as the patient's needs.

Many relied on home remedies or patent medicines purchased from the chemist's shop. People of all classes employed the dubious and unlicensed ministrations of herbalists, bonesetters, homoeopathists, and quackery had an excellent time of it.

David considered applying to be a hospital houseman but personal recommendation was important here as well, as it was mostly only the fortunate young men with relations in senior hospital positions who were granted junior appointments. Ability appeared to be no substitute for connections in attracting patients and income.

His first years were likely to be lean and aspiring young doctors needed funds, even when patients came they did not usually pay cash. The time between the doctor's service and the payment of the bill could be hungry months without a supplementary source of income.

Mr Herbert still provided his allowance but now David had rent to pay and food to buy. Money was also needed to spend on drugs to dispense and valuable earning time was taken to mix prescriptions as well as bottling and labelling them.

David's ideal solution would be to purchase a practice, the best way a financially solvent young doctor could get a foothold in the community, but that would be in the future, he did not yet have the capital. What he needed right now was a visiting list with a high ratio of prosperous middle-class patients – the higher the income of patients, the higher the fees he could charge and the fewer visits required. A wife would be a useful asset as women patients were reluctant to seek advice from a bachelor, but marriage at this time without an assured income would be imprudent.

Some patients would come by sheer circumstance – street accidents, people fainting in shops, personal recommendation – otherwise he had to be content with whoever attended open surgeries at his house and they were usually poor. Although David preferred treating them as they were grateful and less likely to cause a fuss, the poor could not help his financial situation. He turned for help to his friend John Travers, Resident Medical Officer at Charing Cross Hospital.

Mrs Anne Cooper Buckley lived in Cleveland Square, Paddington, with her five children and servant household, her husband was an East India broker and spent many months abroad. He had just returned to India after a short time home on leave and Mrs Buckley found herself pregnant again, which had not greatly pleased her.

Her children, ranging in age from two to twelve years, were a lively bunch, filling the house with noise and chaos, while their exasperated nurse attempted to control them. Mrs Buckley was a woman of buxom build and exuberant good humour, well known in London society for her delightful dinner parties.

Mrs Buckley's trusted doctor of many years had recently retired and her children one by one succumbed to croup. John Travers was an old friend and when he recommended David to oversee the family's treatment, Mrs Buckley agreed to give him the opportunity. David proved to be a skilful practitioner, charming the children who liked him enough to obey his instructions without question and soon they had all recovered.

On several occasions during his visits, David was invited to take his meal in the servants' quarters where his eyes caught those of Mrs Buckley's personal maid, Mary Kelly. Soon he plucked up courage to invite her to spend a day with him and to his surprise she agreed.

Mary was a beautiful, twenty year old Irish girl with large eyes the colour of a spring sky and an agreeable mouth which when she smiled revealed two dimples. Her mass of curly black hair stole from under her cap in dark delicate rings on her forehead and round the nape of her slender neck.

David was not experienced with women and was keen to make a good first impression. He asked friends to advise him on where he should take her and they suggested the Royal Cremorne Gardens at Chelsea.

With a pounding heart, he called at her parent's small terraced house in Star Street, Paddington and Mrs Kelly answered the door. She had the same blue eyes as her daughter but her face looked worn, her hair was grey and pulled back into a bun at the back of her head. Mary's two brothers peered round their mother's skirts, keen to catch a glimpse of their sister's new doctor friend.

Mary was wearing a purple checked muslin dress with a flounced skirt supported by a crinoline and little buckled shoes. Her white bonnet was tied with ribbons under her chin and in her gloved hands she carried a fringed blue cotton parasol. Her face was radiant, her dress perfect. David caught his breath, she looked so beautiful.

The couple travelled by omnibus to the Kings Road and spent the afternoon promenading through the colourful gardens amongst crowds dressed in smart clothes and bright hats, admiring fountains, flower beds and statues. As they stopped beside a lavender bush, its scent filling the air with delicate perfume, a large tortoiseshell butterfly landed on a flower stem and sat languidly stretching its wings in the warm sun.

David said, 'My father once told me that butterflies are the souls of our dear departed come back to tell us they are safe.'

'How wonderful,' replied Mary. 'That's something I'll always remember.'

The two of them marvelled at the sparkling Crystal Grotto, the Hermit's Cave and the Marionettes' Theatre, the circus and Japanese jugglers. David showed off his skills in the bowling alley and the shooting gallery. They watched in amazement as a manned red and white striped hot air balloon rose majestically high into the air and then landed down again.

As evening fell, they chose one of the many restaurants in the park and, while eating a supper of devilled kidneys and white wine, Mary told David the story of her family's life in Ireland.

'My little sister Bridie, dad, mam and me lived on a farm in beautiful County Mayo in the west of Ireland. Our cottage was of white stone with a thatched roof, t'was really pretty. Chickens and a pig lived in the yard and our three cows grazed on a patch at the back.

'My dad grew enough potatoes to pay the rent, some for us to sell, some for the pig and the rest for the pot. There was a lake and the sea nearby. We collected big mussels from the strand and bought fish fresh from the boats.

'Our rent was paid to Michael Quinn from the big house up near Westport – he leased all the land around us from an English lord in London. Mr Quinn was a good baliff, not like some who evicted as it suited. On rent collecting days he and my dad would chat by the fire – fine friends they were.'

David leant forward and filled Mary's glass, listening attentively to her story.

Mary took a sip of wine. 'Are you sure ye want to hear more?' she asked. 'Dad often says I've a runaway tongue.'

'Please go on Mary, I'd like to know all about you,' said David.

'Life was good,' she continued. 'We were poor but we got by. One autumn day when I was six years old, Da came home from the fields and broke the bad news. When he'd put his spade in the ground a terrible stink came up – all the potatoes were black, our crop was ruined. Mam crossed herself and started to cry. Winter would be hard – we prayed there'd be food enough to last us through and next year would be better.

'They said it was a fungus caused by the wet which came off American clipper ships from potatoes fed to passengers, all Europe was suffering. There was food to be had but most went away to line the landlord's pockets and what was left we couldn't afford, not even bread. Dad killed the pig – she lasted us the winter. The hens stopped laying, so one by one Mam wrung their scrawny necks 'til the yard fell silent.'

Mary paused for a moment. 'What a terrible time for you all,' said David.

'T'was a really bad winter, rain, rain splashing down,' she went on. 'At night we huddled together in the big feather bed. Everywhere mothers begged for their children, we gave what we could but soon had nothing more to give.

'Still the rains came, endlessly pouring into spring. Da had no seed potatoes to plant – floods made the fields useless anyway.

Summer came and still it rained. Our little Bridie got sick – we'd no medicine and no money for doctors. When she died, Da built a wooden coffin and carried her five miles to the cemetery – we saw bodies laid in graves with just dirt thrown on top. Then my mam was expecting; another mouth to feed and we knew we had to leave.'

David covered her hand with his. 'You poor darling,' he said. Tears rolled down Mary's cheeks, she pressed her handkerchief against them and continued with a tremble now in her soft voice.

'Mr Quinn came to collect the rent. My daddy told him we'd no money – we couldn't give what we didn't have. Mr Quinn wanted our land, he'd to pay rent on plots like ours and t'would be better if we left. Da struck a deal, we'd go if he gave us money for our passage to England and he agreed. Uncle Mick fixed Da a job in London – we packed up and left, mightily pleased to do so.'

When Mary had finished speaking, the two of them sat in silence for a few minutes. Nearby a band struck up and couples began to dance on a wooden circular platform.

Mary wiped her eyes and said, 'Oh, I love to dance, come on David.'

'I don't know how,' he resisted.

'Oh come on now, I'll help ye.' Despite his protests, she took his hand and as the band played a waltz, showed him how to hold her and the steps he needed to avoid crushing her toes. And soon they were whirling round like everyone else, laughing with delight.

When darkness came a magnificent firework display lit up the London sky. On the way home David plucked up courage to hold Mary's hand and the thrill when he kissed her goodnight stayed with him for days to come. David thought he'd found the perfect woman and was overwhelmed by his feelings for her, while Mary told her mother no one could be more in love than she was.

From then on they spent all the time they could together. They picnicked in parks, walked by the river, talking endlessly of their lives and hopes for the future. David took her back to his house in

Harrow where the maid Jane prepared them simple meals before disappearing to her room.

Weeks went by and on one cold December night, when the dark sky was thick with stars, Mary told David she was expecting his baby. She wanted them to be married straightaway but David was not sure he was ready – he still needed to build his career and was not yet financially able to support a wife and child. Together they broke the news to her parents.

Gerard Kelly was a large, good-humoured man with a mass of dark greying hair, big hands and a heart to match. He'd first come to England as a young lad with his brother Mick to work as a navvie building the canals. When his father died, he'd returned to Ireland to help his mother run the family farm and soon married Ava, his childhood sweetheart. Mick stayed on in England earning enough money to buy himself a public house, where Gerard began working when the family fled the famine.

Ava was a mild-mannered woman who busied herself to make sure her husband and two sons had a clean shirt each day, a hot meal on the table and a warm, welcoming home to return to.

The Kellys were a Catholic family but their experiences had made them question their religious beliefs. What they'd seen during those terrible years taught them there were worse sins in the world than intimacy before marriage between two grown people in love. Gerard and Ava were fond of David and trusted his intentions to marry Mary as soon as he was in a position to do so.

Mary worried about telling Mrs Buckley about the baby and being dismissed from her post as lady's maid, so David decided to take into his confidence Jesse Gilbert, Mrs Buckley's butler. Jesse was distressed by the news but liked the couple and wanted to help them.

'I'm prepared to tell Mrs Buckley. I'm afraid her reaction may not be favourable but I'll do my best,' he warned.

'We're both indebted to you, Mr Gilbert,' said David.

Mrs Buckley was at first stern and disapproving, demanding

Mary should leave her house at once. But after some persuasion, her attitude softened – she knew quite well how easily these things could happen. Mary was a pleasant girl, an honest and conscientious worker who would be hard to replace.

When her time came, Mary would be allowed a maximum of six weeks' absence but with no pay. The rest of the staff must be sworn to secrecy, her household was not to be the subject of dinner party tittle tattle. Mrs Buckley was confident her generosity would be repaid with devoted service.

She was not, however, so benevolent in her views towards David. Before long, the word was spread amongst her considerable circle of friends that Dr David Herbert Llewellyn was of dubious moral character and should not be trusted with their servants or families.

After discussions with David and the Kelly family, a decision was reached. Mary would give birth in secret and afterwards return to Mrs Buckley in Cleveland Square. Her mother, Ava, agreed she would take care of the baby until the lovers were married and could look after their child.

David met once more with Jesse Gilbert and together they planned Mary's confinement. Jesse's father, Philip, was a lawyer living in Great Bedwyn, not far from David's home in Easton Royal. After hearing of the situation, he arranged with the landlord of a nearby inn, The Pelican, at Froxfield, for rooms to be available and a local midwife, Sarah Waite, to be on hand.

In June 1860 the couple arrived by coach at the inn where Sarah was waiting. Nothing happened for several days and the two women spent time chatting about their lives. Mary proudly told Sarah how David was the godchild of Mr Sidney Herbert, the politician, and that Mr Herbert had even introduced him to the famous Florence Nightingale.

Sarah had lived all of her married life on the Wilton estate and was acquainted with the Herbert family. Her husband had worked there as a gardener and she'd been kept busy delivering the babies of estate workers and tenants. After her husband's death, she'd moved to Great Bedwyn to live with her daughter.

When the birth pangs began, Mary started to feel frightened. 'Oh Sarah, I'm so scared.'

'Everything will be fine, dear,' Sarah reassured her and sent for the maid to bring hot water and towels. The pains came and went – when the pains were strong, Sarah rubbed her back.

Mary wept and whimpered. 'I can't stand it.'

'Yes you can – you are standing it – you're doing well.' She held her hand and Mary gripped her harder. Three hours passed, then the pain was bad and she screamed.

Sarah said, 'Good girl – coming along nicely. Baby will be here in no time.'

A great gush of water came and a strong pain, which had her moaning like a soul in torment.

'Easy dear, steady now.' Sarah waited until she knew it was time then softly whispered 'now push'. It took a few more good pushes and out he sailed. He cried sharply and looked round with wide open eyes. Mary started to laugh weakly.

Sarah put her arms round mother and baby and they laughed together. Then the afterbirth came, she cut the cord with the birthing knife and dropped it in a bucket. She took the baby, tenderly washed him, wrapped him in a blanket and handed him back to Mary. David was waiting in the next room, Sarah called to him. He came at once, smothering mother and child with gentle kisses, tears streaming down his face.

Sarah took the bucket out to the yard where a place had been prepared, tipped the contents, sprinkled them with salt and murmured a short prayer. She sat quietly on a bench, feeling the fresh evening air on her hot face, all emotions drained from her.

After paying for the coach and board and lodgings at the inn, David had no money left for the midwife. He reluctantly handed over his godfather's gift of gold watch and chain to Sarah as payment for her services and the couple returned to London with their son to the Kelly's house in Star Street.

The chance encounter at the Pelican Inn resulted in Sarah that night confiding to her daughter a story she had kept to herself for over twenty years. How Mr Sidney Herbert had paid her handsomely to take a trip by ferry to France, collect a baby and return with the child to the Llewellyn family in Urchfont. She'd travelled in the Herbert's coach to Southampton, joined the Nightingales on the ferry to Le Havre, then on to Rouen where she'd stayed until the baby was ready to leave.

The trip had been an amazing adventure, her first and last time in Europe but her excitement had been tinged with sympathy for the young girl who'd had to give up her child. Sarah was not a well-educated woman but she knew the legend of Florence Nightingale and how Sidney Herbert had been involved in sending her to the Crimean war.

The situation appeared to Sarah that the couple had been closer at one time than anyone else knew about and now it seemed she had delivered their grandchild.

Chapter 20

With the proposed army reforms slowly churning through the tedious procedures of government, Florence turned her attentions back to medicine and wrote a book entitled *Notes on Nursing*, outlining her suggestions for new habits of hygiene.

Published in December 1859, the book caused a mild sensation – it was not cheap at five shillings but 15,000 copies sold within a month. The second edition sold firstly at two shillings and then was reduced to seven pence. Thousands of copies were distributed to factories, villages and schools and later on were translated into French, German and Italian.

One evening when Sidney was visiting her at the Burlington, Florence remarked, 'The Trustees of the Nightingale Fund have written to ask my plans for the money still sitting in the bank. Apparently the total has now reached £45,000 and they're anxious to spend it.'

'And what have you decided?' Sidney asked.

'I want to tell them I didn't ask for a fund in the first place and therefore have no plans for its use,' she replied.

Sidney laughed. 'My dear, I think you would be most unwise to step away from this important responsibility,' he said. 'The public donated the money for you to start a nursing school and without your name as figurehead, the success of the scheme could not be guaranteed. What a terrible waste of a marvellous opportunity, not to mention the goodwill of all those generous people.'

Florence took Sidney's advice and proceeded to agree with the trustees' arrangements for investing the fund to set up a training school for nurses at St Thomas' Hospital.

The school opened in July 1860 with the objective of producing nurses capable of supervising others. Fifteen probationers were selected to help in the wards and receive training from the sisters and medical staff. If at the end of the year they passed their examinations, they would be registered as certified nurses. The probationers lived on an upper floor of St Thomas', each had her own bedroom and there was a common sitting room. Board, lodgings, laundry and a brown uniform with a white cap and apron were provided, plus ten pounds for personal expenses.

The first year of the scheme was an anxious one for Florence but was considered to be a success when six probationers were recruited as nurses and two took work in infirmaries. There was a special need for staff in workhouses and also for some to be trained in midwifery, so a decision was made that two thirds of the fund should continue to support training at St Thomas', with one third to be used for specialist training at King's College.

As a relief from military and medical matters, Florence spent time writing a philosophical paper entitled *Suggestions for Thought*. After years of seeking forgiveness, Florence had started to reject conventional religion. To her now, God was a benevolent being of infinite goodness and wisdom, inconsistent with eternal damnation and atonement. She suggested that Christians should behave as she had done – redirect their energies more productively, go out into the world and make a difference. Instead of praying to be delivered from disease, people should make efforts to ensure clean water and proper sanitation was available.

Florence sent out a number of copies of her draft paper anonymously, although most recipients recognised the style of the author. Comments were not favourable, the paper was never printed but one person aroused by its contents was the Reverend Benjamin Jowett.

Benjamin Jowett had arrived at Balliol College, Oxford with a classics scholarship from St Paul's School, was soon elected to a Fellowship, appointed tutor and ordained into the Church of England. His radical theological views outraged clergy and conservatives who regarded them as an attack on religion. Jowett was intrigued by Florence's writings, recognising a kindred spirit and a regular correspondence began between them, although they were not to meet for some time.

During the summer of 1860, Florence rented ground floor rooms in the fresher air of Hampstead to escape the stifling heat of the city. Now confined to bed or the sofa, she seldom walked and rarely went out, finding solace in the company of cats lying on her pillow or twining round her neck.

'My cats are such a comfort,' Florence observed to Sidney, who'd been forced to stay in London for the second summer in succession to deal with the work piling up around him. 'Dumb animals understand us so much better than human beings.'

One evening after parliament had resumed session, Sidney rode over to Hampstead feeling particularly weary, feverish and dispirited. The warm dusky air, laden with the smell of late summer roses, entered through the window near where Florence chose to lie on a red velvet chaise longue, with a large tabby cat sleeping on her lap.

'Good evening my dear, how are you?' Sidney asked, kissing her cheek.

'Oh much as usual, weak as water – you look tired, are things getting on top of you again?'

Slumping into an armchair, he said, 'I swear to you Florence – every day I keep the War Office with the House of Commons is one day off my life. My strength is ebbing by the day.' Sidney sighed and closed his eyes for a moment.

'Any movement on the reforms?' she asked, offering him a glass of cool lemonade.

'We know that to work effectively they're going to cost a great deal of money,' he replied. 'Palmerston is a supporter but William Gladstone as Chancellor is keeping his hand firmly on the purse strings.' Sidney sipped the drink, leaning back in his chair, looking anxious and pale.

Florence was exasperated. 'Surely he must realise the

importance of spending money for the defence of the country?' She pressed together her thin, blue-veined hands in a gesture of frustration.

'As you know,' replied Sidney, 'William and I have been friends since Oxford. We've had many arguments over the years but have never really fallen out. However, this is different. He has an intense dislike and distrust of the military and a great eagerness to reduce expenditure – any suggestions for spending money will not be favourably received.'

'We cannot allow him to overturn the reforms after all our work. You must find a way to persuade him.' As she spoke she banged her hand on the side of the chaise longue, waking the cat who jumped down and ran out of the room.

'Yes my dear, I'll do my best,' but Sidney knew he was in for a bumpy ride.

'Poor Florence,' he thought later on his journey home. 'She has given up so much and is still doomed to fail.'

To appease the Chancellor, Sidney suggested that some of the worst barracks should be sold off and the proceeds used to improve the remainder. Gladstone did not agree; he was of the opinion that any money raised in such a way should be placed at the disposal of the government in the main revenue pot. The refusal was the last straw for Sidney – he wrote to Palmerston asking to resign from the War Office but his resignation was not accepted.

As the year of 1860 drew to a close, Sidney's health finally collapsed. The pain in his side that had started as an occasional twinge now enlarged and developed. He had at first ignored it, telling himself most men of his age get little pains that they cannot account for, but when the fiery piece of anger began to wake him at night he knew he must see a doctor.

Dr Henry Bence Jones, a distinguished chemical pathologist at St George's Hospital, diagnosed Sidney with diabetes and renal sclerosis, a hardening of kidney tissue known as Bright's Disease, which he said was incurable and at an advanced stage.

Three courses of action were open to Sidney – retire altogether, give up the War Office and remain as an MP, or go to the House of Lords and keep the War Office. For the sake of his health, the first was best, the doctors advised complete rest and he longed for the peace and quiet of Wilton but that choice was not allowed him by either Liz or Florence.

It was the worst time for him to break down – everything depended on the War Office reorganisation which only he could push through.

'One more fight, the last and the best,' pleaded Florence. He must not fail now, let him complete this final task and then relax at Wilton. Resentment against life and fate blinded her; she'd proved that serious illness need not interfere with work – now he must do the same.

Sidney knew he had to keep working but he would much rather just keep his seat in the Commons. He was well thought of as an MP, the work of the War Office he detested, it did not suit him and his talents were wasted.

Sidney went to see Florence to discuss the options and she persuaded him that for the sake of all the work they'd already done, he must continue with the reforms. The shock of the doctor's verdict was great but doctors were sometimes wrong and people with so-called terminal diseases often lived on for years.

The terrible thought of the possibility that she might survive him was only consoled by Florence's conviction that she too was declining fast.

Florence suggested Sidney should try the water cure at Malvern, sleep out of town and take plenty of exercise, wear a flannel belt, eat beef and drink beer. Instead he experimented with a concoction called Christchurch Remedy, a mixture of camphor and chloroform inhaled through the nostrils, followed by several glasses of brandy. None of these remedies had any beneficial effect and Liz began to drag her husband on a melancholy round of doctors, trying treatment after treatment, each one to be soon discarded.

A visit to Wilton raised his spirits. Sidney went hunting and slept well for the first time in months. Early in January, he issued a simple and dignified farewell address to the electors of South Wiltshire, announcing his resignation as their MP after serving his constituency for nearly thirty years. Many of his colleagues wrote letters expressing regret and sympathy at his departure.

Shortly afterwards, Sidney was created a Baron with the title Lord Herbert of Lea and took his seat in the House of Lords, which he described to Florence as *'addressing sheeted tombstones by moonlight'*. But Sidney was still convinced he would not recover from his illness and became depressed and despondent.

Weak as she was, Florence summoned her strength and took a cab to confront Dr Henry Bence Jones in his office at St George's Hospital. The couple were already acquainted through his work on the council of the Nightingale Fund.

The doctor rose from his seat to greet her. 'Good morning, Miss Nightingale, how good to see you again. Won't you please sit down?'

'Thank you Dr Bence Jones, but I am afraid my visit is not a happy one,' said Florence as she straightened her bonnet and settled in a chair beside the doctor's desk, removing her gloves finger by finger.

'I am worried that Lord Herbert blames his negative attitude to his health on your diagnosis,' she continued. 'Because of what you have said to him, he is convinced that whatever he does, he cannot expect to live another year and should retire to spend the rest of his life at Wilton with his children.'

The doctor leant forward across his desk, observing Florence with kindly, brown eyes over the rim of his spectacles. 'I am sorry to tell you, Miss Nightingale, that Lord Herbert's condition is extremely serious and there is really not much more we can do to help him.'

'His wife tells me her difficulty now is to raise his spirits,' said Florence. 'He needs a purpose to go on – I'm sure he would collapse and die without political occupation. How often do you see this in professional men who die so quickly after retirement?'

The doctor nodded. 'I have certainly experienced such a thing happening.'

'God forbid I should compare such a pure political life as his to an addiction,' continued Florence, 'but it's like leaving an alcoholic without his brandy. Please say to him that you have known worse cases recover.'

Dr Bence Jones pursed his lips and hesitated for a moment before he replied. 'I understand your concerns, Miss Nightingale, but you must realise it would be completely unethical of me to give Lord Herbert a false impression of his condition.'

'I hope you will not think I am interfering between physician and patient,' Florence replied, 'but I'm sure just the right words from you would give him more hope and vitality.'

The doctor tapped the tips of his fingers together. 'Very well, I will do my best,' he said.

She nodded and continued, 'Whatever you may think right to say to him, please do not let Lord Herbert know I have spoken with you. He is so very peculiar in temperament I think scarcely any man knows him. Thank you for your time, Dr Bence Jones – good day to you,' and with the doctor shaking his head at her temerity, Florence left his office in a flurry of black woollen skirts

The scheme for reorganisation of the War Office was launched – every department was to be changed, each official's duties and responsibilities examined and defined.

Florence feared Sidney was weakening under the pressure but she was still unable to accept he was a dying man, complaining about his lack of decision making and poor administration skills. Although she agreed he was thinner each time she saw him, she continued to dismiss doctors' opinions, calling them "quacks".

Sidney bore her tirades with angelic good temper, frequently expressing his admiration for Florence who, though gravely ill herself, had still worked on. By the end of May her pleas were useless, Bright's Disease was advancing with horrible swiftness.

In June he wrote to say he could not struggle on and must retire, but Florence still refused to accept his health as an excuse. Her work was ruined, the War Office was a wreck – he had failed her.

She cut herself off from him and would not see him or write to him. Sidney was distraught – he could deal with her anger but he could not leave her alone in her unhappiness and, ill as he was, he arranged to face her at the Burlington.

It was a beautiful June morning, Florence's room was full of warmth and light, the sound of birdsong filled the air. Through the open window she could see sunshine falling on rich clumps of summer flowers and the long hedge of leafy laurels, scents crept in from the shrubs in the garden. When Sidney arrived, Florence was lying on her chaise longue holding a book in her hand pretending to read, with two tabby cats curled up by her feet.

Looking tired and gaunt, he walked across to her without speaking, sat down and offered his open hand in the hope she would lay hers within it. She was glad of his appeal for tenderness and wanted to respond but some strange force would not allow her to surrender.

After a few minutes he closed his hand, smiled and said, 'I'm so sorry, my dear, if you think I've failed you but we've all done our best. Sadly our faith could not shift the mountains of government after all.'

Florence was unmoved. Still consumed with rage, her voice choked with passion, she replied, 'Sidney, by failing to carry on, you're dooming the whole British Army and turning your back on me after all we've been through. You must fight your illness and help me see our work to its completion. Please don't throw away so noble a game with all the winning cards in your hand.' It was a bitter reproach.

Sidney stood up and began pacing the room, his hands behind his back. 'Florence, you've given up so much, your pluck and resistance during the Crimea was miraculous, no man could have shown more, but this massive task was hopeless from the outset. I simply cannot go on, please forgive me. I have tried...' He stopped speaking, overcome with emotion and unable to find the right words.

Sidney moved towards her, took her pale face in both his hands and murmured, 'Florence, my dearest Florence.' Her eyes met his loving glance, her heart melted but with enormous effort she deceived him of her true feelings.

She turned her head from his touch, looking blankly through the open window. 'I won't call you a coward but one of us is and it's not me. Perhaps it would be better if you left.' Her unjust words stabbed at him like knives as a clamour of starlings arose from the garden.

Sidney sighed with the finality of helplessness. 'Very well, my dear, if that's your wish. Please don't distress yourself, goodbye for now.' With his usual valediction of 'God bless you', he left her still gazing through the window, pouting and displeased. Yet Sidney bore her anger with kindness and good humour – he'd passed beyond her power to wound him.

When Sidney had gone, Florence dissolved into floods of tears convinced her whole world was collapsing round her, misery filled her heart leaving no room for other people's sorrows. A cat jumped up onto her lap and she buried her face in its warm fur, comforted by the sound of soft purring.

All through the next few weeks, Sidney became more ill. At the end of June, he travelled down to Wilton then decided to visit the spa at Karlsbad, spending a night in London to take leave of his more intimate personal and political friends.

On the 9th July at around 4.00 p.m., he called on Florence at the Burlington Hotel. The couple were not alone – Sidney could no longer walk and had to be assisted up the stairs.

When he entered her room, Florence gasped as she realised the frailty of him – finally she was forced to accept that her lover, her champion, the centre of her world was close to death. Blinking back the tears, she offered Sidney her trembling hand which he raised to his lips with something like a sob and their eyes met for a moment in mutual love and understanding. The two of them exchanged a simple 'Goodbye, God bless you' and she never saw him again.

The party reached the spa on 13th July and at first the change seemed to do him good. Three days later he sent his official resignation to Lord Palmerston. On the following day, he was less well and his doctors urged his immediate return to England if he wanted to die at home. Sidney's favourite horse, Andover, had been brought over for his use and on dismounting he kissed the horse's neck and fed him sugar saying, 'I shall never ride again'.

The party arrived back on 27th July and, after a day in London, the last journey was made. William Gladstone watched him go and wrote to Liz: *'Give him my most earnest love and ask him what I know is needless – to forgive me if I have torn his tender spirit.'*

When they reached Wilton, Sidney was overjoyed to see his beloved home and to spend time with his children. The next day he was well enough to be wheeled in a bath chair to admire for the last time his beautiful gardens in the glory of an English summer afternoon. That evening he said goodbye to his four sons and three daughters, received Holy Communion and with perfect calm and resignation waited to die, watched through the night by his devoted wife.

Early in the morning of 2nd August 1861, he was heard to say, 'Well, this is the end. I have had a life of great happiness, a short one perhaps but an active one. I have not done all I wished but I have tried to do my best.' Then he murmured twice his last words, 'Poor Florence, poor Florence, our joint work unfinished.' A few minutes later he died, one month before his fifty-first birthday.

Florence was in Hampstead when she heard the news of Sidney's death – she was overwhelmed with anguish and despair, the structure of her existence had been destroyed. When her fits of weeping had finally subsided, she sat exhausted, gazing for hours numb and unseeing through her window into the garden beyond.

Aunt Mai and Uncle Sam arrived the next day, trying to be kind and consolatory with sympathetic platitudes when a companionable silence would have provided the best comfort. Without knowing the secrets of her past, the world could not understand the true extent of how much Florence had lost. At forty-one years old, her life seemed over.

WEN came to see her and they threw their arms around each other. 'Oh Papa, I loved and served him like no one else,' she cried, rims of bright red showing round her grey eyes. 'Ours was a silent love, we were identified and no more discussion was needed. How can I go on without him?'

Her father was at a loss to know the right words to console his daughter. 'I'm so very sorry my dear – if only things could have been different for you both. He was a most charming man and stood by you until the end.'

'Papa, I ignored how much he was giving up for me. I made things worse instead of better and never let him see how perfectly I loved him.' Florence clung to her father for comfort as tears poured down her face. 'No wife could be more bereaved, no widow more desolate than I am now,' she sobbed.

'My dear daughter, try not to distress yourself too much. What has happened in the past can never be altered or put right. You must allow yourself time for grief to run its course.' WEN softened his words with a smile and hugged her close until at last her crying ceased.

Sidney's death left her with a kind of stupefaction, so difficult was it to grasp the sudden advent of nothingness and resign herself to believe he was gone. Florence blamed God for allowing

Sidney to die – but in her heart there was guilt about the pressure she'd put on him, knowing he was seriously ill and she tortured herself that she was in some way responsible for his early death.

Cold shivers ran through her as she remembered her cruel words at their last meeting, how differently she should have behaved – he'd died thinking he'd failed her, when the truth was just the opposite. His encouragement and support had meant the world to her, without him she would have achieved nothing. She worried too about how David would cope with losing Sidney and wished they could be together, consoling each other in their misery.

As soon as she was able to do so, she wrote long letters of sympathy to Liz, mingled with her own expressions of grief and desolation at the terrible loss they were both suffering. Liz wrote back saying that even the children were of no comfort to her. *'He was my all and he is gone. You know everything I have to bear more than anyone else.'*

Sidney was buried in the church at Wilton and a great gathering attended his funeral. Florence was not well enough to make the journey, although she managed to send Liz suggestions of readings she would like included in the service.

William Gladstone, Sidney's friend and adversary, wrote to her afterwards describing the day, saying many men were weeping at the loss of such a well-loved man.

Sidney's parliamentary work left little impression, his promising beginnings came to almost nothing, but he did succeed in making the health of the British soldier an important political issue which could not be ignored by subsequent administrations.

Nine months after Sidney's death, news arrived that his half-brother Robert, Earl of Pembroke, had died in Paris. Members of the family hurried over to France and had difficulty in gaining access to the house in Place Vendôme. When they at last entered a forlorn sight greeted them.

The house was in great disorder and Robert's body lay on a

table covered with a sheet, his mistress, Alexina Gallot, was nowhere to be found nor were the children. The house had been stripped of most of its contents and all the valuable furniture, plate and porcelain removed from Wilton more than thirty years previously, was missing.

Robert was laid to rest in the cemetery of Père Lachaise in Paris and Sidney's eldest son George became the 13th Earl of Pembroke at the age of eleven years.

Chapter 21

Sidney Herbert's death was a shattering blow for David; during the eight years he'd lived in London they'd become close and he valued his godfather's support and companionship. Sidney's poor health meant they had not met for some time, so he'd had no opportunity to tell him about his love for Mary or about the baby. Neither had he yet told his parents, deciding to wait until he and Mary were married before breaking the news.

His father had passed on to him from the Marquis the £50 left to him in Mr Herbert's will but the allowance he relied on was now ended. The clothes he'd bought when he first qualified were looking worn and shabby. Bills were coming in and he had nothing to depend on but slow dribbling payments from people who must not be offended.

Mrs Buckley had lost him many promising patients and he was worried that his reputation amongst her wealthy friends was now irreparably damaged. John Tasker had helped him once but David had let him down and he was too embarrassed to ask again.

David calculated that by charging the going rate of two shillings per call, even if he had ten calls a day, six days a week, the most he could earn was less than £300 per year. House visits were made at all times of day and night.

After dark he took a lantern and found his way through densely inhabited parts of town, down dirty narrow streets, lit only by a single lamp with tall, old, neglected houses on either side. The air was impregnated with filthy odours, drunken men and women fell around in the mud, unpleasant looking figures skulked in doorways. Fog often shrouded the buildings, making the place seem even more menacing.

David walked with care down dark passages and up flights of

stairs to gloomy rooms with smoky fires and broken furniture. Limbs were bound, pulses felt, boils lanced and suspicious looking bodily fluids examined in basins.

A few days after Christmas, an advertisement in a local shop caught his eye for the position of assistant medical officer in the union workhouse. Although not an attractive proposition, his pride and self-esteem were now growing dim and this job would at least provide a regular source of income.

The interview took place in a stuffy, dark room at the back of a grocer's shop, where four humourless men sat in disinterested expectation. One was the medical officer who introduced himself as Dr Strange. Two others were members of the union board and the fourth was the master of the workhouse. The grim quartet appeared to David to be men who were perfectly satisfied with their own opinions and considered themselves of paramount importance.

After some perfunctory discussion, the four gentlemen, still without displaying the slightest suspicion of enthusiasm, agreed David's qualifications and experience were satisfactory. As there were no other candidates and it was now nearly lunch time, he was offered the job to begin immediately. No opportunity was allowed for him to speak other than to confirm acceptance but Dr Strange offered to show him round the infirmary the following day.

The workhouse was a red brick, prison-like building, with rows of small, dismal windows frowning down on the street, surrounded by iron railings and with a porter stationed at the gate. Inside, the old and infirm, paupers and vagrants crowded together in a dreary and comfortless life; poverty was generally perceived by those in charge to be the result of personal weakness. The greatest economy was exercised and little comforts that might be considered a luxury were carefully excluded to discourage all but the neediest.

It was a bitterly cold day in January, snow lay on the ground frozen into a hard crust. Dr Strange was a fat little man of fifty with a red face and watery blue eyes, wearing a rusty brown coat with a threadbare velvet collar and a black bowler hat. He'd toiled at the workhouse on his own for some years and was now finding the increasing number of inmates too taxing for one man.

'Well, here we are, Dr Herbert Llewellyn. As you can see, the infirmary is separate from the main building. Six wards, two male, two female and two for infectious cases, plus a lying-in room and mortuary. Most inmates are suffering exhaustion from the burden of their years – chronic bronchitis or incurable diseases like paralysis or tuberculosis. Many die soon after they arrive.'

The two men entered one of the male wards. David saw thirty or so narrow wooden beds crowded together with hardly space between them. A terrible stench came from a recess containing one lavatory and a water closet. Some patients smiled as he passed, others held out bony hands asking for help or lay on their backs gazing at the ceiling with unseeing eyes, their thin fingers clutching at worn blankets. In the fireplace there burnt a miserable fire, the cold air was filled with the sounds of moaning and cries of pain.

Dr Strange saw the look on David's face. 'The overcrowding is not acceptable but what can we do? I reported the problem of no water supply over a week ago but nothing has been done about it.' The doctor shrugged his shoulders and dropped his hands in a gesture of helpless apology.

'So who's in charge here?' asked David.

'Mrs Jackson, the matron – she does her best but she's never been trained as a nurse,' Dr Strange replied. 'She gets help from female inmates but most of them can't read which leads to problems when dispensing medicines.'

David tried not to show his horror. 'Be careful when you prescribe alcohol,' the doctor continued. 'It's often purloined in transit, or traded by patients in return for extra food or favours. Drunken carers on the wards are a common sight I'm afraid.'

By the time they'd completed their tour, David was overcome with a hopeless state of despondency – this was no way for an aspiring young doctor to earn a living. He must find a better way to buy a country practice so that he and Mary could be married and start a new life; things were getting desperate.

A few weeks later, following Sidney's instructions, David wrote to Henry Pelham-Clinton, Duke of Newcastle-under-Lyme.

Dear Sir: I am writing to you on the recommendation of my late godfather, Lord Herbert of Lea, to ask for your help. I qualified two years ago as a general practitioner but am finding difficulty in making a living in London because my expenses have been much greater than anticipated.

I am engaged to a wonderful lady but we cannot marry until my situation improves by ideally accumulating sufficient capital to purchase a small country practice. The only way I can see to better my future is by being paid for my medical skills in perhaps the military. If you have any suggestions on how my ambitions could be achieved I should be very pleased to consider them.

I remain, yours sincerely – David Herbert Llewellyn LSA

Henry was now Secretary of State for the Colonies. He'd recently returned from a trip accompanying the Prince of Wales to the United States and Canada to discuss the effects of the American Civil War on the British economy.

Henry dismissed the idea of sponsoring David to join the British military services. He was aware that medical men were poorly treated compared with officers and badly paid for their considerable skills.

Instead he wrote to the Confederate President, Jefferson Davis, whom he'd met on his recent visit, to explain David's background and circumstances. President Davis was only too happy to encourage British involvement in the Civil War and used his influence to arrange what appeared to be a satisfactory solution to

David's search for a new beginning.

When he received Henry's letter and instructions for what to do next, David was relieved but now he had to explain to Mary. He would organise a happy day out and break the news about the plans which he hoped would finally secure their future together.

On their son's second birthday, a fine day in June 1862, David, Mary and William took an excursion on a steam train from the railway station in London and journeyed down to Brighton. The platform was packed with excited Londoners eager to escape to the seaside with picnic hampers, rugs and all the paraphernalia necessary for a day out with the family.

The train stood waiting, its great black engine noisily belting out smut and sparks. They climbed into a crowded wooden carriage. The guard blew his whistle, the boilers hissed, wheels started to turn, chains clanked and then they were off, whirling along at twenty miles an hour through the fresh green countryside. William pressed his nose to the window, exclaiming with delight and pointing his finger at fields with sheep and cows he had never seen before.

The crowds pushed down from the station along the promenade. Brighton was a pretty picture – the beach, the bathing machines, the long line of rocks and buildings were blushing and bright in the sunshine. Bands played, there were organ grinders and Punch and Judy. Then there was the sea – a vast expanse of shimmering blue water disturbed only by small white crests of waves breaking on the shore.

David and Mary found a place to sit, laying out their rugs and picnic. David carried William down to the water's edge, dangling the little boy's fat bare legs in the sea and laughing as his son squealed with delight when white topped waves came leaping over the blue. David soon turned away – the sea looked serene and welcoming from a distance but the power of the waves and the depth of the water frightened him.

They dug in the sand and collected stones, building up high

towers and knocking them down again. Soon they were hungry and tucked into bread and cheese, pork pie and chutney, then fruit cake, apples and lemonade. After lunch, with their young son sleeping, David knew the time had come to break his news to Mary.

'Listen, my darling – I have something important to tell you,' he said. Seagulls screamed overhead.

Mary looked at him with her large blue eyes and smiled her sweet smile. 'Yes dearest, what is it?'

David hesitated a little, looking vaguely towards the horizon as she sat in silent expectation. 'You know there's nothing more I want than for us to be a family and live together?' Mary nodded.

David continued, 'Although I've tried my best to make a living as a doctor, I've slipped into difficulties. It seems that in no other career has a man to work harder for what he earns, or do more work without earning anything. I can see no way out unless I do something to make a great deal of money in a short period of time.'

'And how will ye do that?' she asked.

'Before he died, Mr Herbert gave me instructions to contact a certain Mr Pelham-Clinton if I needed help. He has kindly arranged for me to join a Confederate ship as assistant surgeon. The money will be very good and I'll be able to save for our future together.'

Mary's lower lip began to tremble. 'Does that mean fighting in the war?' A cold shiver ran through her in spite of the warmth of the day.

'I suppose it does – but the ship is built of the strongest construction and manned by a most experienced crew.' David held out his hand and she placed her own within it.

'How long will ye be away?' she asked, her face was now as white as paper.

'That I can't really say – probably around two years – it's unlikely the war will last much longer.' The sound of the sea was like a sigh.

'So when do ye go?' her voice was low and faint, barely a whisper.

'Next month,' said David, there was no easier way of telling her.

A large tear which had for some time been gathering, rolled down Mary's pale cheek as she looked up and tried to smile. 'How will we manage without you?' she asked.

'Try not to grieve darling,' he said. 'I know it will be difficult at first but I need you to be brave and understand this is for our future. The time will soon go by, then we can be married and start our life together with William in some little country town. Wouldn't that be wonderful?'

She agreed it would and wiped away her tears. 'Oh David, I'm very sad ye have to go but please love me always, promise me you will love me always?'

'Of course I will dearest – you are my one true love,' he replied, close now to tears himself. David put his arms around her and they sat together in silence, lost in their own thoughts until William awoke and demanded attention.

The little family group strolled to the end of the great Chain pier, then back along the promenade. A troupe of black faced musicians dressed in brightly coloured tailcoats, striped trousers, spotted bow ties and straw hats, cracked jokes and played plantation songs on banjos and concertinas.

Mary laughed at the show and did her best to appear cheerful, but David's news had sent a stab of fear through her heart. She wished there could be another way for them to be together but David was doing his best and she must be happy and brave for him. The couple returned to London with their child wondering when would be their next family outing.

The American Civil War had begun in April of the previous year with British support split between the bossy, bureaucratic Federal North and the plucky underdogs of the agricultural Confederate South.

William Gladstone was of the opinion that Britain should support the South but the government was chiefly concerned with not becoming involved at all in the conflict. There was too much at stake, the livelihood of one million mill workers depended on the import of raw Southern cotton, while British investors held five hundred million dollars' worth of US stocks and securities.

Queen Victoria issued a proclamation forbidding British subjects from entering the war but Britons still volunteered in their thousands to join both Federal and Confederate armies.

The North began blockading Southern ports, cutting off commercial advantages and resources vital to military power and domestic comfort. The South needed a navy to draw away Northern ships but the Confederacy had no shipyards capable of building such vessels.

A Confederate agent, Captain James Bulloch, contracted Lairds of Birkenhead to design and build a ship that could survive the harshest conditions for years on end. The whole transaction had to be kept between private parties to avoid interference from the English authorities and Fraser Trenholm & Co, cotton merchants of Liverpool, assumed responsibility for payment.

The result was *No 290*, a steamer of the most perfect symmetry with full sail power, equipped with three masts, two engines and cabins that could comfortably accommodate twenty four officers and a crew of one hundred and twenty.

First Lieutenant Kell was responsible for recruiting the initial civilian ship's company. The seamen were almost all British, picked up from the streets of Liverpool, given new shirts and a good clean up with soap and water. Officers were already appointed, experienced Confederates, but with two exceptions – the Master's Mate, twenty-one year old George Townley Fulham from Hull and Assistant Surgeon, Dr David Herbert Llewellyn.

Seizure and detention of the vessel was only hours away and she must leave England under a British flag with a British captain. The gentleman chosen was Captain MJ Butcher of the Royal Naval

Reserve.

On Saturday 29th July 1862, *No 290* was steamed down the Mersey, supposedly on a trial and boarded by influential friends of Lairds keen to show off their latest craft. Later that day, the passengers disembarked to another vessel and returned to Liverpool, while *No 290* steamed on out to sea, much to the consternation of officials on shore who were too late to prevent her departure.

Two weeks later, *No 290* moored at Terceira in the Azores where she was equipped with all the requisites of an armed steamer, including eight powerful guns. Captain Raphael Semmes arrived with his officers and loved the ship from the moment he saw her, describing her to his men as 'sitting on the water with the lightness and grace of a swan'. During his thirty-seven years in the navy he had never sailed on such a well-crafted vessel.

On Sunday 24th August, the crews of *No 290* and the accompanying two ships, *Bahama* and *Agrippina*, were summoned to the deck. The officers were dressed in full uniform of an attractive shade of grey with a conspicuous abundance of gold braid, contrasting with the crew in regulation blue.

Commander Semmes mounted a gun carriage and read his commission from the President of the Confederate States and the order of the Secretary of the Navy, directing him to assume command. The reading over, a flag and pennant were hoisted to the breeze, a gun boomed and *No 290* became the *CSS Alabama* to the cheers of all on board.

Semmes then addressed the men: *'Good morning, gentlemen. It gives me great pleasure to greet you today as the captain of this beautiful ship, in the hope you may be prepared to join us on our two-year mission. The Alabama is a man of war, governed by the rules of the Confederate Congress – for any man to disobey these rules would mean certain and perhaps severe punishment.*

'We shall be cruising in mixed climates with sometimes perilous conditions. Men will be required to work the ship in all weathers by

day and night. We cannot rule out capture by our enemy and the failure of our cause. Our work to be done is definite, our itinerary prearranged with exactness, to be carried out without deviation. We must remain mysterious and uncertain in our whereabouts to our enemy and be a terror to his commerce on all seas.' There was a murmur among the men.

Semmes continued: *'To reward their efforts, our crew will receive double the wages paid by the English navy and in gold, plus a share in prize money equivalent to half the value of destroyed and bonded ships. Grog will be issued twice a day, rations will be generous and you will be well treated. Now it is up to you to decide whether you wish to commit to our wonderful ship and help serve the Confederate cause during this most unfortunate war. Thank you for your attention.'*

The captain finished speaking and stepped down from the gun carriage. The boatswain piped the carry on and the men scattered into groups, discussing the pros and cons of the situation. One by one they lined up by the paymaster, until a crew had enlisted, forfeiting the protection of the English government, fully realising the gravity of what they were doing and binding them to their officers with hooks of steel.

Some chose to leave the ship, no doubt concerned about the ability of the *Alabama* to achieve the task before her. Finally there was a ship's company enlisted of 26 officers and 85 men.

Semmes had initially not been keen to recruit David, due to his lack of experience at sea but when he'd heard from Jefferson Davis that the young surgeon was the godson of a peer, he had been intrigued and decided to give him a trial. To be on the safe side, he had brought with him Francis Galt, an experienced surgeon who had recently served with him on another ship.

The officers were mostly young men and the crew had in them the dare devil spirits of pirates; they would need a great deal of training and careful handling. *Alabama's* appropriate motto was 'Aide-toi et Dieu t'aidera' – help yourself and God will help you.

Captain Butcher, his job completed, gave Captain Semmes a hearty shake of the hand, wished him 'God speed' and stepped up the gangway of the accompanying ship, *Bahama*. Their crew gave three hearty cheers, answered by the remaining men and then turned to head back to England, leaving the *CSS Alabama* alone on the ocean.

David had been stirred by Captain Semmes' address but was also disturbed by the dangers that lay ahead and had to concentrate on the reasons he had taken this huge step – for Mary and William. He told himself that two years would soon go by then they would be together again with enough money for a wonderful new start.

Even the sight of the massive ocean and his fear of water could not swerve David from his determination to see this uncertain venture through to the end.

Chapter 22

In the autumn of 1861, when the health of Florence's valued assistant, Arthur Clough, deteriorated, he was advised to take extended leave and set off for a walking tour in Europe. Some weeks later, his wife Blanche and their new-born baby travelled to meet him in Italy but after a few days of sightseeing, he collapsed and died. In her misery, Cousin Blanche caused more family ill-feeling, blaming Florence for killing her husband by making him work too hard.

Florence was still heavily in mourning for Sidney, comparing herself with Queen Victoria who was nearly mad with grief at the recent loss of Albert. Now the death of Arthur and the family bitterness instigated by Blanche were almost too much for Florence to bear – lonely and in pain she desperately needed someone in whom she could confide. She wrote to Reverend Benjamin Jowett requesting he travel from Oxford to the Burlington and administer communion for her. He agreed to visit her on one Sunday each month and a special friendship began to develop between them.

Jowett was three years older than Florence, short in stature, handsome and cherubic in features, with a high-pitched voice resulting from a childhood glandular complaint. As a boy he'd been delicate, possessing little physical strength but unusual intelligence. His appearance, wit and eccentricities were university legends – in the stronghold of Oxford he represented a new rebellious religious order.

Benjamin admired Florence's independent and enquiring mind, holding her in high esteem as a critic of his work – the closeness of his relationship with such a famous woman flattered him. Florence, in turn, leaned on his devotion and was grateful for his advice; she was in need of masculine protection and he comforted her in her isolation.

One cold rainy afternoon in February 1862, some months after their first meeting, the couple were relaxing by the fire when Florence said, 'You know, Benjamin, since Sidney Herbert died, I seem to have become such a bad tempered person. Not one of my family visits any more, I've upset them all with my demanding ways and have only myself to blame for my loneliness and ill health.'

Benjamin poked the coals on the fire then rested both his feet on the firedogs. 'Oh come on now Florence, I'm sure you're exaggerating. You have suffered a great deal over the last years – it's not surprising you've a tendency to become depressed and unhappy.'

'But how can I make amends for all the terrible things I've said and done?' Florence asked.

Benjamin smiled and took her hand. 'Please don't be so hard on yourself, try to be more cheerful. Your family loves you and I'm sure needs only small encouragement to renew your closeness. Look back on your achievements and be proud and positive about the future. If you like I'll visit your parents, Aunt Mai, as well as Cousins Hilary and Blanche to tell them how much you miss them.'

'I should be most grateful, thank you Benjamin,' she said and he leant down to put more coals on the fire as outside a fierce wind blew the rain in pattering drops against the windows. True to his word, Jowett successfully interceded and soon members of the family were once more calling round.

Late in the summer of 1862, Florence received a letter from Henry Pelham-Clinton.

'Dear Madam – I am contacting you as advised by the late Lord Herbert of Lea.

Doctor David Herbert Llewellyn recently wrote requesting my advice on obtaining a position which would promote his career as a doctor. I was happy to help secure him the post of Assistant Surgeon on the CSS Alabama which he has now joined and will be at sea for two years. I hope this news is of interest to you.'

The letter perplexed Florence. Why had David turned his back on a medical career in London to join a foreign ship fighting a war in which he had no concern? She was angry with him for putting his life unnecessarily at risk.

Florence didn't altogether trust Henry's judgement in orchestrating David's departure – he had, after all, resigned from the government one year after the start of the Crimean War in the wake of his disastrous decisions at that time. She wasn't sure either that Sidney would have approved of David undertaking such a dangerous mission. Florence wanted in some way to intervene and prevent him from leaving, but it appeared to be too late.

Then she remembered the plans she'd desperately wanted to achieve and her frustrations when her parents had objected, David must have had good reasons for his actions. Florence was aware of the silent mills of England, supplies of raw cotton blockaded from leaving the Southern States causing terrible hardship to thousands of workers. She could only pray that the war would soon be resolved and David would return safely home.

Florence and Liz Herbert wrote and sent flowers to each other on the first anniversary of Sidney's death. The marble effigy of Sidney commissioned by Liz had been unveiled in Wilton church and below the recumbent figure, at the base of the tomb among the bas relief scenes from the Crimean war, was included one of Florence at Scutari.

During her year of mourning, Liz had spent time in the south of France and then travelled on to Rome. Her religious doubts had increased and it was widely rumoured she was considering becoming a Catholic, but her husband's family cautioned that if she took such a step they would make her children wards of court.

Soon afterwards Liz was received into the Roman Catholic Church in a private ceremony in Sicily and, as she'd been warned, her conversion resulted in estrangement from her family and friends, including Florence. Liz remained in the Herbert family home in London and never returned to live with her children at Wilton.

Florence was haunted by the loss of Sidney, vivid and terrifying dreams ambushed her sleep, one in particular she often experienced. She was standing in the desolate battlefields of the Crimea surrounded by blood split from disembowelled and limbless bodies – desperate moans of the dying filled the air. Then a figure appeared out of the mist, walking towards her with arms outstretched.

As the apparition grew closer, she recognised the smiling face of Sidney and moved forward to embrace him but, before they could touch, the vision had melted away, leaving her alone in the carnage of war. Florence woke screaming, lying restless and unhappy until dawn, afraid to sleep and wondering how she could ever find peace again.

She turned for help to the Spiritualism movement that had recently caught the public imagination and become part of Victorian subculture. Promises of a new era, a more just, equitable and loving world appealed to many believers who were seeking an alternative to traditional religion. Queen Victoria herself had become a devotee.

One afternoon while they were having tea, Florence asked Jowett for his views. 'Benjamin, wouldn't it be wonderful to believe the living could communicate with the dead?'

'Spiritualism could be seen as an American plot concocted by those promoting their own religious views,' he replied. 'But supporters of all shades of opinion seem to have a shared set of beliefs. Those who accept the divinity of Christ see Spiritualism as the triumphant vindication of their faith.' He helped himself to a slice of cake. 'Alternatively, Christian faith is not necessary to understand the rationale for a soul's survival and everlasting life.'

Florence nodded, 'I should like to believe that life is merely a necessary preparation for entrance to the spirit world,' she said. 'Maybe death is a state through which we must all pass on the journey from one world to the next. Can I pour you some more tea?'

Benjamin held out his cup, saying, 'It seems the ability for communicating with the unseen world is facilitated by feminine passivity – another lump of sugar, please. Spiritually gifted females are taken seriously and given privilege and power not normally allowed in this world by others of their gender.'

Florence laughed, 'Well, that's a small blessing. So what would you say if I wanted to speak with a medium?'

'My dear, you must be sure of your reasons. Death is indisputable and irreversible – nothing can bring them back, this we must accept. I think the spirits of the dead survive in the hearts of the living.' He sipped his tea, making little storms in the teacup.

'Does that mean you don't approve?' asked Florence, worried about how he would respond.

Benjamin thought for a moment. 'Speaking with the dead could be a therapeutic way of communing with our loved ones but you can do this at any time for yourself. I wouldn't want you to be disappointed if a medium didn't come up to your expectations.'

'I would still like the experience,' said Florence.

He nodded. 'In that case you should go ahead but don't believe everything you're told. Although the unseen world must contain wise and discerning spirits, I'm sure there are also many charlatans.' Then he added, 'You'll be in good company, even William Gladstone attends séances and he has a genius akin to madness.' They both laughed and finished their tea.

Mrs Maria B. Hayden was an American woman of some education and accomplishment. She discovered her powers soon after the Fox sisters had become a national sensation by beginning the phenomenon, known as Modern Spiritualism, in upstate New York. Although only aged twelve and thirteen, the sisters claimed they had communicated with the ghost of a pedlar, murdered at their house and buried in the cellar years before the family moved in.

Mrs Hayden had travelled to London and began to advertise her services as a medium, charging a minimum of half a guinea for each consultation. She proved an almost immediate success, attracting an affluent and influential following and finding herself in great demand for private sittings and evening parties.

When Mrs Hayden received a letter from Miss Florence Nightingale inviting her to conduct a private consultation at her house, she had no hesitation in agreeing. She was familiar with Miss Nightingale's great achievements and was interested to meet her.

The date arranged was for the evening of the 2nd August, the second anniversary of Sidney's death. Mrs Hayden arrived at the house in Hampstead to find Miss Nightingale alone, dressed in black silk and seated in an easy chair with her hands folded in her lap. No agitation was visible in her, only a deep, concentrated calmness. She sat without lamps in the twilight, the French windows stood wide open, looking out towards the garden.

'Good evening Mrs Hayden. I'm very pleased to meet you.' Florence's grey eyes critically assessed her visitor.

Mrs Hayden walked across the room, smiled and took the hand proffered to her. 'And I am delighted to meet you, Miss Nightingale.'

'Won't you please sit down – where would suit you?' Mrs Hayden motioned to an upright upholstered chair opposite Florence and settled herself down. The room slowly lit up as three candles, shining like dazzling halos, were brought in by the maid and placed on a round table beside a bowl of fragrant white roses.

Mrs Hayden was a fine looking woman of nearly forty with large brown eyes, her dark hair coiled into a thick roll at the back of her head and covered by a small net cap. She wore a white muslin Garibaldi bodice braided in black, with matching braid in geometric patterns round the hem of her long cream linen skirt. Florence had not been sure what to expect and was relieved Mrs Hayden appeared to be a friendly person with no sense of ghoulishness.

'So Mrs Hayden, you have acquired an excellent reputation as a medium. Please tell me something about your gift,' Florence said.

'Well, Miss Nightingale, I'm fortunate to possess the ability to receive and pass on messages from the spirit world, but we can all connect and feel a loved one's presence. Mediums only exist because people do not yet accept the continuation of life.'

'So how can you tell when you are connected?' Florence leant forward in her chair.

Mrs Hayden explained. 'We cannot yet measure psychic energy or spiritual vibrations – we have to use our faith and listen to what our hearts tell us is true. It's important before we start to focus on positive feelings and open ourselves up to the spirits. Tell me, Miss Nightingale, what is your reason for communicating with the spirit world?'

'I'd like to contact my late dear friend Sidney Herbert. I've had disturbing dreams which make me wonder if he's trying to send me a message.'

'When we dream, our relaxed meditative state connects us with the spirits,' said Mrs Hayden. 'Dreams are the voice of our intuitive self, revealing feelings linked to past events. The departed looks well and happy because that's how he is in the afterlife.'

'But what is the afterlife?' Florence asked.

'A bright, loving place full of kind and caring energy, where our worldly worries, pains and problems are left behind,' Mrs Hayden replied. 'The end of the body does not destroy the living soul. When a loved one passes into the spirit world, their life essence transforms into energy which doesn't die but simply moves around.'

'I'm worried my behaviour helped to cause Sidney's death. I said things I regret and wish for his forgiveness.' Florence's voice began to break.

The Spiritualist reached forward and placed her hand on Florence's for a moment.

'Guilt is natural, a normal part of human nature,' she said. 'Do you have someone with whom you can share your experiences?' Florence nodded, thinking of Benjamin.

'Then I think we are ready to begin.' Mrs Hayden took a deep breath and closed her eyes, spreading her long, white fingers flat on the round table in front of her.

She spoke in a soft voice, as though talking to herself. 'With love and light, I welcome the spirits and invite them to use my body as a channel to share messages of love.' She paused, then continued. 'Sidney Herbert, we are here tonight in the hope we will receive sign of your presence. Please feel welcome to join us when you are ready.'

After a few moments, with a voice now clear and bold, Mrs Hayden asked, 'Is there anyone who wishes to speak with us?'

The candles flickered as the still evening air moved slightly. The black cat, sleeping on a cushion near Florence, woke with a start and looked round the room with wide dark eyes. The fur on its back rose, it jumped down from the chair and bolted through the open windows into the garden beyond.

'Sidney, are you with us? Do you have a message for us?' A short pause.

'He's saying he's in a happy place. You're not to blame. He's proud of what you've achieved. You must not give up your work.'

Tears poured down Florence's cheeks. 'Please thank him for the part he played in my life – I shall never forget him.' Mrs Hayden relayed her message.

'He says, "God bless you".' Sidney faded away from her – the connection was over. Mrs Hayden thanked the spirits and said three times, 'Now is done, leave in peace.'

After a few minutes, the two women opened their eyes and smiled at each other. Florence wiped away her tears. 'May I offer you a glass of port wine?' she asked.

Mrs Hayden nodded. 'I should like that very much.'

Later Florence said, 'I'd no idea what to expect from tonight – I feel emotionally exhausted but surprisingly calm. Thank you for all you did.'

Mrs Hayden smiled. 'Everyone has to make peace with themselves in their own way. I hope now you can come to terms with the past, eliminate your doubts and regrets, concentrate on the positive and move on with your life.'

'Oh I shall – tonight, on the second anniversary of Sidney's death, I shall celebrate his life and his memory.' Florence felt a great weight of sorrow lift from her.

Mrs Hayden reassured her. 'What you witnessed this evening was a divine experience. You haven't really lost Sidney, you just can't see him anymore. If you keep him in your heart and mind, you can still have those special moments of closeness.'

Florence was relieved. She needed no more messages from Sidney, he was at peace. She would enjoy the rest of her time on earth without worrying about dying, certain now that when her time came she too would be welcomed into the spirit world.

Encouraged by Sidney's words, Florence approached Lord de Grey at the War Office and offered her services. Soon she was once again immersed in statistics, minutes, letters and reports, becoming a valued advisor to the government for problems affecting the health and sanitary administration of the British Army. Florence was back in her element, driving herself to work as she had never worked before.

Chapter 23

5th September 1862:

My Darling Mary – here I am on board *CSS Alabama* twelve days into our adventure not knowing where we're headed or when this will reach you. We expect to be on the oceans for months at a time, only seeking a port when coal is needed for our boilers. The days have passed rapidly with all hands busy preparing for our cruise.

The motion of the sea affected me at first but now I'm getting used to it. My cabin is comfortable although a little cramped and the ship's surgery is well equipped to handle most situations.

Our mission is to cripple the commerce of the North by destroying vessels carrying cargo. Enemy ships will be on the lookout for us but please don't worry, we're the fastest on the ocean and will do our best to avoid trouble.

We've a good company of officers and men on board. Captain Semmes is a sailor of many years' experience and respected by all the crew, his nickname is "Old Beeswax" on account of his highly waxed moustache. I'm a little afraid of him as beneath his mild exterior lurks a stern and relentless fighter. My fellow officers are friendly Southerners, full of generous spirit and good humour, most served in the United States navy before the war.

Another Englishman, who joined with me in Liverpool, is George Fulham, late of the Royal Naval Reserve and now looking for a new adventure. He's a little younger than me, not tall but broad shouldered and muscular with blue eyes, brown hair, huge side whiskers and a happy disposition. He spins the best yarns of anyone on board. I'm sure you'd like him and I think we'll become good friends. As prizemaster, he'll board captured ships to assess their cargos, selecting stores and valuables to be removed.

The surgeon is Francis Galt, a Virginian by birth, a handsome man with brown eyes, dark hair and a fine drooping moustache. He served with Semmes from the start of the war on *CSS Sunter* before they joined the *Alabama*.

First Lieutenant John Kell is a fearsome looking chap, very tall, strong, lithe and straight as a willow, with kind, dark blue eyes that can flash lightening on occasions. He looks like a Viking with a phenomenal auburn moustache meeting behind his head and a beard flowing to his hips.

The enlisted crew is an unruly bunch of hard characters gradually being licked into shape, but the highest wages of any fleet and the promise of prize money help to keep them in order. The decks are a hive of activity with the crew under instruction learning the rigging, polishing guns and setting sails.

At eight bells the boatswain pipes to dinner. We officers are served our meal in the wardroom mess where tales are swapped of the events of the last weeks and opinions given on what may be coming. It's time for lights out, so I'll finish for now – thinking of you constantly my darling love.

10ᵗʰ September 1862:

We've arrived in the whaling grounds of the Western Islands and boarded our first capture, a whaler *USS Ocmulgee*. A prize crew went on board, her officers and crew were transferred to the *Alabama* and next morning the ship was fired.

We witnessed for the first time the hauling down of the Stars and Stripes, almost a desecration for those who served in the old navy. The sight of the burning ship brought sorrow to the heart but war is cruel and what can seem ruthlessness soon becomes a matter of course.

So we set sail round the Azores. Within one month we board and burn eight more USS whaling vessels, for days the skies are lit up with fierce bonfires – a whaler makes a grand blaze.

Please don't worry, Mary, about the men on the destroyed

ships. Aside from the captains who are mostly part owners, they seem well pleased with their adventure. Prisoners are given boats, whaling equipment, provisions and traps, allowed to help themselves to what they fancy and their expenses paid by the American consul. Private property is never taken and both officers and men are always treated with dignity and respect.

Our captures provide us with every requisite for our comfort and health. Our prizemaster laid in a carefully selected assortment of clothing, provisions and small stores including a large amount of Virginian smoking and chewing tobacco, much appreciated by the crew. Also saved are the flags and valuable chronometers – flags are kept under the care of the signal quartermaster and the chronometers wound every day to keep them in good order.

The storm season has begun and as we've destroyed most of the whaling fleet, we move on to the Banks of Newfoundland.

Last week we experienced the terror of a cyclone and I have to admit to you, darling, those few hours were the worst of my life. The barometer dropped drastically, the wind quickly increased to hurricane level. The rigging broke and the sails were torn to shreds, leaving only bare masts. The fury of the wind was so great the sea could not get up, the ocean surface stayed completely still.

Most of us sheltered under the weather bulwarks and some lashed themselves to sturdy stations, the wheel was manned by two men, until its violent lurching knocked one of them straight over. The air was white with swirling spoondrift like a snowstorm and the dark green clouds twisted and squirmed as the whirlwind whipped through the sky.

The ship behaved so nobly. Pressed down by the force of the tempest, she lay still and comfortable, making little water in her hold, although the decks were wet with spray and rain.

Suddenly the wind died to dead calm – we entered the dreaded vortex of the cyclone. The seas mounted to appalling heights and the violent roll of the ship threatened to jerk the masts out of her. The storm approached again sounding like thunder – then it struck us, screeching and howling.

For two terrifying hours the *Alabama* struggled for her life, her timbers groaning and creaking. Lieutenant John Low was officer on the deck and showed superb seamanship, had he hesitated for an instant and allowed the wind to catch the port tack, we'd probably have gone down. The barometer rose rapidly, the seas calmed, giving us time to look round at the destruction and thank God for our survival.

A week later, we're sailing under close canvas headed towards the coast just off New York. Our mission now is to complete the destruction of ships carrying cereals and provisions to European markets.

The capture of a ship carrying the latest newspapers is a great event as we gain insight into the whereabouts of enemy cruisers and how the tide of battle is flowing. There are stories calling us "The Pirate" and threats to annihilate us. It's strange that the enemy looks for us where we were last reported, instead of anticipating where we may be headed.

15th October 1862:

Now bound for the West Indies, repairs completed and weather improved. In Martinique we find *CSS Agrippina* lying at anchor with coal for us and take on supplies of all kinds, with the luxury now of fruit between meals. My job has been easy so far with no disease and only minor sickness, cuts and bruises to deal with.

Free evenings are spent on the forward deck where song and dance, improvised plays and yarn spinning is encouraged. The young officers have formed a glee club, delighting us all with songs sentimental, nautical and national. Mary, how I wish you were here to enjoy these times with me.

It's now December and we're headed round South America to Cuba, skirting the coast of San Domingo. The wonderful ability of our lookout Evans to identify flags means we don't waste time chasing foreign ships; we enter the Gulf of Mexico and up to the coast of Texas.

We've time for relaxation – there's an excellent library of books with chess, backgammon and other games in the wardroom. Gambling and card games are strictly forbidden but the sailors are masters of draughts and talented in sewing embroidery on the collars of their frocks in silks of many colours.

Arriving in Galveston, we find the enemy blockading the harbour – one ship *USS Hatteras* came close to running us down and shots were exchanged, until she sent signals asking for boats as she was sinking. Two were killed and five wounded on the enemy ship while only our carpenter's mate received a slight wound on his cheek from a fragment of shell.

20th January 1863:

On to Kingston, Jamaica where officers and crew of the *USS Hatteras* are disembarked. We drop anchor and are given a hearty welcome from many visitors coming on board.

Captain Semmes went off to visit a friend for a few days, leaving Lieutenant Kell in charge. In his absence our paymaster was found consorting with the enemy and spending on drink, money intended to pay the ship's bills. He was arrested and when Semmes returned, dismissed from the service and drummed off the ship.

Galt became paymaster and I was promoted to surgeon, which is a great honour. The sailors are enjoying themselves on shore in varying degrees of intoxication. When time comes for them to return, a party of officers is sent to round them up.

Kingston port has a mail boat leaving for Europe so I'll send this letter now and hope it reaches you soon. Remember, my dearest Mary, I love you and miss you more than I can say. Please give William a big hug and tell him his Papa will be home soon.

With all my love for ever – David

4th February 1863:

Darling Mary – we're now on our way to Brazil approaching the equator with light winds, calm seas and frequent heavy showers. The ship's condenser provides us with only one gallon of fresh water each a day. Boatswain Mecaskey improvised a rainwater bath by spreading out a sail, weighting it down and pulling up the sides to make a large bag – this is luxury under the tropical sun.

Our mission is continued for many weeks, we're busy boarding vessels, mostly neutrals and constantly on the look-out for enemy cruisers. Deep feelings of regret are experienced at the destruction of so many splendid ships and valuable cargos, but knowledge of the devastation going on in the South strengthens our resolve.

I admit I knew very little of the war before I joined the *Alabama* but the more I hear about the injustices inflicted on Southerners, the more my sympathies lie with them.

We continue round the Cape of Good Hope to the safe anchorage of Saldanha Bay, a British possession on the west coast of Africa, sixty miles from Cape Town. Fresh provisions are plentiful with beef, mutton, fish and game.

Arriving in Cape Town, we're overwhelmed with our welcome by the English who appear to support our cause and invite us to balls, parties and country outings.

14th August 1863:

Cape Town is behind us and we're busy in the stream of commerce from the East Indies, boarding many vessels but none of them Yankees. Now steaming due east, headed for the straits of Sunda via the South Indian Ocean where winds and currents should be in our favour.

Oceans have channels of greatest flow where the commerce of the world tends to travel, one or two hundred miles is a mere ribbon of width and a ship at sea is like a needle in a haystack. We select our channels carefully to make sure we're in the busiest commercial areas.

10th October 1863:

The run of five thousand miles is quickly made – weather is stormy and we're rollicking along under full sail, dolphins and flying fish are plentiful. The ship is sparkling clean with new paint, polished brasswork and constant drilling takes place.

We anchor in the mouth of the strait close to the Sumatra coast, looking at the most beautiful views on earth – luxurious tropical foliage, flocks of birds with colourful plumage flying over the sparkling green sea. Mary, my darling, you would love it here.

Our island paradise is left behind as we steam into the China Sea, where we overhaul many vessels. We visit the coast of Borneo then on to China. Currents are rapid and navigation difficult around the dangerous reefs and shoals of the lower China seas.

Captain Semmes is day and night poring over charts, beginning to show the wear of months of anxiety. Most of the crew is young and fit but Semmes is twice their age, lack of sleep and the weight of responsibility start to take their toll.

We spend two weeks relaxing on the small island of Condore, a French settlement, where our ship's bottom is repaired. Then shipshape and rested we steam seaward towards Singapore.

9th December 1863:

We've crossed the Gulf of Siam and anchor in deep waters at the mouth of the Malacca Straits, quickly surrounded by native trading boats. Next morning we set off for Singapore, a British possession with a large mixed race population.

We're moored in the docks of the Peninsular and Oriental Company who generously sell us coal at a reasonable price. The ship becomes the scene of hustle and disorder, overrun by people of all climes, chatting and gesticulating.

I hope to catch the mailboat with this letter – it won't arrive in time for Christmas but remember I'm thinking of you and William and counting the days when we'll be together again.

My love to you, darling Mary – your own David.

28th December 1863:

My dearest love: On Christmas Eve we left Singapore ready for the long pull back to the North Atlantic. Christmas Day was spent relaxing and toasting all our loved ones back home, our wonderful ship *Alabama* and the Confederate cause.

The year of 1864 has come and it looks like our work is done. On reaching the island of Ceylon, along the coast of Malabar, we captured the *Emma Jane* of Bath but she had no cargo, so after removing supplies, crew and passengers, she was torched.

Now we're stretching over for the Arabian Sea in the embrace of the NE monsoon blowing a fresh breeze. It's so quiet at night you might suppose the *Alabama* to be a phantom ship, like the *Flying Dutchman*. Nothing breaks the silence as we travel under full sail, with stars scintillating in the heavens and clouds drawn out in long ribbons of gossamer.

14th January 1864:

We entered the Mozambique Channel and dropped anchor off the island of Comoro where the inhabitants are Hindus, African and Arabs.

Local people crowd on board and I'm constantly called on not only for advice and treatment but also for medicines. Disease was introduced to the islands by men of the American whaling fleets and its spread has become a national calamity. We take on plentiful provisions and leave, southward bound for Cape Town.

21ˢᵗ March 1864:

No results on this commercial highway – ships are scarcer than hen's teeth. We spend three days at Cape Town but this time the crew is not allowed ashore.

Newspapers tell of the utter demoralisation of American commerce and the South sadly appears to be in the last throes of dissolution. Now off to the North Atlantic via St Helena where we will linger for a few days.

12ᵗʰ April 1864:

Approaching the equator once more – in a few weeks we'll be home. We run down the clipper, *Tycoon*, from New York – our last capture.

Cross the equator in usual style, down the Brazilian coast remembering how things were when we first started, how high our aspirations and pride in our ship.

10ᵗʰ June 1864:

We arrive at the entrance of the English Channel, take a pilot and next day enter the harbour of Cherbourg, France. Our cruise is ended and you and I, dearest Mary, will soon be together again to start our new life.

Chapter 24

In June 1864 the *CSS Alabama* arrived in Cherbourg harbour for a much needed refit to her hull and engines, the repairs would take at least one month. David was excited to be home again and keen to travel to London without delay. The money he'd earned in the last two years would be more than sufficient to provide Mary and his son with a happy future, now he was ready to be married and settle down in his dream of a country practice.

News of the arrival of the *Alabama* had reached Captain John Winslow of the *USS Kearsarge* lying at anchor off Flushing in Holland and within two days the ships were positioned only a few hundred yards from each other. Rumours passed amongst the crew of the *Alabama* that Captain Semmes had issued a challenge to Captain Winslow, a surprising move as he was usually keen to avoid conflict of this sort.

Semmes wrote in his journal, *'The two ships are so equally matched that I do not feel at liberty to decline it.'* But the *Alabama* was in a poor state, the *Kearsarge* superior in armament, speed and size of crew, her midships protected by bights of chain hung over her side. Semmes took a gamble – he could stay in port, refit and be ready to take on any USS warship in a few weeks' time, but the chances were that by then a fleet of American cruisers would have arrived to blockade the *Alabama*.

The next five days were spent in frantic activity, preparing for the inevitable conflict. The officers were allowed ashore, determined to make the most of their few days of freedom to enjoy the French bars and cafes. An air of feverish excitement and nervous tension ran through all the crew.

David finished his letter to Mary, wrote to his parents saying he would visit them soon and sent a letter to John Travers, his friend, the Resident Medical Officer of Charing Cross Hospital:

'Dear Travers: Here we are, I send this by a gentleman coming to London. An enemy is outside. If she stops long enough we go out and fight her. If I live expect to see me in London shortly. If I die give my best love to all who know me. I remain, dear Travers, ever yours DH Llewellyn.'

He bought some new clothes, had his hair cut, beard trimmed and a fine daguerreotype portrait taken as a present for Mary.

On the morning of Sunday 19th June, the *Alabama* left the shelter of the harbour; the day was bright and warm with a light breeze blowing. Reports of the impending fight had been widely circulated and a large crowd arrived to witness the event.

Captain Semmes summoned all hands on deck and delivered a stirring address.

'Officers and Seamen of the Alabama: you have at length another opportunity of meeting the enemy, the first that has presented to you since you sunk the Hatteras. In the meantime you have been all over the world and it is not too much to say that you have destroyed and driven for protection under neutral flags, one-half of the enemy's commerce which at the beginning of the war covered every sea. This is an achievement of which you may well be proud and a grateful country will not be unmindful of it. The name of your ship has become a household word wherever civilisation extends.

'Shall that name be tarnished by defeat? The thing is impossible. Remember you are in the English Channel – the theatre of so much of the naval glory of our race and that the eyes of all Europe are at this moment on you. The flag that floats over you is that of a young republic who bids defiance to her enemies whenever and wherever found. Show the world you know how to uphold it. Go to your quarters.'

The *Kearsarge* had withdrawn from the harbour and was lying three miles offshore in international waters. The lookout shouted that the *Alabama* was sailing straight for them – Semmes' plan was to set close enough to board *Kearsarge* and overwhelm her crew but Captain Winslow turned his ship, luring the *Alabama* out to sea until they were a mile apart. Then at 10.57 a.m., battle commenced as both ships turned broadside and started firing. The effects of *Kearsarge's* guns were severely felt, while *Alabama's* shots were unable to pierce the enemy's hull.

David was operating on a wounded sailor when a shell burst open the wardroom, sweeping the table and patient from under him. Two more shells struck the *Alabama's* pivot gun, killing its crew, another entered at the waterline and exploded in the engine room. The ship trembled from the blow, water flooded in and she could float no longer. The colours were hauled down and the pipe given, "All hands save yourselves". The *Kearsarge* demolished the *Alabama* in less than an hour.

A gang of men helped David to move the wounded up on deck and load them into the only two dinghies that had survived the engagement. When the boats were full, an uninjured sailor tried to jump in but was held back by David who said, 'See I want to save my life as much as you do but let the wounded crew be saved first.'

George Fulham urged David to go with them in the dinghy but he replied, 'I will not peril the wounded men.' George and other crew members set off rowing towards the *Kearsarge* without him.

Two French ships, the *Kearsarge* and an English yacht, the *Deerhound*, all lowered boats and were actively saving as many men as possible. Here and there, a human head appeared amongst the long line of wreckage seen winding like a snake from the stern of the *Alabama*.

When David admitted he could not swim, crew members secured two wooden shell boxes, one under each of his arms, to serve as an improvised life preserver. He took to the water with this arrangement and appeared to be making good progress in the calm sea, but the boxes slipped their position.

David disappeared into the trackless deep and was seen no more. The brave surgeon drowned with a boat from the *Deerhound* only a few yards from him – had he taken a moment's thought for himself and let it be known earlier he could not swim he might easily have been saved.

The *Alabama's* death throes were dramatic – she shot out of the water bow first and descended on the same line. Carrying her two remaining masts, she disappeared under the sea, causing a whirlpool of considerable force and the scourge of the oceans was no more.

Semmes was badly wounded in his right arm and due only to the loyalty of Kell supporting him in the water, was brought to the deck of the *Deerhound*. The yacht steamed on to England, carrying forty two survivors and evading Captain Winslow who would have dearly loved to take Semmes prisoner. Three of the crew of the *Kearsarge* were wounded and one died, while the rescue boats were unable to save seventeen of the crew of the *Alabama*.

The newspapers the next day were full of stories of the battle in the Channel and the sinking of the *Alabama*. Florence read with horror and grief the loss of David and the other crew.

Now the worst had happened – her son was gone, why had God allowed it? Had she not been punished enough? This terrible tragedy was like losing Sidney all over again.

Florence took little consolation from reading that David had died an honourable death, sacrificing his life for the sake of others, she needed help. Parthe was the only person in whom she was prepared to confide and she sent a note to her sister's London home asking her to come at once.

'Well, what's the urgency?' Parthe exclaimed, as she bustled in through the door. 'We have dinner guests tonight and cook and I were discussing menus... why Florence, whatever is the matter? Have you been crying?'

Florence's tearstained face was ashen and her lips trembled. 'Oh dearest Pop, it's David – he's dead.'

'David, who's David?' Parthe asked.

'My son, our son, Sidney's and my son – he's been drowned,' and Florence dissolved into heavy sobbing.

Parthe was silenced with shock while Florence laid her weary, aching head on her sister's shoulder, seeking a comforting pillow in this desperate moment. Parthe held her until she quietened and was able to speak, then the whole story came out – how Sidney had become their child's godfather, the secret reports, their meeting and now this cruel disaster.

Florence cried, 'I loved that boy with the utmost love of which my soul is capable, now he's been taken from me and he never knew how much I loved him. Oh Pop, perhaps I shouldn't have met him – is it better to have the pain of remembering or never to have the memory?'

Parthe said little, listening with increasing astonishment as the story unfolded, she was not a mother, never likely to be and could only imagine the emotions Florence was experiencing. How could the two of them have lived together for so long without sharing this shattering secret? She never had been able to tell what was going on in her sister's heart. Parthe helped put Florence to bed, explaining to the servants she was unwell and not to be disturbed.

Florence remembered the Spiritualist medium's words and knew she must be positive but how she wished for Sidney to be here with her now. She attempted to recall every memory of the happy evening the three of them had spent together – what David had said, the sound of his voice, the way he'd looked, his brave attitude and the pride she'd felt in him.

A letter arrived from Henry Pelham-Clinton, sending his sincere condolences on her sad loss. Florence stayed in her room not speaking or eating for three days, until slowly she began to come to terms with her grief.

Mary Kelly was in the basement kitchen at Cleveland Square humming to herself while she prepared Mrs Buckley's breakfast tray, when there was a loud hammering on the door. Jesse Gilbert, the butler, opened it to find Mr Kelly looking pale and agitated with a newspaper clutched in his hand.

'Why Da, what are you doing here?' his daughter asked. 'Has something happened? Is it William?'

Her father walked towards her, his arms outstretched and said, 'Oh my darling girl – you must try to be brave – there's been a dreadful catastrophe – it's David, he's dead.'

'David? No you must be wrong – David's in France, he's coming home soon – look I just had a letter.' She pulled a folded paper from her apron pocket.

'My dearest child, I'm so sorry, David has died.' Mary's eyes opened wide in one terrified look at her father's face, before she fell to the floor in a deep faint. Jesse and her father sat propping up her head while the cook brought smelling salts and a glass of water.

Soon Mary revived. 'Tell me it's not true Da – please,' she pleaded.

Her father put his arms round her. 'Listen sweetheart – there was a battle – the *Alabama* sank and David was drowned.'

Her blue eyes filled with tears. 'He hated the water – he couldn't swim – he should never have gone – my poor, poor love.' She started sobbing and wailing and nothing could console her.

Mary Caroline, Marchioness of Ailesbury, sat at her breakfast table in the dining room of Tottenham House reflecting on her plans for the day.

Her husband sitting opposite her reading the morning newspaper suddenly exclaimed, 'Good Lord, I think you should have a look at this, dear.' He handed her the paper with headlines about the sinking of the *Alabama*.

As the Marchioness read the news, her hands flew to her face knocking over her cup and spilling coffee on the white damask tablecloth. 'Please call for the carriage,' she cried. 'I must go to Easton Royal.'

During the short journey to the vicarage, Mary Caroline thought over the years when she'd watched David grow up in the village. She and George Frederick had not been blessed with children, David had been special to her and she had shared in her brother Sidney's pride when his son had qualified as a doctor. How sad that such a fine young man with a promising future ahead of him should have died in such a tragic and needless way. She wondered how Miss Nightingale would be coping with the terrible circumstances.

The news came as a double tragedy to the Llewellyns after the death of their eldest son John, eleven years before. David had not been a frequent visitor since he'd left home but his letters had told them how difficult it was to make a living in London and that he was going to sea to make money to secure his future. He'd just written from France saying he would soon return to England and had something important to tell them.

With no coffin to bury or grave to weep by, all they could do was to arrange a memorial service, thank God for his life and pray for his soul. Reverend Llewellyn ended his address that day to the sombre congregation by saying, 'In the midst of life we are in death – the present moment is all we can call our own for works of mercy and family tenderness.'

A letter from a fellow student was published in *The Standard* under the heading, "Hero of the Alabama":

'The surgeon of the Alabama was Mr DH Llewellyn, formerly of Charing Cross Hospital College of Medicine, son of the Rev D Llewellyn, rector of Easton, Pewsey and also godson of the late Lord Herbert of Lea.

He was beloved by all his fellow students and those with whom he came into contact for his good heartedness, as well as for his genuine disinterestedness carried out as we now see not only in everyday occurrences of life but in the midst of danger and in the face of death itself.'

Captain Semmes issued a statement acknowledging David had served with the *CSS Alabama* throughout the whole of her eventful career and was much respected by all on board.

A meeting was held at the Charing Cross Hospital Medical School to discuss a suitable memorial. Contributions came not only from students but also from doctors in the Indian Army who were sympathetic to their fellow medical man, members of the public sent money as did some of the *Alabama's* surviving officers.

The most important part of the memorial took the shape of a perpetual scholarship to be awarded annually to the student achieving the greatest distinction in final year examinations. A plaque erected at the medical school bore an inscription framed inside a wreath resembling a ship's cable, commemorating the self-sacrificing courage and devotion of former student, the late David Herbert Llewellyn.

Chapter 25

The village of Easton Royal remained much the same in 1864 as it had been when the Llewellyns had arrived with their three young sons some twenty-five years earlier. The curate had either christened, married or buried most of the villagers during that time and knew them all by name.

A number of his congregation recently moved to worshipping in an old thatched stable designated as the Wesleyan chapel and when Elizabeth showed concern over the dwindling church attendance, her husband declared he wouldn't meddle with people doing as they liked in religion. People should follow their consciences; their preferences were between themselves and God.

Dissenting preachers were notorious for their enthusiastic sermons and often accused of whipping up their congregations into frenzies, but the Reverend Llewellyn was not willing to compete, he was weary and ready to retire. His son, Arthur, had taken holy orders after completing his BA at Oxford and was now preparing to take over from his father.

Since 1847 Holy Trinity had become part of the Salisbury Diocese which had meant a new employer for the Reverend Llewellyn, but not much else had changed in the running of the parish. The church had been kept in repair with difficulty, too often pervious to the rain and damp and in 1852, a scheme financed by the Marquis, Church Building Societies and the parishioners resulted in extensive alterations to the Gothic fashion of the day.

The work lasted for over a year and the Reverend Llewellyn grumbled continuously about the disruption to church services. He considered the money would have been better spent on repairing the vicarage, which he complained was the coldest and most uncomfortable parsonage house in the whole of the Diocese.

On the death of his father in 1856, George Frederick had succeeded as 2nd Marquis of Ailesbury, taking great pride in his position as owner of the Savernake Estate and Warden of the Forest.

The Bleeding Horse alehouse was closed on the recommendation of his wife, Mary Caroline, after reports of frequent fights between the locals and the navvies employed on the construction of the nearby railway line. The Gammon of Bacon inn, site of the revels for so many years, burnt down soon afterwards and the Marquis generously built a new public house across the road naming it the Bruce's Arms, although the locals stubbornly still referred to it as "The Gammon".

Mary Caroline was keen to improve the health of Easton Royal tenants with fresh fruit and vegetables, setting aside land for allotments and planting rows of fruit and nut trees along the village street. She was not to know that in the autumn, villagers collected apples, made strong cider from them and spent the long winter evenings becoming uproariously drunk, singing rowdy songs with choruses like "Oh when apples be ripe and nuts be brown, 'tis petticoats up and trousers down".

Soon after David's death, Mary Caroline had been surprised to receive a letter from Miss Nightingale requesting her help. Florence had decided she needed to commemorate David's life in a way she thought Sidney would approve and wrote outlining her plans for a memorial to be erected in Holy Trinity Church at Easton Royal. *'I will pay all the costs and my involvement must remain anonymous,'* she wrote.

The Marquis obtained permission from the Diocese for the work to go ahead and WT Hale of Baker Street, London was commissioned to produce a marble tablet from Florence's design while stained glass window specialists, Messrs Lavers and Barraud, installed a new east window.

The memorial consisted of a black marble slab with a white

Latin cross, at the foot rested a naval anchor and cable with cannon shots of varying sizes. Leaning against the side of the cross was a snake-entwined staff – the rod of Asclepius, the Greek god of medicine, healing, rejuvenation and physicians. The inscription read:

'David Herbert Llewellyn, youngest son of Rev D Llewellyn, minister of this Parish. He was surgeon of the Confederate War Steamer Alabama and after her engagement with the Federal Steamer Kearsage (sic) off Cherbourg nobly refusing to imperil the escape of the wounded he sank with his ship on the 19th June 1864 in the 26th year of his age. Erected by voluntary contribution in admiration of his self-sacrificing courage.'

The beautiful stained glass window showed scenes from the Bible of healing miracles and two small yellow shields near the top carried black anchors.

The Llewellyns were honoured but bemused by the extravagance of the memorial and the mystery of the unknown benefactor. Mr Herbert had died three years before so who else could have been so profoundly affected by the loss of David?

On a gusty raw morning at the end of April in 1866, a one horse gig pulled up outside the vicarage, followed by a knock on the door which was answered by Martha, the young housemaid. Elizabeth Llewellyn was making pastry in the kitchen while her husband was reading in his study. Their son Arthur had recently taken over the curacy from his father and was out with his sister Sarah on parish business.

'There's a Mr and Mrs Gilbert to see you ma'am,' Martha announced.

'Well show them into the parlour and I'll be there instantly.' Elizabeth wiped her hands, removed her apron, straightened her dress and pushed her hair back under her cap.

Waiting in the warm front room where a bright fire blazed was an attractive well-dressed woman of around thirty, with a mass of black curly hair and large blue eyes. She was accompanied by an older man with a pleasant face and side whiskers and also with them was a young boy of five or six. The child looked up as Elizabeth entered the room and she thought she detected something familiar about his pale oval face and intelligent grey eyes staring intently at her.

'Good morning, I'm Mrs Llewellyn. Won't you please sit down?' she said. When they were all seated, Elizabeth asked, 'Now, how can I help you?'

'I am so happy to meet you,' the woman replied, her soft voice had a pretty Irish lilt. 'My name is Mary Gilbert and this is my husband, Jesse. We are staying with family in Great Bedwyn and couldn't leave without visiting you. You see, Mrs Llewellyn, we have brought William to meet you – he is your grandson.'

Elizabeth's face drained of colour. 'My grandson?' Her voice was hardly audible.

'Yes, he is my child and your son David was his father. We were to be married when he came home from sea and he planned to tell you then.' Mary paused to allow Mrs Llewellyn to understand the full impact of her words.

Elizabeth regained her composure. 'I think we should have some tea and you can tell me the whole story.' She left the room to speak with Martha and returned with her husband. 'May I introduce my husband, Reverend David Llewellyn – dearest, this is Mr and Mrs Gilbert and William our grandson.'

The Reverend Llewellyn was frail now in his slippered years, his chest was weak and he needed a stick for support. He sat down in a large chair by the fire with his black scarf tied like a muffler round his neck, looking round the room with bewilderment as though listening to a language he did not understand.

'I'm so sorry to shock you both like this,' continued Mary. William sat on his mother's lap, immersed in a picture book Elizabeth had found for him.

'The fact is that Jesse and I are emigrating to America in a few weeks with William, to start a new life. We've both been in service and are now looking for the opportunity to perhaps set up a business of our own and buy a house. I have family in New York who will be able to help us, but we didn't want to leave without introducing you to your grandson.'

Elizabeth nodded. 'I see, that was kind of you,' she said. The teapot with cups and saucers arrived on a large tray with a glass of milk and biscuits for William.

Once the tea was poured and handed round, Mary began to tell of her time with David, the arrival of William, David's need to earn money and buy a practice so they could get married, leading to his decision to join the *Alabama*. The Llewellyns were moved, fighting back their tears at the sadness of Mary's story.

'Jesse was so kind to me after David died – for a long time I just wanted to die too. But soon I realised William needed his mother and my strength returned. My friendship with Jesse grew into love and we were married last December.' She smiled across the room at her husband.

'That's wonderful, I am so pleased you are happy now and planning a new life,' Elizabeth said. 'But we shall be sad to lose you all after such a short time of acquaintance. David was a delightful child, a pleasure to be with and I'm sure William is the same.'

Elizabeth and her husband reminisced with the Gilberts about David's early life in the village and the adventures with his brothers. 'We were so proud of his achievements. Of course, Mr Herbert was a great help in his upbringing – without him he would never have become a doctor.'

'Yes I know,' said Mary. 'David talked a great deal about Mr Herbert but sadly he'd died before I could meet him and he knew nothing of William.'

'Now before you leave, I must show you David's memorial,' said Elizabeth.

Elizabeth and the Gilberts, with William holding his mother's hand, walked the short distance to Holy Trinity Church where the brasses shone and the pews gleamed. The still air was filled with perfume from vases of lilies standing by the altar.

Elizabeth showed them the black marble memorial with the inscription and the beautiful east window. Mary and Jesse were overwhelmed by the generosity of the anonymous donor who had provided such an elaborate tribute to David.

Before they left the church, the four of them knelt together, each lost in their own thoughts. Rays of late morning sun streamed through the stained glass window, showering them with patterns of red, yellow, blue and green light.

High above their heads, amongst the beams of the chancel, fluttered a lone tortoiseshell butterfly.

Chapter 26

The new St Thomas' Hospital was formally opened by Queen Victoria in 1871 – Florence had overseen and approved plans for the building from an early stage. Although not well enough to travel there herself, she had sent Dr Sutherland, an expert on sanitary matters, to carry out inspections on her behalf.

The hospital was the most expensive in Europe, designed to the pavilion principle, providing maximum fresh air and light. The windows were large and the airy wards plastered in special washable and non-absorbent cement, with three open fireplaces in each ward giving additional ventilation.

In return for the Nightingale Fund's payment for the cost of training probationers, St Thomas' agreed to provide a suitable course of instruction, but recent criticism in the press of this training had galvanised Florence into taking a more active part in the running of the school.

She asked her cousin, Henry Bonham Carter, Secretary of the Fund Council, what was going wrong so she could decide how to improve the situation.

'Training schools are being established at other hospitals,' he explained, 'and we're all competing to recruit the small number of suitable applicants willing to devote their lives to nursing. Also I'm afraid there's very little supervision over the standards of teaching.'

'I know there's a problem with attracting the right kind of women,' said Florence. 'The idea still exists amongst the middle classes that nursing is akin to being in service and only for those disappointed in love, but I must find out more about how the school courses are run.'

While at home lying on her couch, dressed in black silk and

wearing a white net cap edged with lace, Florence began to conduct personal interviews each day with the sisters, nurses and probationers.

Florence soon discovered that the Resident Medical Officer at St Thomas' was often the worse for drink, rarely delivering the lectures and ward training as promised, the matron was frequently ill and had little contact with her staff. The probationers were given menial tasks on the wards rather than being taught to be professional nurses, and there were no promotional structures in place to encourage the supervisory staff of the future.

At Florence's instigation, John Croft, a senior surgeon at St Thomas', was recruited as the new Resident Medical Officer. He took his duties seriously, delivering weekly lectures providing vigorous instruction with practical guidance and theoretical background for the year of the probationers' training. John Croft's contribution made a significant difference and gradually the Nightingale Training School regained its reputation for excellence.

Florence approached Sir Harry Verney, Parthe's husband, who was now chairman of the Nightingale Fund. 'I'm keen to be involved somehow in the training of these young women but am not well enough to visit them at the hospital,' she said to him. 'Do you think if I wrote some words of encouragement, you would be prepared to deliver them on my behalf?'

'Certainly,' Sir Harry agreed. 'A message from Miss Nightingale herself would be an enormous boost to morale. Perhaps a printed version could also be prepared to hand out for the nurses to read at their leisure afterwards.'

Florence knew she must write her words with care in a way to be easily understood, as some of the pupils had not had the benefit of satisfactory schooling.

'My dear friends,' she began. *'I've had experience of many different hospitals in different countries but if I could recover*

my strength, I would come for a year's training with you at St Thomas' and learn something new each day.

The purpose of our instruction is to teach us how to train ourselves, how to observe and think things out, this is the time to sow the seed for your future in nursing. The more experience you gain, the more progress you can make, which will continue even when your training is over. Learn self-control, have a strong sense of truth about yourself and a golden sense of love and charity for others. Think less of what you might gain and more of what you may give.'

She continued by emphasising the rules to be kept – to be trustworthy, punctual, quiet, orderly, clean, neat, patient, cheerful and kind.

'We must do good to those who are not good to us, behave well to those who behave badly to us, serve with love those who do not receive our service with good temper and instantly forgive any slight we may receive.

The acts of a nurse are keenly scrutinised by young and old patients. If she is not perfectly pure and upright, believe me they will know. A nurse is in charge of people at times when they are most vulnerable and impressionable, she leaves her stamp on them whether she likes it or not.'

Then she concluded: *'We must be grateful to the Medical Instructor for the pains he has taken with us. If when I was young there had been such opportunities of training for hospital work, how eagerly I would have made the most of them. Please do not throw away this year, as it can never be recovered.*

God bless you all – Florence Nightingale.'

Her words were well received and the Nightingale address to nurses became an annual event.

Florence was now living in a house her father had bought for her on South Street in Mayfair and from the windows of her bedroom she had a fine view over Hyde Park. Parthe's London home was nearby and she developed a habit of dropping in unexpectedly, which was not always appreciated by Florence who liked to work all day with no disturbances.

Florence employed a cook, kitchen maid, a housemaid and a personal maid. She was particular about hygiene and loved food – alcohol she enjoyed in moderation, especially ginger and port wine. Details of ingredients for the cook were written out to make sure what she was eating was nutritious and her mother was asked to send boxes of fresh fruit, vegetables and flowers from Embley.

Cats were still Florence's constant companions and she had many of them. Pedigree males were carefully selected for the females but annoyed her when they tended to prefer the local toms. The resulting kittens were sent off to homes with members of the family, whether they wanted them or not.

On hearing of the death of her beloved cousin, Hilary Bonham Carter, from cancer after a long and painful illness, Florence berated herself that she'd been unable to rescue Hilary from the self-sacrifice of domesticity that had swallowed up her life. She broke into a rage of anger and despair at her cousin's wasted talents, the stupidity and indifference of her family and the unfair system that allowed such injustices to exist.

Benjamin Jowett's friendship was the only one that Florence wished to fit into her life, providing consolation in her solitude. There were no demands, only intimate communications by letter although he would occasionally spend an afternoon with her when he was in London.

Then one day she received a letter from her father:

'I have urgent business to attend to in Lea Hurst and must go very soon. Your mother is not well enough for the journey, she had an accident last week leaving her bruised and shocked.

Please, dear daughter, would you be able to leave your work for a short time to come and look after her? It's so long since we have seen you and things here are in a pretty poor state, we really need your help.'

Florence was not sure she wished to face her mother, the differences between them were still so great and she was at a loss to know how to heal the wounds.

When she asked Benjamin for his views, he wrote and advised her:

'Your father and mother are fond of you, it's not their fault they can't understand you. Don't dwell on their failings or despise them. Please visit them in their hour of need and do what you can to ease the worries and helplessness of old age, in the way that only you can do best.'

It was on a hot July day in 1872, six years after her last visit, when the invalid carriage Florence had hired for the occasion pulled into the driveway at Embley. The gardens looked unkempt with weeds growing through the gravel, hedges uncut and overgrown flowerbeds. Arriving at the front door, Florence was helped out by a surly, sallow-faced footman in a shabby uniform and shown to an unfamiliar guest bedroom which smelt musty and disused.

Her mother's personal maid came to help her unpack and Florence was pleased to recognise a friendly face. 'Lily, it's good to see you again, are you keeping well?'

'Yes, thank you Miss. Can I say what a pleasure it is to welcome you back to Embley?' Although she'd worked for the family since a young girl and known Miss Nightingale in different circumstances, Lily was still a little nervous in the presence of the heroine of the age.

'That's kind of you, Lily, it's good to be back. But may I ask why I'm in this room?' Flies began buzzing on the closed windows.

'Miss Julia has your old bedroom – I hope you won't be too inconvenienced, Miss. Most of the house is shut up now and Mrs Nightingale scarcely has any company these days. I can't remember when we last had a party.'

'I suppose we're all getting older and less sociable,' Florence replied, opening the window to let out the flies and allow in a summer breeze to stir the stale air of the room.

'Things are very different here now, Miss, especially with no housekeeper.'

'I was sorry to hear of Mrs Watson's death, you must miss her.'

'We do, Miss, that's for sure. I hope she'll soon be replaced 'cos I can't run the house on my own for much longer.'

'I'll do my best to make sure you don't have to.' Florence smiled reassuringly.

'Mrs Nightingale is resting at present, Miss, but she would like you to join her for tea.' Lily bobbed a curtsey and left the room.

Fanny Nightingale's sitting room was stuffy and dark, no sunlight was allowed through the tightly drawn curtains. As her eyes grew accustomed to the gloom, Florence saw her mother sitting in a favourite tapestry covered chair, she crossed the room and sat beside her.

Florence was shocked at how small and frail her mother appeared but was touched to see the obvious effort she'd made to prepare herself for the occasion.

The outline of Fanny's sharp shoulders showed through the fine silk mauve fabric of her dress, the circular lace yoke of the bodice was trimmed in purple velvet with a matching band round the skirt. Her thin grey hair was wound into a neat knot at the back of her head, covered by a white lace cap ornamented with loose purple ribbons.

'Florence, is that you?' Her voice sounded faint and tired.

'Yes, Mama, I'm here at last.' Florence bent down to kiss the soft powdery down of her mother's sunken cheeks.

'How are you, my dear?' Fanny asked, her dark eyes half closed in an effort to assess her daughter. 'You look a little peaky, working too hard as usual? Such a shame you always dress in black, a little colour works wonders for the complexion.'

'I'm having problems with back pain but otherwise keeping well,' Florence replied. 'But how about you? Papa tells me you had an accident.'

'A wheel came off the carriage and we landed in a ditch – no broken bones but bruising and a great deal of shock. Aunt Julia had hysterics when they carried me back but anything sets her off these days.'

A maid Florence did not recognise brought in the tea. When they were alone once more, Florence remarked to her mother, 'It seems you've had a few changes since I was here last.'

'We've been in a bit of a pickle since Mrs Watson died – frankly dear, we don't need so many staff and have let a lot go. We no longer entertain and money is tight, your father is at Lea Hurst sorting out problems there.' Fanny indicated to Florence to pour the tea.

'Is Aunt Julia not able to help you?' Florence asked.

Her mother shook her head. 'She's worse than useless, spends most her time in her room weeping for hours on end. My eyesight is not good which makes it hard for me to check the accounts.'

'Perhaps while I'm here I could give you a hand?' Florence offered.

'Your father and I would be most grateful.' Fanny leant towards her daughter. 'You know Flo, you and I've not always seen eye to eye but I tried to do my best for you. After the trauma of the baby, I just wanted to help you find someone you could marry and not become a sad old spinster like my sister Julia – lonely and depressed, always relying on the goodwill of others.'

'Mama, I'm sure that's true but I think you could have been more understanding about what I wanted. You must have realised how unhappy I was.' She placed her mother's cup of tea on a small table in front of her and cut her a slice of cake.

'Florence dear, I'm sorry if you were unhappy but it all turned out alright in the end,' Fanny said, stirring her tea. 'We're very proud of your success. Thousands of girls have been named after you, everyone has heard of you. I understand Mr Herbert was a great help, he must have felt very guilty about what he'd done.'

'I couldn't have achieved anything without him. Next month is the eleventh anniversary of his death and I still think about him every day.' Florence looked down and studied her hands for a moment.

Fanny sipped her tea and picked at the cake. 'I often wonder whatever happened to your child,' she said. 'Such a pity, I'd have loved grandchildren.'

Florence changed the subject. 'Have you seen Parthe recently? She tells me she's writing novels these days.'

'She's too busy at Claydon to visit, still worrying about her health and behaving as if money, butlers, carriages and housekeepers grew on blackberry bushes.' Fanny put down her cup, brushed crumbs from her skirt and patted her hair. 'And what about your nice Mr Jowett? Is there any chance he might ask you to marry him?'

Florence smiled. 'Mama, you are incorrigible. Benjamin is just a good friend – marriage is definitely not an option for us. Now I think I'll go and have a nap before dinner.'

'Very well, dear, but don't expect too much of the food – your father's always complaining about the cooking these days – as you can tell from this cake.' Fanny pulled a face and for the first time in many years, the two women laughed together.

A sudden and significant change came over Florence. She no longer saw her mother as an antagonistic, hurtful, unfeeling person, refusing to forget her daughter's misdemeanours. Instead she recognised her as a woman of her time, living her life and bringing up her children in the only way she knew how, simply because that was what the world had expected of her.

Now aged fifty-two years, the conflict that had embittered

Florence's life was over. The resentment against her mother that had been such a poison working inside her, melted away and at last they were reconciled. Florence became gentler and calmer, the storms had passed and tolerance replaced her uncompromising desire for perfection.

Once again she was drawn into organising the family's affairs. In place of a life filled with matters of vital interest and national importance, she was in a neglected country house with her aged parents and hysterical aunt, spending her days satisfying their requests, resolving difficulties with servants and straightening out the family finances.

Eight months passed. When she had recruited a new housekeeper and Embley was running smoothly once more, Florence made her excuses, returned to her house in South Street and resumed her work. Matters concerning hospital statistics, district nursing, lady health visitors, the troops in India, the English barracks, the Nightingale Training School – all once again came under her close scrutiny.

Two years later, WEN died suddenly after a fall at Embley and under the terms of Uncle Peter's will, both houses passed to Aunt Mai who decided to live at Embley but without Fanny. After the death of her husband, Fanny's confusion had increased and she could not understand why she now had to leave her home.

Shore, Aunt Mai's son, rescued the situation by inviting Fanny to live with his family in London during the winter months, allowing her to enjoy summers at Lea Hurst. Florence spent a great deal of time looking after her mother, until she died a month before her ninety-second birthday and was buried next to her husband at East Wellow. Aunt Mai continued to live at Embley until her death in 1889 and seven years later the house was sold.

Parthe became seriously ill and died on Florence's seventieth birthday in May 1890. Sir Harry Verney was now nearly ninety so Florence travelled to Claydon, took over his household and stayed on to look after him. Benjamin Jowett, Shore and Sir Harry all died within six months of each other.

Florence returned to South Street and spent the rest of her life in her bedroom. A crimson damask chaise longue stood by the open windows through which her favourite scent of summer roses drifted in on the breeze. The long casement windows had no coverings and Florence could watch the moon and stars from her iron bedstead covered by the patchwork counterpane lovingly stitched by her sister.

In the tall wardrobe hung her black silk day dresses with white collars and cuffs, her bonnets and lace caps on a ledge above. Shelves holding her favourite books lined one wall of the room and framed watercolours by Parthe hung on the others – a view of Embley, a portrait of her spaniel Venus and a landscape of the rolling Derbyshire hills seen from Lea Hurst.

The black grate held a bright fire blazing through all but the high days of summer. On her desk tidily placed were a cut glass ink stand, pens, a silver paper knife and a pile of white paper. In a secret drawer, she kept a black velvet box containing a turquoise and pearl heart-shaped pendant on a fine gold chain, together with a bundle of letters tied up with a blue silk ribbon.

During her long lonely hours, Florence often reflected on how different things might have been if she had not conceived David. On that day at the Burlington, when she had given herself to Sidney, a new life had begun for her, utterly different from the one a woman of her background should have been destined to lead.

There was no one now with whom she could speak of those who were gone; first her eyesight and then her mind failed her.

August 1910, Pennsylvania, USA:

The doctor bade 'good night' to his last patient of the day and closed up the consulting surgery. After removing his jacket, he entered the kitchen and kissed his wife as she prepared supper for their three children who were fidgeting in expectation at the large pine table.

'Where's grandma?' he asked.

'She's on the back porch,' answered David, his eldest son.

As the doctor approached his mother, he thought how beautiful she looked, dressed in cool white cotton, relaxing amongst cushions in a bentwood rocking chair with her grey hair softly swirled up into a bun, tendrils of curls escaping on to her forehead and round the nape of her slender neck. Her lovely face was etched with stories of a difficult life but behind gold-rimmed spectacles her large bright eyes were still the colour of a spring sky.

She looked up at him and indicated to the newspaper on her lap. 'I've been reading that Miss Florence Nightingale has died in London at the age of ninety. What an extraordinary woman she was, so brave and determined, devoting her life to others. It says here that *"her achievements helped to break down the walls of prejudice and encouraged other women to lead more fulfilling lives".'*

'The image of the Lady of the Lamp attending the sick has become iconic all over the world,' her son said. 'She must have had a will of iron to succeed as she did.'

'Your father often talked of the time they met,' his mother continued. 'Miss Nightingale's words that night inspired him to carry on with medicine, even when he was struggling to make a living as a doctor.'

William leant down and put his arms round her. 'Dearest Mam, I can never say too often how grateful I am for all the sacrifices you made to send me to medical school.'

'Running the guest house was difficult at times to be sure, but at least Jesse died knowing you had qualified,' she said. 'We were both so proud of you and your father would have been too – it's wonderful that you've achieved his dream of owning a country practice,' and Mary Gilbert smiled, happy and content now in the autumn of her life.

Epilogue

In June 2009 representatives of the Sons of Confederate Veterans from the United States arrived at Marlborough College to present a Medal of Honour awarded to the college's former pupil, the late David Herbert Llewellyn.

The flags of America, the United Kingdom and the Confederate States were paraded into the Adderley Hall, each accompanied by the appropriate anthem.

The master, Nicholas Sampson, spoke words of welcome which were followed by a brief resume of the story of the *Alabama* by David Du Croz, former Head of History. The audience was addressed by Henry Kidd, Commander-in-Chief of the Sons of Confederate Veterans, splendidly dressed in an elaborate uniform, offering an invitation to the college to accept the medal he had unveiled.

The master formally accepted the medal which he undertook to hold in David's honour and display securely to remind pupils of his bravery. *The Last Post* was sounded, followed by prayers, a short period of silence and then *Reveille*. The Honour Guard saluted the medal and marched out, the ceremony completed.

Visitors to Holy Trinity Church at Easton Royal still admire the ornate marble memorial and glorious east window commemorating the life of David Herbert Llewellyn. They must wonder why the son of a humble clergyman who died in unfortunate circumstances serving a country other than his own, should have been honoured in such an elaborate way.

Although Florence Nightingale had been offered a national funeral and burial in Westminster Abbey, she chose to be laid in the family plot at East Wellow, near to Wilton and the grave of her beloved Sidney.

When the Nightingale Memorial Fund was formed, plans for a commemorative statue were suggested and given public approval. The selection of a site took some consideration but finally Waterloo Place, near the Crimea Memorial, was decided as the most suitable.

At the inspired suggestion of Sydney Holland, the Treasurer of the Fund, the decision was made to move the statue of Sidney Herbert from Pall Mall to stand next to her.

Holland wrote: *'I believe Sidney Herbert wanted to marry her. Anyhow it is a pretty thought to put them side by side – he, who had the bravery to send her out and stick by her when there, and she who went.'*

So now they stand for perpetuity, the three statues forming one of London's most impressive sculptural groupings with Florence to the west, Sidney to the east and the larger Crimea Memorial standing solidly behind them.

Author's Notes

The idea for this story came by accident. Whilst sorting through papers for a village archive, I found a letter written some years before by local stonemason, Ben Lloyd, introducing himself to our newly-appointed vicar. Ben wrote how well he knew the church of Holy Trinity at Easton Royal, including the impressive marble memorial and east-facing stained glass window, both dedicated to David Herbert Llewellyn, who had died in tragic circumstances in 1864.

Then followed Ben's revelation that David was in fact the illegitimate son of Florence Nightingale and Sidney Herbert, not the son of Reverend Llewellyn as recorded. The story had been passed down from Ben's great, great grandmother, Sarah Waite, a midwife who had apparently delivered David's own illegitimate son.

I contacted the Lloyd family. Ben had recently died but his son John confirmed that although his father was full of stories, mostly the products of his own mind, Ben was convinced the one of David Herbert Llewellyn was true and had told it many times. His family still possesses the gold watch and chain given to Sarah Waite for her services.

The story was too compelling to ignore and I became a detective, searching for facts to link the lives of Florence, Sidney and David. Here are some of the results which encouraged me to complete the book:

- It was common practice at that time to include the birth father's surname into that of their illegitimate child.

- Sidney was tutored by the vicar of Chilmark and Reverend Llewellyn worked in the neighbouring parishes.

- Ben wrote that Florence's seduction had taken place during Christmas festivities in December 1836 – her recorded vision from God took place in February 1837 – six months later the family travelled to Rouen – David's birth was in September 1837.

- Mary Caroline, Sidney's sister, was married to the Marquis of Ailesbury's son and thus able to influence Reverend Llewellyn's appointment to Easton Royal.

- The cost to educate three boys at Marlborough, followed by university and medical training would have required a wealthy benefactor.

- An early biography of Florence published in 1913 describes Florence and Sidney as childhood friends, whereas later biographers record they did not meet until after Sidney's marriage. Could private documents referring to an earlier relationship have been deliberately destroyed or hidden?

- Florence's early life is described by biographers as being full of anguish and frustration with an overwhelming desire to achieve redemption by serving others.

- Richard Monckton Milne's poem, *Shadows*, describes observations of a couple close to him who could well have been Sidney and Florence.

- Jesse Gilbert was recorded in the 1861 census as being a butler in Mrs Anne Cooper Buckley's house and born in Great Bedwyn where Ben Lloyd's family lived.

- Ben stated David had an illegitimate child with a Matilda Kelley.

- Matilda Kelley (I changed her name to Mary Kelly) registered an illegitimate child in 1860 called William.

- Matilda and Jesse Gilbert were married in 1865, the year

after David's death.

- In his published will, Sidney cancelled Henry Pelham-Clinton's debts – what better way to repay a favour?

- Henry Pelham-Clinton was Secretary of State for the Colonies at the time of the American Civil War.

- The published letter from a fellow student after David's death describes him as "the godson of the late Lord Herbert of Lea".

- Captain Semmes recorded a comment that David was "the grandson of a peer".

- No record exists of the name of the benefactor of David's memorials in Easton Royal church.

- There is no doubt that Sidney and Florence shared a close and caring relationship.

- Sidney put his personal and political reputation at stake by sending Florence to the Crimea.

- Sidney's reported dying words seem to convey his feelings of guilt and regret.

- Florence's grief after Sidney's death is described as genuine and long lasting.

What I have done is to use dramatic licence to weave together the fact and fiction of the lives of these three Victorians with whom it has been a pleasure to become acquainted – kind, brave David who died placing others' needs before his own and charming, honourable Sidney whose life was devoted to fulfilling his political and personal responsibilities.

Finally, the remarkable Florence Nightingale, whose passion for social reform and resolute purpose to achieve redemption, led her to demonstrate extraordinary courage and steely determination whilst helping to improve the lives of countless others.

BIBLIOGRAPHY

Wardens of the Savernake Forest by the Earl of Cardigan

Life of Sidney Herbert, Lord Herbert of Lea by Lord Stanmore

Florence Nightingale by Cecil Woodham Smith

Florence Nightingale by Mark Bostridge

The Herberts of Wilton by Tresham Lever

An Englishman's View of the Battle between Kearsarge and Alabama by Frederick Milnes Edge

David Herbert Llewellyn from *Wilts Archaeological and Natural History Magazine Volume 68* by Mark Baker

Florence Nightingale – a Biography by Annie Matheson

A History of Marlborough College by AG Bradley, AC Champneys and JW Baines

Early Days of Marlborough College by Edward Lockwood

Collected Works of Florence Nightingale by Lynn McDonald

The Medical Profession in Mid-Victorian London by M Jeanne Peterson

Getting a Medical Qualification in England in the Nineteenth Century by JJ Rivlin

The Criminal Conversation of Mrs Norton by Diane Atkinson

Two Years on the Alabama by Arthur Sinclair

Queen Victoria's Journals – online

Florence Nightingale – to her nurses

The Darkened Room by Alex Owen

The Oxford Dictionary of National Biography – online

PRINTED AND BOUND BY:
Copytech (UK) Limited trading as Printondemand-worldwide,
9 Culley Court, Bakewell Road, Orton Southgate.
Peterborough, PE2 6XD, United Kingdom.